TIMMINS RINGS
THE CHANGES

J E HORTH

ISBN-13: 9798654868183
ISBN-10: 147712356

Cover design by: Geoffrey Bunting

Printed in the United States of America

To my beloved parents, Peggy and Leslie Moore. I wish you could have read it.

CONTENTS

TIMMINS RINGS THE CHANGES

J. E. HORTH

CHAPTER ONE

THE BISHOP WAGS A FINGER

"Never again!" exclaimed the Reverend Mr Samuel Timmins, after an afternoon spent giving a tour of his church to children from Quillington Parva Primary school. The little beasts had been uncontrollable, screeching with laughter each time he said the words "Saint Uncumber". "Saint Cucumber!" they insisted, despite their exhausted teacher's pleas for good behaviour. When it was over, Timmins made a beeline for the vestry, eager to resume an exciting encounter with the ravishing Amélie Delacour.

The icy February wind howled, and the church had been freezing, but the vestry, with its big old mahogany cupboards, faded rugs and aroma of books and dust, offered sanctuary and warmth thanks to the "Sun God", a most effective oil heater which he had purchased several years previously. True, the Vicarage was only a step away, but nobody was likely to disturb him here. He took up his book, 'The Amours of Amélie," the latest in a series of rather racy novels by Blossom Madgwick. It concerned the adventures of Amélie Delacour, a sultry, raven-haired French spy and favourite of King Louis XIV. In this volume, Amélie had arrived back in France as a heroine, having escaped capture by Spanish pirates. It was thrilling stuff and he was looking forward to immersing himself once again in her adventures, but first, he required sustenance.

He poured a cup of tea from his flask and settled back in his armchair with a slice of Mrs Whibley's moist, sticky date loaf. "This should last you several days," his housekeeper had said yesterday, as she put the cake to cool in the pantry. "Don't you go eating it all at once."

Just four slices remained by the time he had gone to bed that evening, and these he had smuggled out to enjoy as a reward for enduring the schoolchildren's visit.

"Better save the rest for later," Timmins told himself, when two slices had quickly disappeared. He took up his book and read, but his eyelids grew heavy and soon the familiar cottages and honey-coloured Georgian buildings of Quillington Parva replaced the streets of seventeenth century Paris. Instead of the crowds of adoring Parisians which had acclaimed Amélie, he saw the cardigan-clad ladies who did the flowers cheering him, with one voice; "Timmins! Reverend Timmins!"

Strange how deep that voice was. Timmins frowned. It sounded like a man's voice! Odd!

"Timmins, old lad! Stir your stumps! It's me, Bishop Archbold. Need to chat with you so I thought I'd pop in and introduce myself."

Bishop Archbold? Good Lord, what on earth was he doing here? A tall, broad-shouldered man with an unruly mop of ginger hair and a fiery ginger beard stood before him, a cheery expression on his face.

Archbold was new to the diocese, but Timmins had heard through the grapevine that he was far more demanding than his predecessor. The venerable Bishop Ogden, a distant relative of Timmins, never troubled his clergy overmuch; each one of his few visits had been a pleasant occasion involving a generous afternoon tea, an idle hour spent listening to the wireless and a glass or two of sweet sherry. Archbold, people said, meant business.

"Er, Bishop Archbold! So pleased to make your acquaintance. Please take a seat."

Archbold looked around him. Timmins had the only adult-sized chair in the room, so he picked up a small wooden Sunday School chair, positioned it to face Timmins and threw himself on to it with more gusto than Timmins thought wise. The chair creaked in the most alarming fashion but held firm. One eyebrow raised, the Bishop pointed to the book which had fallen to the floor, its lurid cover glaringly obvious. "That yours?"

"Er, no. I... that is...my housekeeper, Mrs Whibley, has a taste for romantic fiction."

Archbold grinned. "Just as you say. Any tea in that flask?"

Timmins poured out a cup and passed it to Archbold, who was eyeing the cake. "Would you like a slice?"

"Don't mind if I do." Archbold drained his tea, took the larger of the two remaining slices and demolished it in three large bites. "Scrumptious! You must give me the recipe." He fixed Timmins with a piercing blue gaze. The clock ticked away the seconds.

Timmins' mouth was dry. Bishop Archbold"s first act had been to deal with Reverend Jenks, vicar of the neighbouring village of Abbots Tump. Jenks' fondness for the bottle was common knowledge, and there had been some unpleasantness at a jumble sale which had led to his being required to resign his living. "I," Timmins reassured himself, "have done nothing for which the Bishop can reproach me". Aside from the Sunday services and the odd wedding or funeral, he kept a very low profile.

"Cosy little nest you've got here, Timmins. Nice spot for a lazy afternoon."

"I...I just popped in for a breather. It's been a busy day - no time for lunch. You were lucky to find me here."

The shadow of a frown crossed the Bishop"s face. "Hmm. Whatever you say, Timmins. I called at the Vicarage first, and that housekeeper of yours told me I might find you here. You are in demand. I was not your only visitor. A Miss Bellamy called to see you just as I bid good day to Mrs Whibley. Delightful woman. She asked me to tell you she will pop in tomorrow"

Timmins' heart fluttered at the mention of her name. Lavinia Bellamy? What brought her back to the village after so many years?

Archbold's voice cut through his thoughts. "Now then, Timmins. To business. Tell me, what success have you had in your work over the last few years?"

Aha. So that was it. Old Bishop Ogden must have been singing his praises. Could promotion be on the cards? It had never concerned him - he was very happy where he was. ("No ambition, that's his trouble!" had been his late father's constant criticism). Was Archbold looking to replace the current Dean, who was due for retirement. Yes, that must be it.

"Well?"

"Forgive me, Your Grace." Timmins stretched out his legs and sat back in his chair. He would not, in the ordinary run of events, have put himself forward for promotion, but if Archbold was determined to offer him the post, perhaps he should accept. To refuse might be seen as churlish. And the Deanery was a very large and beautiful building, to be sure. He could be quite comfortable there... "To answer your question, I can say things have... changed since I took up the reins here. The previous incumbent, Reverend Bellamy, was a dear soul, but between you, me and the gatepost, he inclined to self-indulgence and was not the most dynamic of people. He ..."

"The question was not about Bellamy, but about you." The Bishop's tone was sharp, his stare piercing.

Timmins sat up. His mouth suddenly felt parched. "Yes. Of course. Well. Ahem. I... I am not one to sing my own praises, you understand, but I am sure that if you were to ask around ..."

"Could you say, for example, that you have grown the congregation in your time here?"

"Well, there are some regulars and..."

"Have you taken your ministry into the heart of the community? Visited the sick and needy? Taken steps to welcome the villagers into the fold? Promoted the church hall as a means of generating income and gathering in your flock?"

Timmins flushed. The Bishop"s tone suggested that promotion was most definitely not what he had in mind. He bit his lip. "Well, I think I..."

"I believe I can give the answers." Archbold leaned forward, the little wooden chair creaking ominously. "You have done none of these things, Reverend Timmins, none. This is a comfortable living, and you have become rather too comfortable within it. My sources tell me you enjoy an easy time of it here and that you are far from dynamic."

Just then, the ancient bells rang, the sound ruined by the thud of several dissonant notes. "And there is yet another example of your failure. Your efforts in this parish have been minimal. Bells are the voice of the Church, ringing out across our English countryside, calling the faithful to prayer and reminding us of God's joyous presence. However, according to a report in my possession I note that at least one bell of St Uncumber's is not in full voice. Reliable information informs me that you have carried out little or no proper maintenance and that at least one of them is cracked." He raised an eyebrow. "What plans have you made to afford the repairs?"

Timmins' heart was beating so that he was sure the Bishop could hear it. "Well, Your Grace, I..."

"No, Reverend Timmins. Do not utter a word. There is nothing you can say that can excuse your ... I hesitate to use the word ineptitude... your, shall we say, complacency?" He reached out and took the last slice of date and prune loaf. "You don't mind? Thank you.' He wolfed down the cake.

Archbold wagged his finger.

"You, Timmins, must raise your game. You must grow your congregation, involve the Church more fully in the life of the village, and get those bells fixed! Raising money for that will give you an ideal opportunity to reach out to the wider populace. What say you?"

"I... er..."

"I give you until the end of August, Timmins. Six months. I intend to keep my beady eye fixed upon Quillington Parva, and if I do not see a significant improvement in the state of affairs here, I shall remove you from this parish."

"Remove me?" Timmins squeaked. "What can you mean?"

"I mean," the Bishop said, standing and brushing crumbs from his cassock, "that I will uproot you from this comfortable environment and transplant you to a more challenging parish where you will work under supervision. I intend to test you, Timmins, as they tested our dear Lord, for your own sake and for the sake of this parish. Do I make myself clear?"

"Y...yes, Your Grace. You do."

"Good. I'll see myself out and leave you to contemplate what I have just said." He wrenched open the door, allowing a blast of icy air to sweep in. "Oh, and next time we meet, I look forward to hearing your opinion of "The Amours of Amélie". I believe it to be the finest of Blossom Madgwick's oeuvre to date. Goodbye." With that, he turned and strode off along the path, shoulders hunched against the bitter wind.

Timmins, watching him, had the same sick sensation he used to get when his prep school Headmaster, Septimus Clissold, threatened him with the cane if he did not "Step things up a gear, boy!" How he had hated school.

Teeth chattering, Timmins reached for his tweed overcoat. His stomach was rumbling; it was time he went home for tea. He wound a long lambswool scarf around his neck and put on his hat. He gathered up his book and keys, locked the ancient iron-studded door and picked his way along the gravel path that led through the churchyard to a small arched gateway in the surrounding wall. Lifting the latch, he stepped through the gate into the front garden of the Vicarage. He had been most comfortable here for twenty-six years. Why must the Bishop spoil everything? And what could Lavinia want?

The freezing evening air prickled his nostrils and pinched his cheeks. "What, oh, what am I to do?" The moon had come out from behind the clouds, its pale light highlighting the buff-coloured stone of the handsome Georgian Vicarage, with its five white-painted windows, stone portico, gravelled carriage-sweep and neatly trimmed lawns. "This is my home. I cannot, and will not, leave it to confront who knows what dangers!"

The sudden mocking caw of a rook startled him, and he fumbled for his front door key. He vowed to face whatever challenge came his way if it meant that he could stay in Quillington Parva.

CHAPTER TWO

LAVINIA HAS AN IDEA

Timmins passed a restless night, plagued by nightmares in which an unknown menace pursued him. He awoke, sweating, to find the bedclothes twisted about him in an untidy muddle. Where was he? The terror of the night lingered, and his heart raced.

Pale sunlight filtered in through the thick curtains of his dear old bedroom. Pulling the blanket over his head, he curled up, foetus-like, and revelled in the warmth of the little nest he had made for himself. The world could go hang! Neither Bishop Archbold with his demands and threats, nor Lavinia Bellamy, could touch him now. How comfortable he was! If only he could stay here, snug, cosy and protected.

"Vicar? Vicar! Are you awake?" Loud banging on his bedroom door jolted him and Mrs Whibley's shrill voice pierced his eardrums. "It's past nine o'clock! There's bacon and eggs waiting for you - cold now, but you've only got yourself to blame for that, staying in bed until this hour. It's in the pantry. I'm popping to the grocers. Shan't be long."

"Thank you, Mrs Whibley. I will be down directly." She did not reply,, and he heard her heavy, flat-footed tread on the stair. He had annoyed her, that much was obvious, and he would have to clear the air later. "Bother!" He clambered out of bed and shivered his way to the chilly bathroom. Jack Frost has been, he thought, noting patterns of ice in feathery fronds on the inside of the bathroom window.

When, twenty minutes later, he arrived in the sitting-room, it was to find a blazing fire crackling in the hearth. He ate his breakfast and drank three cups of tea. Outside, the wind was blowing a gale and despite the hour it was still dark, the room lit only by the glow of the fire and the warm pink light of the standard lamp. Timmins decided against venturing out. He took up "The Amours of Amélie" but could not concentrate. Instead, as the clock ticked, and the fire crackled, his book slipped to the floor and he thought back to the day when he had arrived in Quillington Parva as a young curate, eager to make his mark on his first parish.

It had been a golden Autumn afternoon in 1904, just over a quarter of a century ago. The trees were a fiesta of red, gold, green and yellow when the omnibus had dropped him, a slim, dark-haired youth of twenty-four, at the end of the High Street outside the Fat Rascal Tearooms. Struggling to alight and hindered by a heavy Gladstone bag, he had been grateful when a kindly voice greeted him, and a strong arm steadied him.

"Reverend Timmins, I presume?" His rescuer was a small, round, bald clerical gentleman with a shining red face and a mischievous expression.

"Reverend Bellamy?"

"Guilty as charged, young sir! Ambrose Bellamy, at your service. How fortuitous that I was here at exactly the right time to meet you! I should be at a meeting of the Parish Council, but I cancelled it as it was such a lovely day. I confess I have spent the past hour indulging myself in the Fat Rascal." He winked at Timmins and tapped the side of his nose with his index finger. "Don't tell my daughter, dear boy! Lavinia is forever castigating me for my overindulgence, but the Fat Rascal serves the most delicious treats. I am inordinately fond of their Eccles cakes, and I have just consumed four!" He winked and patted his stomach. "Lavinia would be so vexed with me."

"In that case, Reverend, might I suggest that you brush the crumbs from your clothing?"

"I say, what a good thing I bumped into you, dear boy! Good grief, Lavinia would have spotted the evidence at once and known me for the glutton I am! I can see that you will be a real asset, dear chap, a real asset! Now, come along, let us go home, and I shall introduce you to Lavinia."

On their arrival at the Vicarage, Reverend Bellamy ushered

Timmins into the sun-filled sitting room where a young, dark-haired woman was sitting at a little mahogany Davenport. "Lavinia, my dear, here is our young curate, come to lighten my load. Put away your pen, my love, and say hello to the Reverend Samuel Timmins."

She stood and smoothed her skirt, then held out her hand. "I am sorry." Her voice was gentle and welcoming. "I was away with the fairies! Forgive me. We have been looking forward to your arrival, Reverend Timmins."

Her grey eyes reminded him of the sea on a winter's day. He shook her hand, noting its soft warmth, and felt his heart leap. There was something about her that gave him a sense of belonging. "Delighted to meet you." He knew he was blushing.

"I hope you will be very happy in Quillington Parva. May I get you some tea?" She disappeared into the kitchen, leaving a faint scent of Lily of the Valley.

"Oh, I say! Scones and jam! That's the ticket, my dear!" Reverend Bellamy said, as she reappeared with a laden tea tray. He winked at Timmins. "She's taken such good care of me all these years since my dear wife departed this earth. She'll do the same for you, now you are to be a part of our little family, won't you, my dear?"

What happy days those had been! Yawning loudly, he closed his eyes and stretched.

"Reverend?" The voice was soft and familiar. "Reverend! Samuel, dear."

Samuel? Dear? Nobody had ever called him dear – except Lavinia. He was about to heave himself out of the chair when a great weight landed on his chest and although he threw his arms up to shield his face, there was an onslaught of wet, slobbering kisses. This was not the Lavinia Bellamy he remembered! She appeared to be suffering from a heavy cold; the snuffling and snorting that accompanied the kisses were disgusting beyond belief!

"Ugh! Stop it!" Good Lord! What was the woman doing? He twisted and turned to stave off her passionate embrace. This was too much! After the way she had treated him all those years ago, she dared to accost him in this manner!

"Miss Bellamy, let me be!" he said, but it was no use. What strength she had! And what damp kisses she was bestowing upon him! "No more!" He bellowed the words, all went silent and still, and he opened his eyes.

He was staring into the deep amber gaze of a great, lolloping, hairy dog; a damp, dripping dog standing on its hind legs, resting its front paws on his chest; a dog whose tongue flopped from the side of its mouth, whose warm breath smelt rather meaty, and who gazed at him from beneath shaggy eyebrows, panting. "Poffley?"

Poffley belonged to Mrs Prout, a wealthy widow and sometime benefactress of the church. An invalid, she was used to getting her own way and must have persuaded Lavinia to walk her beloved pet for her. Timmins detested the beast. The feeling was not mutual. Poffley, a creature of unrecognisable parentage and vast proportions, lunged forward again to lick his face.

A peal of laughter rang out. "Oh dear! He likes you, Samuel! You two are clearly old friends!"

Timmins pushed the dog away and stared at the woman standing before him. Despite the grey hair, she was still recognisable as the girl he had loved all those years ago. "Lavinia," he began, then stopped. He did not understand the turmoil of regret, resentment, anger, and love that her presence stirred up in him. To think she could have been his wife! "Lavinia, I..."

At the sound of his voice, Poffley launched another amorous attack, and before he could stop himself, Timmins swore. "Damn you, pestilential creature!"

"Naughty boy!" Lavinia said, and Timmins recoiled. Her tone instilled in him the same fear that his mother had aroused when, as a child, he had committed even the most minor misdemeanour.

"I was only..."

Before he could make his excuse, she grabbed hold of Poffley's collar. "Naughty Poffley! Get down!" She attempted to detach the animal, but without success.

Summoning all his strength, Timmins pushed Poffley away and heaved himself out of the armchair. He fumbled in his trouser pocket for his handkerchief and wiped away all traces of the dog's damp kiss. "What on earth," he demanded, brushing dog hairs from his clothing, "is that animal doing in my drawing-room?" He glared at Poffley who, undeterred, sprang at him again, tail wagging.

"Oh dear, Samuel! I am so sorry," cried Lavinia. "Poffley! Leave him alone!"

The dog took no notice.

"Enough! I will not have it. Poffley! Get down this instant!" There was steel in her voice; it had an immediate impact on Poffley. He curled up beside her. "What that animal needs is discipline," she remarked. "He's spoiled rotten." She hesitated. "Are you all right, Samuel?"

Timmins, stifling a yawn, nodded. "Yes, yes. I believe so, thank you."

"Good. Good. I met Mrs Whibley, and she kindly gave me the back door key so I could let myself in. I am very sorry for disturbing you, but ... "

"I was enjoying a few moments' peace to consider my sermon for this Sunday."

Lavinia glanced at the floor beside him and raised one eyebrow. There lay 'The Amours of Amélie', its front cover depicting the generously endowed heroine in a very low-cut gown.

"'Mrs Whibley is an admirer," Timmins said, scooping up the book and placing it on the coffee table. "Now, Miss Bellamy! How can I help you?"

Picking at a loose thread in her skirt she replied, "Must we be so formal? Will you not call me Lavinia? At least, in private?"

Timmins bit his lip. Her request seemed to hark back to their previous intimacy, but they were different people now. "Well - Lavinia. What can I do for you?" He looked at his watch. "I am a very busy man."

Before she could reply, words tumbled out of his mouth. "I admit it surprised me to hear of your return, Lavinia, after so many years. Quillington Parva is your home, but if you have come here hoping we might rekindle what once was between us..."

"You mistake my intentions, Samuel," she said. "It is simply that I have realised life is too short to waste in holding on to old hurts and disputes. I have returned to the village for good, since my cousin has died, and have bought Meadowsweet Cottage where I shall be quite comfortable. I intend to involve myself in the village community, and the church, although I shall, from time to time, have to go away on business."

There was a short pause and when she resumed, her tone was more serious, her voice quieter. "We cannot avoid each other, Samuel; it will make things very difficult if we allow matters between us to remain unresolved, so I have come to offer once again the hand of friendship.' She paused. 'Just friendship, Samuel - nothing more. Father would have wished it. I wish it."

Timmins flushed. She was right. He glanced at a silver-framed photograph on the mantelpiece. Dear old Ambrose! He felt ashamed. She had devoted her life to caring for others, first her father, and then her cousin. If it concerned her now to seek his hand in friendship, then what right did he have to deny her?

"Miss Bellamy... Lavinia...forgive me. It was, perhaps, thoughtless of me to speak to you in that fashion. I can only offer as an excuse the fact I am a trifle out of sorts today, having had a most unpleasant shock yesterday evening."

"There is no need to apologise. Please, won't you tell me what has happened?"

Timmins went to the window. Should he confide in her? It could not do any harm. Pulling the red brocade curtains back as far as they would go (Mrs Whibley would insist on leaving them half-closed), he gazed out at the garden. A thick, freezing fog shrouded it, riming the plants with needles of ice. Shivering, he crossed to the fireplace, picked up the poker and gave the coals a stir. A little burst of sparks danced up the chimney as he told her what the Bishop had said the previous evening.

"I have, you see, been very preoccupied since that meeting." The relief that came with unburdening himself took him by surprise. "I told myself my long years of service in this parish are witness enough to my dedication, but I did not pass a restful night, my dear Miss Bellamy... Lavinia. You see before you today a broken man. Even Blossom Madgwick cannot make me forget my troubles."

She smiled. He stiffened. He had opened himself to her in a way he rarely did, and this was her response? To laugh at him? A flicker of rage flared in his soul. He had too often been the object of ridicule - both at home, as a small child who did not live up to his father's expectations, and later, at the hands of his schoolfellows. And now Lavinia dared to mock him when he had confided in her.

"You find my predicament amusing?" He straightened and clasped his hands behind his back.

"No, far from it. Forgive me. It pleased me to learn that you enjoy a historical romance. I like... that is, I gain a great deal from the adventures of Amélie Delacour." Her expression was serious. "I assure you I was not laughing at you. I wish I could be of help. I know how much this place means to you, Samuel." She hesitated. "But Samuel, is there no truth in the Bishop's criticism?"

Before he could reply, Mrs Whibley came in with a loaded tray. "Got my shopping done quicker than I thought I would, Reverend, so I've made a pot of tea. Thought you and Miss Bellamy might like a cuppa." She deposited the tea tray on the coffee table and straightened up, pushing a stray wisp of grey hair back under her cap. "Ooh, you're reading 'The Amours of Amélie!'" she remarked. "My sister gave me a copy for my birthday last week. It's saucy! Have you got to the part where old Alphonse tries to have his wicked way with Amélie in the stable? Shocking, I call it!"

"Thank you, Mrs Whibley," he said. "That will be all." The housekeeper was altogether too prone to chatter, but it was a fault he was prepared to overlook for the sake of her superior skills in the kitchen.

Lavinia, smiling, winked at him and he flushed.

"I am afraid I shall be rather busy this morning," he snapped, "so our meeting will have to be short but at least allow me to pour you a cup of tea." With an exasperated "Tut!" he removed the knitted doll tea cosy, one of Mrs Whibley's more fanciful creations. How many times had he told her to use the best cosy when guests were present? This one, with its orange curly hair, rictus grin and ludicrous purple and black striped crinoline, was repellent.

Lavinia sipped her tea, deep in thought. "I didn't mean to offend, Samuel," she said, "but you have been the vicar here for a long time. It would be no surprise if you had slipped into something of a routine." When he did not reply, she continued. "I see you are in a pickle, Samuel, and I would like to help you, if I can. No, do not refuse me. You cannot afford to allow pride to stand in the way of a solution."

Ignoring Timmins' affronted glare, she continued. "Mrs Prout would, I am sure, wish to help. I suggest you pay her a visit."

"Ask her for money, you mean?" The thought was shocking. Mrs Prout, an elderly widow, was, at the best of times, intimidating. "I could not presume upon her generosity in that fashion."

"I am sure she would understand. She has always supported the church and although she tells me that she has not been well enough to attend services for some time, I know that she still takes a great interest in it."

Timmins thought for a moment, stroking his chin. Mrs Prout was very wealthy, and it was not as if he wanted the money for his own personal use. Besides, he needed to explore all options. He could not afford to stand on his pride. "Hmm. Yes, I take your point, Miss Bellamy' Lavinia. I take your point. I shall pay Mrs Prout a visit. It can do no harm."

"I must go, Samuel," Lavinia said, glancing at the bracket clock on the mantelpiece, "I have an appointment in Quillinghampton and I have to return this animal to his mistress before I catch the bus. Come along, Poffley."

The dog, who had been snoring in front of the fire, yawned and shook himself, then trotted over to Lavinia, who fastened his lead.

"Do not allow me to keep you. I, too, have things to do." Timmins said, looking warily at Poffley.

The dog returned his gaze, unblinking.

"I understand that the Parish Church Council has not been active for a while. Why not call a meeting? You could report your conversation with Bishop Archbold, say that you are both keen to get things moving again? No need to mention his exact words..."

"Yes! Of course! I shall write the letters at once. Perhaps I have allowed things to slip. It is about time I took charge. Why did I not think of this beforehand instead of wallowing in self-pity?" He strode across the room, lifted the lid of the roll top desk, switched on the desk lamp against the gloom of the morning, and picked up his pen.

Lavinia stood for a moment in the doorway, watching him, before she spoke again. "Goodbye then, Samuel. We shall meet again soon, I am sure."

"What? Oh, yes! Goodbye Lavinia. Now, excuse me – I must get on!"

She slipped out of the room, leaving behind a faint aroma of Lily of the Valley.

CHAPTER THREE

TIMMINS GOES CAP IN HAND

The following afternoon Timmins made his way warily to the front door of Tall Trees, Mrs Prout's enormous Arts and Crafts house on the edge of the village. He was on the lookout for Poffley, who delighted in springing out of the bushes on unsuspecting visitors, knocking them off their feet. Although his devoted mistress insisted that it was only "Dear Poffley-Woffles having a little fun," Timmins did not trust the creature. He was not fond of dogs.

Today he arrived without incident at the heavy oak front door and jangled the brass bell. Edna Dobson, Mrs Prout's housekeeper, usually appeared at the door within a few moments, but today nobody came. He pulled the bell again; still no response. Mrs Prout was expecting him, so she must be in, and she was not a woman who liked to be kept waiting.

He grasped the big brass doorknob and pushed. The door did not move. Bracing himself against it, he shoved with his shoulder as hard as he could. There was a click, the door flew open and he stumbled into the wide, tiled hallway, struggling to keep to his feet. "Oo-er." He collided with the hat-stand, which went crashing down.

'Is that you, Vicar?' Mrs Prout's voice boomed from the drawing-room.

"Er, yes, it is I," he replied, righting himself.

"What are you doing out there? Shut the door behind you, come into the drawing room, and stop shilly-shallying!"

Timmins hastened to do the old lady's bidding. He picked up the hat-stand, reinstated the various items of clothing that had fallen from it and brushed himself down, taking a moment to compose himself. He might not like Mrs Prout, but pandering to her was, unfortunately, a tactical necessity. "Here I am, Mrs

Prout!" he called, making his way to the enormous drawing-room where she usually spent her days.

She was sitting on one of the two sofas facing each other in front of the fire, reading the latest copy of The People's Friend. This month's edition, he noticed with interest, boasted 'A Tender New Love Story by the celebrated Blossom Madgwick' He made a mental note to purchase a copy on his way home.

Mrs Prout put down her magazine, folded her hands on her lap and peered over her horn-rimmed glasses. "You're a little later than expected, Reverend," she said. "However, I shall forgive it on this occasion." She sniffed. "It has been some time since we last met. Visiting the sick does not appear to come high on your agenda."

Timmins flushed. "I..." he began, but she held up her hand.

"No, do not, I beg, seek to offer apologies or excuses; they would demean you. You are here now. I presume that you have come here to offer me spiritual comfort and therefore I propose that we shall spend an hour in quiet prayer and study of the Good Book - if you can spare me the time?"

"Yes, Mrs Prout." Timmins hurried to reassure her. Bother. She would want to pick over the nitty-gritty of some obscure theological argument - the last thing he wanted. He had hoped to broach the subject of the bells, have a spot of tea and get back home to his book.

"Good. We shall have tea first. Kindly make your way to the kitchen and fetch the things. Mrs Dobson has the afternoon off to visit her elderly aunt in the care home. Very inconvenient for me but I suppose one must make allowances for one's staff from time to time. It's quite beyond me to understand why she would visit a relative with whom she has never got on and who now barely recognises her, but that is her choice. What she hopes to gain from it I do not know. However, I believe that she has left for us some ham sandwiches and a Victoria sponge. Did you hear me, Vicar? Vicar! Are you going to fetch the tea or stand there all afternoon?"

Timmins had been gazing out of the diamond-pane windows at

a blackbird busily making a meal of a large black slug. "Ugh!" he thought, with a little shudder. "Tea? Yes, I shall fetch it straightaway, and after we have finished our readings I have another little matter I would like to discuss with you, if that is acceptable?"

"Yes, yes, yes," Mrs Prout replied.

As Timmins reached the door, a sudden thought occurred to him. "Will Poffley be joining us?"

"No," came the reply. "I believe Mrs Dobson has taken him with her. The old people adore him. He is such a gentle, loving little man, and he entertains them so."

"Yes, indeed," Timmins agreed. Thank the Lord for that - no Poffley! Relieved, he made his way to the kitchen and opened the door.

There was a noise.

Timmins' heart missed a beat. Was it an intruder? A burly burglar in a striped jumper and mask, wielding a cosh? What should he do? He saw himself bravely challenging the felon and wrestling him to the ground. He would be a hero! His fame would spread far and wide, bringing people flocking to hear his sermons! Bishop Archbold would be in awe of his heroism....

But what if the burglar beat him with his cosh? He shuddered at the imagined pain of the blow; saw himself unconscious and bleeding on the kitchen floor; conjured up images of Lavinia weeping by his hospital bed. No, he would not risk his own safety. He would tiptoe back to the drawing-room and tell Mrs Prout to call the police. Carefully, he closed the door.

Woof!

This was no burglar! This was Poffley in the kitchen! Timmins contemplated his next move. He had no excuse for returning without the tea tray, but he really did not want to face Poffley. 'Timmins, be a man!' he told himself as he stepped into the kitchen.

There, gazing up at him from the detritus of the promised tea, a slice of ham dangling from the corner of his mouth, was Poffley. His hairy face was powdered a ghostly white with a liberal sprinkling of ... icing sugar? Flour? Mrs Dobson had not, it seemed, taken him with her. Damn the woman!

He gulped as, in one quick movement, Poffley jerked back his head, swallowed the meat and launched himself forward, leaping up at the vicar with a deafening bark.

"Oh! Get down! Oo- er!" Timmins backed out of the kitchen, Poffley leaping and dancing around him. "Good Poffley! Help!"

Timmins flew off down the corridor with Poffley in pursuit, his claws skittering on the ceramic floor tiles. He felt the wretched animal's hot breath on his legs as he reached the cloakroom just ahead of Poffley, slammed the door shut and slid the bolt. He slumped down on to the lavatory, panting, while his hairy pursuer barked and scraped at the door.

That was a close thing! His heart pounded, and the blood rushed in his ears. The cloakroom was cold and there was a strong smell of disinfectant. The tap dripped slowly. Timmins shivered. Now what was he to do? The little leaded light window with its gaily coloured panes would not permit an exit, yet to venture out again into the hallway would be folly. "Bother!" he thought. "I shall have to call for help. How very humiliating!" He was about to speak when Mrs Prout's voice resounded from the drawing room.

"What's going on out there?"

For an invalid, she certainly had some powerful lungs. What should he say? How to tell her that Poffley was holding him hostage?

"Vicar? Vicar! What are you playing at, and where's my tea? Come in here at once!"

"Er, I...Um.."

"REVEREND TIMMINS! WHERE ARE YOU?"

"I'm just in the lavatory," he cried, opening the door a crack to make his voice heard. "Poffley was in the kitchen and when I opened the door, he chased me. Is it safe to come out now?"

"Safe? Of course it's safe! Stop playing the fool, Reverend, and come back here. At once!"

Timmins poked his head round the door. No Poffley. He tiptoed back to the drawing room, his heart pounding. Poffley, curled up at Mrs Prout's feet, raised a hairy eyebrow and stared at him. Timmins could swear that the dog was grinning. "He...." Timmins began. Why attempt to explain? Mrs Prout would think him a fool. "I am afraid that there is no tea."

"No tea? What ARE you talking about? Mrs Dobson has left it on the tray in the kitchen, as I told you. What on earth is going on?" Before he could explain, Edna Dobson entered the room with a laden wooden tea tray. "Here we are! I've brought cups and saucers and so on, and I'll pop back in a tick when I've made more sandwiches."

Mrs Prout frowned. "I don't understand. Why do you need to make more? You told me you had already prepared sandwiches for us... And why are you here at all, Mrs Dobson? Surely you and Poffley were to be absent all afternoon?"

"Well, I would have been," Mrs Dobson replied, putting down the tray on the coffee table. "However, a certain animal was not on his best behaviour today, and wasn't in the mood for visiting. We got to Twilight House, said hello to Auntie and then his Nibs went racing off. I searched all round the place, thinking he'd gone off to visit one of the other old dears, but he was nowhere in sight. I was in a right panic, I can tell you. Then someone said he'd seen Poffley heading back this way, so I said cheerio to Auntie and came back as fast as I could and there he was, sitting on the back doorstep. I'd just let him in when I noticed the butcher's boy out on his bicycle and I wanted a word with him about the sausages he delivered last week, so I went back down the garden to flag him down."

Mrs Prout tutted. 'Yes, yes, but where are our sandwiches, Mrs Dobson?"

"Well, I forgot about them, didn't I? Didn't cover them up." Mrs Dobson said. "When I got back into the kitchen, the blasted dog had been at them. He's ransacked the larder too. Sorry madam, but he's in the doghouse today and no mistake. I'll make you a few more sandwiches." She shuffled out of the room. Poffley followed her, casting a triumphant look at Timmins as he left the room.

Mrs Prout sighed. "Switch on the lamps, Reverend if you please." Timmins switched on the various standard and table lamps dotted about the room. A warm, pinkish glow replaced the grey afternoon gloom, and he drew the brocade curtains in the three large square-paned windows before taking his seat opposite his hostess.

There was an awkward silence. Timmins bit his lip. Should he ask Mrs Prout about the money now, or wait until later? As he pondered this problem, he was all too aware of her scrutiny.

"You seem a little distracted this afternoon," she said. "Since Poffley's high spirits seem to have delayed our tea, I see no point in sitting here wasting time while you stare into the middle distance. Shall we begin our study of the Good Book?"

She picked up her Bible. "Where shall we begin?"

A short while later, Mrs Dobson brought in a tray of sandwiches, accompanied by a rather subdued Poffley, who lay down in front of the fire, gazing mournfully at Mrs Prout.

"Here you are! I'd run out of ham so it had to be corned beef," she said. "And the cake's ruined, so it's just the sandwiches, I'm afraid. I've told that dog off good and proper, I can tell you. He knows he's in the doghouse so don't let him get round you."

Mrs Prout dismissed the housekeeper with a wave of her hand. "Help yourself, Reverend."

Timmins was about to take a bite of a corned beef sandwich when there was a loud jangling sound in the hallway, followed shortly after by a braying laugh. Millicent Gore-Hatherley, thought Timmins gloomily. Millicent was the last of the Gore-Hatherleys who had lived in Hatherley Court for generations. He had always got on quite well with her, but did not relish asking Mrs Prout for money while she was present.

"Daphne, old love!" she said, bursting into the room and striding across to plant a loud kiss on the other woman's cheek. She brought with her a strong odour of horses and fresh air. "Been out hacking on dear old Bingo. Mrs D told me you were busy, but I said, "Stuff and Nonsense! I've come to see my old chum and I'm jolly well going to see her."

She sat down on the sofa next to Timmins. "What-ho Reverend! Tea! By Jingo, that looks good; I'm famished!" She reached out and picked up a sandwich which she devoured hungrily, dropping crumbs and brushing them on to the floor. "Jolly good. Ages since I've had corned beef."

Mrs Prout sighed. "Hello, Millicent," she said. "Reverend Timmins, would you mind ringing for Mrs Dobson? We shall need another plate."

Timmins got up and pushed the bell by the fireplace. Now how was he to ask Mrs Prout for a donation to the church fund?

Millicent was in a good mood and over the next half an hour she regaled them with tales of her latest equine exploits, gossip about County folk and her recipe for apple chutney, admired, she claimed, by none other than the Duke and Duchess of Quillingshire. As she spoke, she ploughed her way through the pile of sandwiches.

Timmins was still pondering how best to phrase his request for money and when, exactly, to do it., when Mrs Prout, looking over her spectacles, interrupted Millicent's monologue to ask, "Reverend Timmins, was there not something you wished to discuss with me?"

Timmins nodded. "Yes," he replied, "but I do not wish to trouble Mrs Gore-Hatherley.."

"Millicent!" Miss Gore-Hatherley said, spraying more crumbs as she spoke, her mouth still full of sandwich.

Mrs Prout, an expression of distaste on her face, watched as her friend brushed the crumbs on to the Aubusson carpet. "Have a care, do, Millicent!" she snapped, waving her stick. "Reverend Timmins, if, as it now appears, we are not to continue our Bible Study, then at least let us conclude one useful piece of business today. What was it you wished to say?"

"Um... Well.." He reached out for the last sandwich, but Millicent got to it before him. How that woman could eat!

Mrs Prout, brows knitted, said, "Well?"

Any remaining courage slipped away. His mouth dried and the

carefully worded request he had rehearsed so many times that very morning disappeared from his memory.

"Er, I... Hrrmmmph!" He cleared his throat. "I..." A loose thread on the cuff of his shirt caught his attention; he picked at it, pulling it out and letting it float to the ground. What was he to say? "It's like this," he began.

"Yes? Yes? What is it, Reverend Timmins?" Mrs Prout frowned at him over the top of her glasses. He noticed the yellowish tinge to her skin, the deep lines etched across her forehead, and the tiny red veins in her eyes. "What do you wish to ask me? You clearly have something on your mind. You have been as jittery as a bucket of frogs all afternoon and, to be frank, it is getting rather tiresome. Come along, man." She rapped her stick on the floor. "What is it you want?"

He told her of Bishop Archbold's ultimatum. "You - pray forgive me for mentioning it - you are so very wealthy and naturally my first thought was that..."

Mrs Prout banged the floor once more with her stick. "Reverend Timmins!" she said, her voice icy and clipped. "You wish me to donate to the church bell fund, is that it?"

"Er, yes. Yes, that is it. If you would be so kind.."

"And you hope to persuade me to do so by alluding to my wealth?"

Timmins felt his face flushing.

"Oops!" Millicent muttered. "Bit tactless, Timmins!"

"Be quiet, Millicent!" snapped Mrs Prout "The Reverend is correct; I am very wealthy. There is no secret about that. I have also, in the past, made donations - very generous donations - to the Church. However, in recent years I have been less inclined to do so. You have done little other than rely on my contributions. You have, I am afraid to say, been singularly lax regarding the care of our beloved Church. People dislike being taken for granted, Reverend Timmins. I dislike being taken for granted."

Her voice drilled into his head. How she reminded him of his father!

"I am astounded, Reverend Timmins, that you should come here, cap in hand, begging for the money. I have bitten my tongue for far too long and now I feel it is only right you know my feelings on the subject. I fully support the Bishop on this matter. It is time, Reverend Timmins, that you got off your backside and worked harder for the good of the parish."

Her words hit Timmins amidships; he recoiled, unable to speak. Millicent slapped her thigh, the retort of palm on tightly stretched jodhpurs reverberating in Timmins' head. Surely she would not join in with the criticism? He braced himself.

To his surprise, she spoke up in his defence. "I think you are being a little unfair on Reverend Timmins, if you don't mind my saying so, old love!" she exclaimed. "He's a good sort at bottom. Besides, it's not as if he is asking for the money for his own personal use, now is it? I, for one, am glad to see that he has taken the Bishop's advice to heart and now seems to be turning over a new leaf."

Timmins stared at her.

Mrs Prout raised an eyebrow. "Oh?"

"Yes. The Vicar has already called a meeting of the Parish Church Council this week, and I'm sure he will have come up with plenty of ideas by then. All he's doing is asking you to do your part. It's easier for a camel to pass through the eye of a needle and all that. You shouldn't just sit on your cash, you know." Millicent winked at Timmins.

Their hostess noticed the gesture. She straightened her back and snapped. "If it comes to the question of sitting on one's cash, as you so vulgarly put it, then I might ask you what your contribution might be?"

"Well," Millicent, unabashed, dabbed at her mouth with her napkin, which she then placed with a flourish on the tray before sitting back on the sofa and folding her arms across her generous bosom. "If you must know, I am great friends with Evangeline Honeybell, the singer, and she is appearing in Quillinghampton shortly, at the Gaiety. I intend to hold a musical soirée in aid of the church. Evangeline will sing for us, I am sure, and we will sell tickets and have a raffle. Should raise a considerable sum for the church." Her expression told Timmins that the idea for the musical evening was as much a surprise to her as it was to him.

"Yes, that's it," she said, nodding as if to confirm it with herself. "A musical evening. What do you think of that, Reverend?"

Timmins resisted the sudden overwhelming urge to clap. "How very generous and public-spirited of you!" he said. "I cannot thank you enough! And thank you too, my dear Mrs Prout," he said, "for your hospitality this afternoon. I apologise if I have been at all indelicate in raising this matter. If I have trespassed upon your good nature at all, then I beg forgiveness."

"Humph!" Mrs Prout snorted. "All very fine, I am sure. I am glad for you, Vicar, that your visit here today has not been entirely without purpose." She looked at him thoughtfully for some time before she continued. "I am disinclined to donate any money as things stand. The failure of the bells is, I fear, synonymous with the decline in attendance at services and both are because of your laziness, Reverend Timmins. However, now that I see you are stirring your stumps, I venture to hope things will change. When I next see my solicitor, Mr Bungay, I will raise the matter of my will with him."

Timmins clasped his hands together. "That is such a relief, dear madam," he began, but she interrupted him.

"Do not think, Reverend, that this lets you off the hook entirely. You cannot go through life waiting for other people to bail you out of difficulties."

"No, of course..."

"You will still have to prove yourself and make up the full sum required," she said. "Besides which, I have every intention of remaining on this earth for a great deal longer." Mrs Prout sank back against the cushions, suddenly breathless and pale.

He stood. "I cannot thank you ladies enough," he said. "You are both truly generous. I assure you I will repay your generosity with renewed efforts on my part. And now I must leave you, I am afraid. I have other duties to attend to."

He left Tall Trees with a spring in his step. Mrs Whibley had promised to make one of her delicious steak and kidney pies for his evening meal.

CHAPTER FOUR

THE MEETING

Later that week, Timmins ventured out into the icy, wind-blown rain and scurried to the church hall for the Parish Council meeting. He was late and very apprehensive. What if nobody came? Then what would he do? If it proved, as he feared, that his own former idleness and apathy had taken hold amongst other members of the community, then he might well find an empty church hall awaiting him.

He need not have worried; the lights were on. A small thrill of excitement whirled up in his chest as he entered the tiled lobby. Steam and an odour of damp wool rose from the sodden coats hanging on the big brass hooks, and he heard the drip, drip, drip of water from the several umbrellas in the large, cast-iron umbrella stand. He took off his own coat, hung it on the only available spare hook, then stepped through into the hall itself.

It was fuggy in the meeting room and his spectacles steamed up. As he polished them, he observed that not only was each member of the PCC present, but several interested villagers had also turned up. Lavinia was serving tea and Harold Bungay, the local solicitor, was in earnest discussion with Millicent Gore-Hatherley. Small groups of people were dotted around the room. Why had he worried? All it had taken was one letter from him, and they had all come out on this cold January night.

"Dear friends," he said, but nobody responded. Not one person had noticed his arrival. He cleared his throat and took a step further into the room. "Friends!" he said more loudly. One or two people glanced in his direction. How vexing! This was not a social gathering! There was important business to discuss; business that might very well affect his future. He would have to be firmer if he was to take control. Filling his lungs, he roared, "Your attention, please!"

As everyone turned, the door opened, admitting a blast of cold air and Poffley, who raced into the room, barking excitedly, followed at speed by Edna Dobson in a gabardine mackintosh and headscarf. She chased the dog round the hall, finally capturing him in the kitchen.

"Sorry, Vicar," she said, winding the dog's lead round her wrist so that he could not escape again. "I had no choice but to bring the dratted animal. Mrs Prout isn't feeling too well this evening, and she wanted Poffley out of the house. He can be noisy, you see. "I'll tie him up to the umbrella stand - he should be all right out there." she said. The two of them disappeared into the lobby.

"Hello, Timmins," chortled Bungay, "kind of you to announce the beast's arrival in that fashion! Ha! At least the dog gets noticed when he walks into a room! How long have you been there? You should have told us you were here, we would have jumped to attention, wouldn't we, ladies and gents?"

Timmins frowned. Why did Bungay treat him with so little respect?

Edna Dobson reappeared. "Sorry again for the disturbance – he's a blooming nuisance!"

"Well, now we are all here, can we not jolly well just get on with things?" Millicent exclaimed. "Don't know about you chaps, but I'd like to get home before midnight tonight. There's a jolly good single malt with my name on it waiting for me back at the Hall, and I'm halfway through the latest Blossom Madgwick novel. Keen to get back to it, don't you know?"

There was a murmur of agreement.

Timmins cleared his throat. "Ladies and gentlemen, Miss Gore-Hatherley is right; we should press on. I see that Miss Bellamy has furnished you all with light refreshments, so might I suggest that we take our seats and embark upon the matter in hand." He waited impatiently until the scraping of chairs and negotiations about who was to sit where had ceased. Finally, an expectant hush fell.

"Spit it out!" Bungay exclaimed. "We're all on tenterhooks here, wondering why you've called this meeting. Can't remember when we had the last one!" He patted his ample belly. "I rushed my dinner so I wouldn't be late, so don't keep it to yourself. Spill the beans!"

Timmins hesitated. How much should he tell them of what the Bishop had said? He could not - would not - tell them that his position as Vicar of Quillington Parva was in danger. "As you may all be aware, a few days ago I received a visit from our new Bishop, the esteemed Bishop Archbold, and he is most keen that I... that is to say, that we... "

"Tea, Reverend?" Lavinia appeared, bearing a delicate china cup and saucer. "Two sugars?" The cup rattled as she placed it in front of him.

"Most kind," he replied. "Most kind. Now," he peered over his half-moon glasses at the expectant crowd, "let us get down to business. Bishop Archbold is most keen that we increase the congregation and that we raise some money. For some time now, two bells have been out of action, and he thinks it would be nice if we could rectify that situation."

"Ha! You mean he gave you a ticking-off, eh? Told you to pull your finger out, did he?" boomed Bungay.

"I beg your pardon?'"

Bungay leaned back in his chair, the buttons of his tweed waistcoat straining across his ample belly. With evident glee, he continued. "I met the fella last week. He's the chum of an old pal of mine, don't you know. They were at Winchester together, apparently, and then again at Oxford. He's a decent sort, but an ambitious blighter, I'd say. Keen to make his mark. Sort of chap who'd give a man a hard time if that man was slacking."

Timmins felt the colour rush to his face. He gave an embarrassed cough, fidgeted, and was just about to reply when Millicent spoke up.

"Well, it's about jolly time for a shake-up around here, don't you know? New broom and all that – never a bad thing. I'm sure the Vicar has plenty of ideas, haven't you, Vicar?" She patted his hand. "Otherwise, he wouldn't have called us all to this meeting now, would he? Mrs Prout has promised to help, although I rather fear we shall have to wait for her to shuffle off her mortal coil before that happens... Mind you, that may be quite soon. She looked pretty grim when we saw her the other day, don't you think, Reverend? Quite yellow, in fact."

Harold Bungay put down his tea and wagged a finger at Millicent. "Now come along, old gal!" he admonished. "That's not quite the ticket, is it?"

"Er, no, indeed," interjected Timmins. Millicent's comments, although reflecting fairly closely his own thoughts, were not in the best taste. He had been trying, these last few days, to banish from his mind any idea that Mrs Prout's passing would solve his problems. "No, we all wish the dear lady a speedy recovery from her current ailments, and a long and happy life thereafter. You are correct, Mr Bungay. It is up to us, as the PCC, and me in particular, to come up with a plan. We cannot sit back on our heels and await the poor lady's demise."

Millicent waved her hand. "No, no. Didn't mean that at all. I've already told the Reverend that I intend to do my bit by hosting a musical soirée at the Hall. Going to get my old chum Evangeline Honeybell to come along and give us a song or two."

There was a buzz of excitement. Evangeline Honeybell was, in the words of the Quillinghampton Gazette, a "local girl made good" and "quite the best singer of light opera ever to emerge from Quillingshire."

Millicent leaned forward. "So, Reverend, what other ideas have you come up with?"

Timmins flushed. What was he to say to them? He had no other ideas.

He took up his cup and drained the last few drops of tea. Ugh! He hated cold tea, but he needed a few moments' thinking time. "Well," he began. "I... I... Miss Bellamy, is there any more tea in the pot?"

"Oh, come along, man!" called Millicent. "We haven't got all night! surely you have something up your sleeve?"

"I have several ideas about how we might go about raising funds. I have thought of little else and I... Ah, thank you, Miss Bellamy."

Lavinia handed him a cup of tea and slipped into the vacant seat at his right hand. While he drank, he tried desperately to think. He had to come up with something else!

"Tsk tsk!" scolded Millicent. "Anyone would think you were stalling for time, Reverend. Do you, or do you not, have any suggestions to put to us? I, for one, have better things to do than to sit here watching you drink tea. Good Lord, man, we're champing at the bit for a project to work on."

Timmins groaned inwardly. Thinking on his feet had never been one of his strengths. He opened his mouth, hoping that inspiration would strike as he spoke. "Well," he began, "I...."

Lavinia interrupted him. "Why do you not tell them about your idea of holding a Beetle Drive, Reverend?"

Timmins stared at her. Beetle Drive? What was she talking about? They had discussed no such thing. "I do not..." he began, but as he spoke, he noticed the tiniest flutter of her eyelid. She was winking at him. Light dawned. A Beetle Drive! Yes! What a good idea! Why had he not thought of it himself?

"A Beetle Drive would be an ideal way to draw in people of all ages," Lavinia was saying.

Timmins interrupted her with a grateful nod. "Thank you, Miss Bellamy." He looked Bungay in the eye. "A Beetle Drive," he said, suddenly full of confidence, "might well be the first of many enjoyable social events through which we could bring people back into the fold." He glanced at Lavinia. They were both complicit in a lie, but he knew that she had rescued him from embarrassment.

"Well, that's more like it!" Millicent said. "Haven't been to a Beetle Drive in years. Good fun. Advertise it round the village. Charge a few pennies per entrant? Sell raffle tickets, refreshments – it'll raise a few bob and give people a good time into the bargain. What do you say, Dorothy? Brenda? Janet?" One by one, the other ladies voiced their approval.

"Jolly good. We'll get cracking on the organisation, Vicar," she said, taking another pinch of snuff. "Something to get our teeth into at last, eh, ladies?"

Timmins felt a glow of pleasure, but it did not last. Bungay's voice cut across the excited chatter of the women. "That's all well and good," he intoned, "but one Beetle Drive will not cut the mustard. You'll raise a few pounds, granted, but not enough to mend the bells. Still, I imagine that you've got some other plans up your sleeve, eh? An intelligent chap like you? Come on, don't keep us in suspenders! Or is that really the only thing you've come up with?"

Lavinia pushed back her chair and stood up. "Would anyone else like more tea? I can make a fresh pot." She gestured towards Dorothy Manifold. "This lovely lady has been kind enough to bring us some of her wonderful flapjacks. I'm sure we can all find room for one of those?"

While Lavinia made and served the tea, and handed round the flapjacks, Timmins racked his brains to think of an idea that would prove he was a man of vision and, better still, would wipe the smug look from Bungay's face. When all was calm again, the members of the Parochial Church Council looked at him expectantly. The clock ticked. Bungay raised an eyebrow.

Timmins opened his mouth.

Poffley, out in the lobby, barked.

"Dog show!" exclaimed Timmins. "Yes, a dog show – in the summer. And a fête. It's been a long while since we have had a village fête; we should reintroduce it, perhaps to coincide with St Uncumber's Day, and we could reinstate the ancient St Uncumber's procession. It was customary, years ago, for the local girls to parade through the village in the guise of St Uncumber..." He pointed to the painting of the saint hanging over the doorway. It depicted a rather hirsute young woman.

"Wearing beards!" Bungay interrupted. "The parade of bearded girls!" He laughed. "A goatee for Miss Bellamy, I think! What d'you say, Timmins? Think it'd suit her? And you, Millicent, I can picture you with a bushy great beard and a droopy moustache! Or perhaps a set of muttonchops!" He took out a handkerchief and blew his nose. "I can just see it now!"

Timmins bridled. Apart from him and Millicent, everyone was

laughing. This was intolerable! "I will have you know," he said, "that such parades were common in Quillington Parva for hundreds of years. It is, in fact, one of our oldest traditions, begun by an ancestor of yours, Miss Gore-Hatherley, back in the sixteenth century."

"Oh, yes?" Millicent's voice was frosty. She glared at Bungay.

"Yes," Timmins continued. "A certain Lady Edith de Gorey, back in the fifteenth century, developed whiskers in her middle years and her husband spurned her. Distraught, she sought solace in the Church, and prayed for help to St Uncumber. She was responsible for the building of the church and its dedication to Saint Uncumber, then created the parade in her honour."

"Yes, I seem to remember my old granny telling me something about it." Bungay said. "Custom died out a long time ago, but it might be rather fun to bring it back. Should attract quite a crowd into the village and be rather a lark into the bargain." He nodded. "Good show, Timmins."

Just then, Lavinia came back into the room bearing a tray full of cups and saucers and a large plate of biscuits.

"Thank you, Miss Bellamy," Timmins said. "I could fancy a biscuit or two now. I rather think this meeting will prove very productive. We shall show Bishop Archbold that he should not underestimate the people of Quillington Parva!" Poffley barked again, and Timmins made a mental note to save him a digestive.

CHAPTER FIVE

THE ENTERTAINMENT

In the following days there was a spring in the step of the Reverend Samuel Timmins. He had left the meeting with a long list of projects designed to fulfil the Bishop's demands, and his hopes were high. The first of the planned events, the musical soirée, took place a fortnight later. On a cold and frosty evening, Timmins motored up the twisting driveway to Hatherley Court. Passing under the turreted gatehouse into the gravelled courtyard, he hummed a few bars from a Stanley Lupino song he had heard on the wireless that morning.

'Some people make a fuss when a thing goes wrong,
Some start to swear and cuss, others sing a song.
I don't do either, that's all naphoo.
When a thing goes wrong with me, this is what I do.

I lift up my finger and I say,
'Tweet tweet, shush shush, now now, come come'
And there's no need to linger when I say,
'Tweet tweet, shush shush, now now, come come.'

Lights blazed from the mullioned windows of the handsome red brick Tudor manor house, and there were several cars parked on the gravel sweep. 'Good-oh! Looks as if it will be a good turnout this evening,' he thought, as he came to a halt next to Harold Bungay's shiny black Morris Cowley. He clambered awkwardly out of the Austin, crunched across the gravel to the porch with its low arch, and tugged at the bellpull. The heavy oak door swung open to reveal a liveried footman who showed him into the panelled entrance hall and relieved him of his coat.
Sproat, the butler, appeared, and Miss Gore-Hatherley's grey lurcher, Gentleman, ambled forward, circling him and sniffing

disdainfully. "Good evening, Reverend," Sproat wheezed, setting off in a rheumatic shuffle towards the Great Hall. "Kindly follow me." Timmins obliged, and Gentleman brought up the rear.

A fire blazed in the huge stone fireplace and a piano tinkled merrily. Women sipped champagne cocktails, gossiped and glittered in jewels and figure-hugging gowns, while the men, like so many oversized penguins in their crisp, stiff white shirt fronts and black tailcoats, quaffed whisky and swapped anecdotes in booming voices.

Sproat cleared his throat and in a thready whisper announced, "The Reverend Samuel Timmins!" His voice went unheard, and, with an apologetic glance, he prepared for a second attempt.

"There is no need," Timmins said, scanning the room for his hostess. A woman in dusky pink crêpe de chine and pearls gave him a little wave. She seemed somewhat familiar, but before he could place her, she had disappeared in the ebb and flow of the crowd. Who could she be?

"Reverend Timmins! I say! There you are at last!"

Timmins recognised Millicent's stentorian tones issuing from somewhere amongst the sea of faces. "Miss Gore-Hatherley?" he enquired. "Where are you?"

"Here I am!" His hostess, clad in a deeply unflattering orange and yellow evening dress, was barrelling her way energetically towards him. Millicent was not an elegant woman, but what she lacked in grace she certainly made up for in enthusiasm and in her wake, one or two people winced from the pain of a trampled foot. She sported a turban from which sprouted a foot high peacock feather that bobbed and danced as she spoke. "We've been waiting for you, Reverend. You're jolly late, you know! And you've brought the beast in with you! Why did you do that? Does 'oo want your tummy tickled? Does 'oo?"

"I beg your pardon?" The offer startled Timmins until he realised that she was addressing Gentleman, who had thrown himself onto his back and lay with all four paws up in the air and his tongue lolling.

Millicent bent to rub the dog's belly, her peacock feather waving wildly. When she straightened up, she was red in the face. "Silly boy!" she said, affectionately, and again, Timmins was not sure to whom she referred. "He's not really invited this evening, but as you've let him in, I suppose he can stay. Now, what do you think, Reverend? Good crowd, eh? And they've all paid quite a whack for the bally tickets! Should boost the old coffers! Tell you what, come and meet dear old Evangeline. She is rather keen to meet you. Between you, me and the gatepost, she's got a thing about men of the church, Lord knows why! Sees them as a challenge, I suppose." She wheeled round and ploughed her way back through the guests who, this time, stepped nimbly out of harm's way.

Timmins followed her, acknowledging those people he recognised. Bungay raised a glass to him and drained its contents, and the woman in the dusky pink dress gave another wave. Now he recognised her. "Good grief! That's Lavinia!" Not only was she most becomingly attired, but - good Lord! - she was wearing lipstick and eyeshadow. And rouge? For a split second he experienced a long-forgotten flutter of excitement. But there was no point in being sentimental; there had been nothing between him and Lavinia for years.

Millicent grabbed him by the sleeve and pulled him towards her. "Come along, man! Don't dawdle! Evangeline, old sprout, allow me to introduce you to our vicar, Samuel Timmins, and Vicar, pray meet my good chum, Evangeline!"

A lumpy vision in sea-green silk and a purple feather boa shimmered before him in an overwhelming cloud of perfume which he recognised as Nuit d 'Amour, a favourite of his mother's. She squealed, offering him her puffy white hand to kiss. He noted the unevenly arched eyebrows, the full lips with their smudged crimson lipstick and the pencilled-in beauty spot by the right eye. Good Lord, she was quite a sight to behold! From a distance, she appeared quite youthful, but a closer inspection showed the truth.

She pouted and fluttered her eyelashes.

Timmins collected himself. "Delighted, I'm sure."

Evangeline giggled. "Millie dearest, our friend here is quite ... overcome!" She gave Timmins a playful push. "No need to be shy, Vicar! You must not allow my fame to overawe you." She reached out a bejewelled finger and tapped him playfully on the chest, glancing at him coyly. "What are you thinking, I wonder? You are such a mystery, you men of the cloth, for men you are, and I know men." For an instant, her face clouded with an expression of great sadness. "And yet the nature of your calling offers such reassurance and promises such a place of safety. Quite a conundrum. Quite a delectable conundrum!" She giggled. "I am sure we shall become quite the best of friends!"

Timmins blushed. "Er, yes. Yes, I am sure we shall," he stuttered, resolving to avoid her henceforward. "Delighted, I'm sure. Hrrmph. Yes."

"Dear old Evangeline has done us the singular honour of ducking out of a rehearsal to come and sing a few ditties for us. She's on at the Gaiety next week, you know, doing that Gilbert and Sullivan thing. What's it called? Something about an apron..."

"Pinafore, Millie, dearest, HMS Pinafore. I am giving my Buttercup once again, by popular demand." She cast a winsome glance at Timmins.

"We are very lucky to have so distinguished an artist with us this evening! Ha! How honoured we are!" He knew he was babbling. "Welcome, Miss Honeybell, to our quiet little village, and may I thank you, on behalf of us all."

"Oh, my dear Reverend – or may I call you Samuel? I am so pleased to be here. Quillington Parva is a delightful village, the church is beautiful, and, may I say, its vicar is devilishly handsome." She glanced at him playfully over the feathered fan, beads of sweat glistening on her top lip.

Could she say nothing without flirting in that ghastly manner? "You are too kind!" he mumbled.

A soft white hand reached out and stroked his face. The intimate gesture made him shudder, and he recoiled with a gasp of dismay which he quickly converted to a loud cough. "Eeugh!

Harr! Hrrmph!"

"My dear man, there is no need for embarrassment! I speak my mind – it was ever one of my failings – and I find you... most attractive. Perhaps we might find a quiet space together for a cosy little drink and a chat after I have given my recital? I think you shall find that I can be most... generous!"

Timmins stared. What could she mean? From the way she ran her tongue suggestively over her top lip, it would appear that she had more in mind than donating money. Good Lord, she was shameless! He blushed. "A drink? Er, yes. Perhaps," he said. "But, er, I long to hear you sing." What he really longed for was the safety of his own cosy sitting-room, out of reach of this predatory female.

"Dear boy!" she replied, fluttering her eyelashes again and blowing him a kiss. "I shall sing for you, and you alone!" She shimmied over to the piano and struck a pose.

Millicent clapped her hands again. "Take a pew, everyone! We are in for a real treat, a musical delight performed for us by a supremely talented singer, one of my oldest and dearest chums, Evangeline Honeybell."

Timmins took up a position by the door. Could he make his excuses and leave early? He would miss dinner, but he was keen to escape before that appalling woman made any more suggestive remarks. He had his reputation to consider, and she was so... colourful, so forceful, and so perfumed.

Millicent's hectoring tones interrupted his thoughts. "Come along, Vicar! You're keeping us all waiting. There's a seat here for you, right at the front, next to me."

There was to be no escape. He made his way to the front of the room and took the only vacant chair, squeezed between Millicent and Harold Bungay. Gentleman, who was sitting in front of the empty chair, got up as he approached, and moved to flop down, paws outstretched, next to his mistress at the end of the row. A faint aroma of dog remained.

"I shall begin my little entertainment," Evangeline announced, "with 'O Foolish Fay', sung by the Queen of the Fairies in

Iolanthe. I do so hope you will enjoy it." She cleared her throat, struck a pose, signalled to the pianist and sang.

"Oh foolish fay
Think you because
This brave array
My bosom thaws
I'd disobey our fairy laws
Because I fly
In realms above
In tendency
To fall in love
Resemble I the am'rous dove..."

While she sang, she continued to gaze at Timmins.

Bungay finished his drink and hiccuped. "I shay," he said, in what he clearly thought was a whisper. "Think she's taken rather a shine to you, what? Think you've got a fan there!"
Timmins did not respond. He had tried to avoid looking at Evangeline and was counting the beats of the music with his index finger.

Bungay, however, was not an easy man to ignore. He had also drunk several large glasses of sherry. "Psst! Timmins! She's giving you the glad eye. I think you are in with a chance if you play your cards right." He nudged Timmins. By now, people were shushing him, and Evangeline glared at him as she sang the closing lyrics;

"Could thy Brigade,
With cold cascade,
Quench my great love, I wonder!"

There was rapturous applause. "And now," announced

Evangeline, "a little song from The Yeomen of the Guard, entitled 'Were I thy Bride." Again, she signalled to the pianist and sang. Again, she appeared to address the song to Timmins and as she sang, Bungay nudged Timmins, chortling quietly. By the time the song was nearing its end, Timmins had had enough; he turned to the solicitor, and whispered, "Kindly refrain from intruding your elbow into my ribs and desist with the ribald comments. It is ungentlemanly of you to speak of a... a lady... in that fashion."

"Whassat? D'you say something? Whattdyousay?" Bungay had taken out a large white handkerchief and was mopping his shiny red face. "She'd give you a run for your money, all right. Hot-blooded filly, that one."

Timmins raised his voice. "I said, do not speak of Miss Honeybell like that! You impugn her honour. One does not speak aloud of a lady in that fashion, whatever one's opinion of her. She is the most talented singer I have the greatest admiration for her."

It was unfortunate that, just as he spoke the final sentence, the song finished, Timmins' voice rang out loud and clear and she heard every word. She gave him another little pout and blew him a kiss. There was a little ripple of laughter and Timmins blushed. Oh, dear!

'And now, I would like to 'Spread a Little Happiness' with my next song. Maestro, please!' She sang again and Timmins, realising that he had no alternative but to remain seated for the rest of the performance, sank back in his chair and made up his mind to enjoy it. As soon as it was over, he told himself, he would thank Miss Gore-Hatherley for her support, plead a headache and make good his escape to the vicarage. Miss Honeybell would be in demand for autographs, and he could slip away without her noticing.

An hour later, the singer took her final bow and Timmins, thankful that the performance was over, turned to Millicent. "I have such a headache. I fear I must return to the peace and quiet of the Vicarage."

His hostess, however, had other ideas. "Oh, you poor old thing!

41

But course there is no question of you leaving - Evangeline's been so eager to have a chin-wag with you. Mustn't let a little thing like a headache stop you from having fun. We can soon get that sorted!" She signalled to Sproat and ordered him to fetch aspirin, then thanked Evangeline for her performance and announced that dinner was served.

Timmins, to his dismay, was to escort the singer. Reluctantly, he approached her and offered his elbow. Placing her plump white arm through his, Evangeline gazed up at him. 'My dear man,' she said, 'how perfectly delightful!' Together they made their way into the dining room.

Candles flickered on the vast table, reflecting in the silver tableware and crystal glasses. Their hostess had placed the singer on her right, and next to her, Harold Bungay. Timmins sat opposite Evangeline with Lavinia on his left. Sproat appeared at his side with the aspirin on a little silver salver.

"This is nice,' Lavinia said. 'Millicent knows how to throw a good party."

"She does,' he replied, swallowing two tablets. 'May I compliment you on your dress? It is very fetching."

Lavinia beamed. "You are too kind!"

"Yes," continued Timmins. "Quite a change from your usual plain attire. I did not recognise you at first. Most refreshing."

A slight frown flickered across Lavinia's face.

"Put your foot in it there, Timmins!" Bungay had overheard his remark. He raised his glass to Lavinia. "Take no notice of him, my dear! You're pretty as a picture! Always are!"

"Oh, Good Lord! I did not mean to insult you, Miss Bellamy! Forgive me - I simply meant... "

"There is no need to apologise, Reverend. I am sure you had no such intention." Lavinia's tone was polite but distant. She turned to speak to the handsome young man on her left, and Timmins sighed. Why was he always in the line of fire? If it wasn't his family telling him he was useless, or the Bishop saying pretty much the same thing, it was Bungay criticising him, Lavinia being frosty or that dreadful woman making fun of him. A footman appeared at his side with a tureen of mulligatawny soup. Timmins ladled some into his bowl, his stomach rumbling and, with gusto, he plunged his silver spoon into the steaming broth.

Millicent coughed. "Reverend Timmins,' she said, 'is there not something you have forgotten?"

What was she talking about? What could he have forgotten? They were all looking at him. Was this some kind of game?

Lavinia raised her hand to cover her mouth in the pretence of a cough. 'Grace!' she hissed.

Of course! How on earth could he have forgotten? " Apologising, he offered thanks for the meal and had had just taken his first mouthful of the spicy soup when there was a stirring under the table. Something nudged his leg. He looked up, surprised.

Evangeline Honeybell was looking at him.

"Dear Reverend Timmins,' she said, 'did you enjoy my little entertainment?"

There it was again! Something had definitely touched his leg - higher up this time, and altogether too intimately. He gulped. "Er, the entertainment?" he squeaked. "Yes, quite..." Another nudge. "MARVELLOUS!" The word came out far more loudly than he had expected. Evangeline gave a trill of laughter and blew him a little kiss.

"Are you all right, Vicar?" Millicent asked.

Just then, Lavinia squealed. "Oh! I say! Something just... that is... oh dear!"

"What is it, Miss Bellamy?" enquired Harold Bungay. "Got a problem?"

Lavinia gave an embarrassed little cough. "No, it's nothing. Just that something... under the table."

Bungay put down his napkin, pushed back his chair and peered under the table. "That dog's - hic - got in here! Ha! Miss Bellamy entertaining a Gentleman under the table - I say! Gave you a shock, did he, old girl? Tickled your fancy? Hic!"

"That blasted animal!' Millicent barked. 'He should not be in here!"

Bungay dragged Gentleman from his hiding-place by the collar, and a footman took him out of the room.

Timmins glanced at Lavinia. Bungay's off-colour remark had clearly upset her. He was about to rebuke the solicitor when something under the table caressed his leg. Across the table, Evangeline winked and blew him a kiss.

The rest of the dinner passed in an agony of embarrassment for Timmins as the singer continued her flirting - winking, making suggestive remarks and, worst of all, tickling his leg with her foot. How could he rebuke her without disgracing her and making himself look foolish? He would have to endure it.

When, finally, dinner was over, the guests adjourned to the Great Hall for dancing. Evangeline, tapping the Vicar playfully on the cheek with her fan, whispered, "I'm just off to powder my nose, and when I come back, I intend to dance the night away in your arms, dear man."

Timmins watched as she waddled uncertainly out of the room. She was rather the worse for wear. Threading his way through the throng of guests, he made good his escape to the quiet of the library, closed the door behind him and leaned against it, relieved. He needed a few moments to recover his equanimity. The silence in the room buzzed in his ears and he felt suddenly dizzy. He needed to sit down for a while. Lowering himself into the comfortable armchair, he reflected upon the evening's events. What had he done to attract the unwanted attentions of that woman? It was unbearable. He must insist to Miss Gore-Hatherley that he needed to go home.

A slight noise told him that someone had come into the library and a strong whiff of Nuit d'Amour confirmed his worst suspicions. He jumped up from his chair.

'So this is where you are hiding, Vicar dear,' Evangeline trilled, advancing towards him. "We... I... missed you." She sat on the arm of his chair and leaned against him, bulky and soft. She put one arm across the back of the chair, thrusting her enormous bosom uncomfortably close to him. "You are a naughty boy to run away from little Evangeline. She's been lonely without you."

She walked her fingers slowly up his arm. "Naughty, naughty boy." The smell of alcohol mingled with the heavy perfume and the faint tang of sweat.

Timmins blushed. "Really, Madam," he gasped, "You should not... er... I... um. Oh dear!"

Before he could say any more, she reached out, lifted his chin and pulled him to her, planting a full and rather wet kiss on his lips. 'Errggghhh!' he spluttered as she let him go for an instant. "Madame Evangeline!!!" He struggled desperately to get out of the armchair, but she pushed him down again, put her index finger on his lips and shook her head.

"No, dearest one, do not utter words of love just yet. Let us revel in the beauty of our shared passion." She picked up his hand and clasped it to her breast. "Oooohhh!" She shuddered, and before he could utter another word, she kissed him again, with even more ferocity this time.

At last, he pulled away from her. "My dear woman!" he exclaimed, horror and anger giving him the strength to get out of the armchair, "What do you think you are doing? I have given you no cause to believe that I admire you in a physical sense, nor that I would welcome such an encounter. Good grief, we have only just met! Besides, I am a man of the cloth! I have my position to consider."

Evangeline advanced towards him again. He stepped back, only to find himself against the wall. She tottered up to him, tripping on the carpet as she came close so that she stumbled against him, her great bosom colliding softly with his chest. "Oops," she giggled, "Naughty!" and tapped him lightly on the nose. "My dear Vicar," she whispered, "I could see, from the moment we met, that your admiration for me quite overwhelmed you, and I feel the same! Our love is writ in the stars! Kiss me again."

"No. No. Absolutely not." Timmins broke free just as Madame Honeybell was about to plant another kiss. Backing away, he gabbled, "I assure you, Madam, that any interest I might have in you is purely as an artiste. I am grateful that you have given up your time to support our fund-raising, but... Ooh!" He had backed into a sofa and sat down with a thud.

"Oh, such delightful modesty!" Evangeline exclaimed. "Do not be shy! Oh, how I yearn for the love of a man like you! I knew, when our eyes met across the crowded room, that you were the one for me." She tottered across to him, collapsing on to his lap. "Oh, if you only knew how those who professed themselves my ardent admirers have betrayed me! It was my fame, or my money that attracted them." Wiping a tear from her eye, she leaned in and clasped his head to her bosom. He struggled, suffocating, but it was no use. She held him firmly. .

"But you - you are a gentleman, decent and true! A man of the cloth. You would never let me down. I would find sanctuary with you. What happiness we could share! What ecstasy!"

Just then the door opened. "Reverend Timmins? Samuel! Are you there?" It was Lavinia.

Evangeline, thrown momentarily off guard by the interruption, let go her hold on him and he thrust her from his lap. She staggered to her feet, and he leapt up from the sofa, straightening his clothes. Evangeline waved a puffy hand in dismissal. "Tell her to go, Sammy," she said. "We were having such a nice little time...Oo-er!" Having used the last of her energy batting Lavinia away, she collapsed into an armchair.

"Miss Honeybell was just..." His voice trailed off. This was most embarrassing. It would be most ungentlemanly to tell her how Evangeline had tried to seduce him, and yet it horrified him to think she might believe him to be at fault. "Was there something you wanted?"

"Well, er...first, you appear to have..." Lavinia tapped her cheek lightly. "Lipstick...?"

Timmins took out his handkerchief and wiped his cheek. "Oh dear! How embarrassing. Please allow me to explain..."

Lavinia touched his arm lightly. "Do not trouble yourself. No need. I see that Madame Evangeline is a trifle... Perhaps she has had a little too much wine?"

The singer was now snoring gently, her lipstick smeared across her face.

Timmins nodded. "Yes,' he said. 'She is rather overwrought, I fear. Perhaps we should leave her - a little peace and quiet might be what she needs."

"I shall stay to look after her, but as for you... Millicent sent me. She is about to draw the raffle and wishes you to say a few words. Evangeline was to draw the first ticket, but perhaps you could make her excuses and say she has quite tired herself and needs to rest?"

"Good Lord, yes! Yes, of course. Thank you, Lavinia, for coming to find me." As he reached the doorway, he hesitated for a moment. Lavinia was making the singer more comfortable in the armchair, placing a footstool under her feet and a cushion behind her head. Timmins felt a rush of gratitude. How could he express his thanks? "May I say how lovely you look this evening. You... you really are the belle of the ball."

Evangeline stirred and attempted to rise. She held out her arms to him. "Oh, you dear man! You like me! Come back to me! I am all yours!"

"Oh, no. Not you! No, I meant... Oh, help!" He hurried out of the room to the safety of the crowd in the Great Hall where Millicent greeted him.

"Where have you been, old sprout? Where's Evangeline?"

"Er, perhaps a little...over-tired," he began.

Millicent seemed to accept the excuse. "Not as young as she was, poor dear, and she finds it difficult to accept." She stepped back while Timmins thanked everyone for their generous support of the musical soirée and expressed his gratitude to Millicent Gore-Hatherley for hosting the event. When the applause had died down, she held out a wicker basket full of folded raffle tickets. "Here, draw the first one, there's a good chap! First prize is a pair of tickets to see Evangeline Honeybell in HMS Pinafore, followed by dinner with the lady herself."

Good God, thought Timmins - pity the poor person who gets that one! A whole evening in the company of that woman! Hastily, he drove the thought from his mind. He should not be uncharitable, but really... Plunging his hand in amongst the heap of folded tickets, he withdrew the first one. "Pink, number 233."

No-one claimed the prize.

"Come along!" Millicent exclaimed. "Somebody must have the blasted thing." Still nobody stepped forward. "Oh, this is ridiculous! Vicar, have you checked yours?"

Timmins handed the wicker basket back to her while he searched his pockets and drew out his raffle tickets. Pink. Numbers 231, 232 and...233.

CHAPTER SIX

A FALL FROM GRACE

It was a raw morning in early April. Pale sunshine glimmered through a thick covering of cloud and frost glistened on the gravestones. White arum lilies and angels' trumpets filled the freezing church, but as yet it was empty of mourners, although Mrs Prout's funeral service should have started fifteen minutes ago. Where was everybody? Timmins looked again at his watch. How long should he wait? He had already instructed the cortège to do a second circuit of Quillington Parva to give mourners time to arrive, and there was a limit to how many times the horse-drawn hearse could keep trundling up and down the same streets without rousing curiosity. Surely Millicent Gore-Hatherley and Edna Dobson would come, and perhaps Harold Bungay too? He had been Mrs Prout's solicitor for many years.

Timmins shivered with excitement. Soon he would find out the contents of Mrs Prout's will. If she had been generous to the Church, he might be able to resolve the problem of the bells! As if on cue, the cracked tenor bell tolled, its sound flattened and dissonant. He had stood here in the porch, shivering, for over half an hour now and was turning to ice. His ears and nose were red and his toes going numb. If only he had worn a vest! Cupping his hands together, he huffed into the hollow created by his palms, but the temporary relief this brought was both minimal and short-lived. He needed to get his circulation going again.

Glancing about to make sure that he was unobserved, he picked up the hems of his cassock and surplice and hopped from one foot to another, singing a Jack Hylton tune that had been going round in his head all week. It was a catchy little number, and as he sang, the hopping became a vigorous little dance.

He stopped. Someone had cleared their throat. He spun round and there before him stood Lavinia Bellamy, Edna Dobson,

Harold Bungay and Millicent Gore-Hatherley, all open-mouthed. "What on earth are you doing, Vicar?" Millicent frowned. "Hopping about like that - not very respectful, is it?"

Timmins gulped. He let go of the hems of his cassock and surplice and bent to smooth them down. "Er, a touch of cramp, don't you know? Yes, that's it. Spot of cramp in my legs. Forgive me."

Millicent glared at him. "That's as may be, Vicar, but I'll thank you to compose yourself. Dear Daphne has arrived."

Glancing over Mrs Gore-Hatherley's shoulder, Timmins saw that the elegant black hearse with its sparkling glass-panelled sides had arrived for the second time at the church gate. Four Belgian Black horses, bedecked in black feathered plumes and drapes, snorted and stamped. Their warm breath curled like little ghosts into the early spring air. Ernie Golightly, tall and spare in his black frock coat and beribboned top hat, stood at the lych-gate, pocket watch in hand, awaiting the signal that he and his pallbearers could unload the coffin.

Timmins beckoned Ernie Golightly, then signalled to the verger who scurried back inside the church. Soon, the strains of Bach's Toccata and Fugue in D minor were rolling around the interior of St Uncumber's as the brass-handled oak coffin entered the church, borne aloft by six pallbearers and preceded by the tall, thin figure of Ernie Golightly. Timmins followed. while the four mourners and Poffley, resplendent in a new black collar, brought up the rear.

The dog padded to the front of the church, sat down beside the coffin and howled.

Timmins jumped back in alarm. "Sssh! There's a good boy!"

Poffley, however, was undeterred.

"Wooooaaawwwww!"

Timmins dithered. If he waited until the music had finished, surely that would put an end to the dog's infernal noise?

"Why did you bring that dratted dog?" Bungay mouthed to Edna Dobson, covering his ears as they took their place in the front pew.

By now Poffley had hit his stride, enjoying the opportunity of exercising his lungs. "WWWAAAOOOWWW!!"

"What?" Edna cried. "I can't hear you over this din!"

Bungay shouted. "I said, why did you bring that beast to a church service? Most inappropriate!"

"I didn't! " Edna was indignant. "I'm not that daft! He must have sneaked out behind me!"

The music ended. Poffley gave one mournful "Woof!" then, pleased with his performance, lay down and gazed up at Timmins, who cleared his throat.

"Welcome, everybody, to St Uncumber's ..."

"Woof!"

Timmins stopped. He frowned at Poffley. "Welcome to ..."

"Woof, woof, woof!!"

Timmins glared at the dog, then at Edna Dobson. She got up, bending double to keep a low profile as she slipped out of the pew, and tiptoed theatrically forwards to collect Poffley. She yanked at the dog's collar. He did not budge. Edna tugged harder. Still Poffley did not move. "Come on, you blasted creature!" she hissed. As she remembered where she was, she crossed herself with a sheepish glance at Timmins, before she gave one final, almighty pull, leaning backwards with the effort.

Poffley chose that moment to spring towards Mrs Dobson, who, taken by surprise at the sudden lack of resistance, let go of the collar. She fell with a thump on to her generous backside, with a loud exclamation of "Oh, cripes!"

Timmins stepped forward to help her up but before she could take his hand Poffley, eager for some rough and tumble, launched himself at the Vicar and hit him amidships. Staggering, Timmins fell back against the pulpit, whereupon Poffley licked his face with great enthusiasm. "Oof! Stop that!" Timmins struggled to regain his feet. "Mrs Dobson! Remove this animal from the church! I am trying to conduct a funeral service!"

When Mrs Dobson, dragging a reluctant Poffley, closed the church door behind her, Timmins regained his composure, wiping his face with the hem of his surplice.

"Upstaged by a dog, eh?" Bungay said. "Whatever next?"

The rest of the service passed without incident, although Timmins, unnerved, stumbled twice over the liturgy. At last, Mrs Prout's coffin was restored to the waiting hearse and the sedate horses clip-clopped away to the cemetery. Lavinia, Millicent and Edna Dobson followed in Bungay's shiny black Morris Cowley.

Timmins was to follow in his little Austin 7. He climbed in and pressed the starter button. No response. He pressed the button again. Again, nothing. This was disastrous! The car, although always rather temperamental, had never failed to start. He tried for a third time, but without success. Blast! Today of all days! He got out of the car, took the starting handle from the boot and located it in the socket. Saying a quick prayer, he turned it. Nothing. He turned it again. Nothing. The car would not start. Bother and blast! He would arrive late for the interment. "Damn!" He did not care who heard. "Damn and bother and blast it!" He would have to walk.

With a sigh, he set off up the High Street at a brisk pace. It was hard work - he had never, since prep school, been fond of vigorous exercise. His heart thumped, sweat trickled down his face despite the cold, and before long he was gasping for air and had a painful stitch. It was no use - he simply had to rest. Bending over, hands on his knees, he panted loudly.

A small group of children in the alleyway between the Post Office and the Fat Rascal Tearoom caught his attention. They were playing hopscotch, and one, a fat, red-faced little boy with a pudding-basin haircut and freckles, was careering about on a beaten-up old push scooter. Light dawned. Scurrying over to the children, Timmins greeted the small boy. "I say, you there! Cyril Pratt, isn't it? Yes? Well now, Cyril, how would you like to earn yourself sixpence?"

Suspicion clouded Cyril's face. "'Ow?" he asked.

"I need to borrow your scooter. Will that be possible, little man?"

Cyril squinted at the vicar. "Um," he said. He was clearly a child of few words.

"Come along my lad," Timmins said, "a bright shiny sixpence. Now, what do you say? I'll bring the scooter back to you this afternoon."

Cyril shook his head. "Nah."

"What?" Timmins' voice was shrill with anxiety. "What do you mean, you little.... I mean," he steadied himself. "Think of the sweeties you could buy with a sixpence. Or perhaps you could have a lovely tea in the Fat Rascal? Wouldn't that be nice?"

Cyril nodded.

"Then will you take my sixpence?"

"Shillin'" came the terse reply.

Timmins glared at Cyril, who stared back, undaunted.

"Very well then," Timmins fished in his pocket for another sixpenny piece. "Here you are, you... you dear child." He tossed the coins at the boy who shot out a grubby hand to catch them. Timmins picked up the scooter, placed his left foot on the running board and set off toward the cemetery, pushing as fast as he could with his right foot, while Cyril pocketed the coins.

It seemed to Timmins that every single villager had emerged from their home to witness the bizarre spectacle of the vicar speeding through the village on a child's scooter. By the time he arrived at the cemetery he was blowing hard, for most of the journey had been uphill. He was also red in the face, both from the physical exertion and because of the humiliation of having to adopt such an undignified mode of transport. Skidding to a halt beside the hearse, he threw the scooter aside, rearranged his surplice, smoothed down his hair, folded his hands across his belly and bowed as the pallbearers lifted the coffin from the hearse. With as much dignity as he could muster and ignoring Millicent's terse "About time too! Where on earth have you been?" he set off behind the coffin on its short trip to the graveside, followed by the little group of mourners.

All proceeded without incident until Edna Dobson, rummaging for a handkerchief, let go of Poffley's lead. At once the dog clasped hold of Timmins' leg and began showing his affection for the vicar. Timmins tried to shake him off, but it was no use.

"Edna!" Millicent barked. "Stop that beast! This instant!"

"Easier said than done." Edna tugged hard at Poffley's collar until he loosened his grip. "I'll take him back to Tall Trees and put the kettle on. Come on, you blithering nuisance!"

Timmins longed for this dreadful morning to end! He said the final prayer at breakneck speed and had just uttered the last words when Poffley pulled away from Edna, raced back and launched himself at Timmins with a joyous "Woof!", hitting him squarely in the chest and catching him off balance. "Wooaaw!" Arms waving and legs flailing, he tumbled into the grave, landing with a heavy thud on top of the coffin.

There was a shocked silence. He gasped, breathing in the damp, earthy smells of the grave while the others peered down upon him. Then Harold Bungay guffawed. "I say, are you comfy down there?" Clapping Ernie Golightly on the shoulder, he roared, "Two for the price of one, Golightly; two for the price of one!"

The funeral director cast him a scornful glance, hitched up his trouser legs, crouched down and peered into the grave. Timmins had hauled himself into a sitting position, a pained expression on his face. "Allow me, Reverend," Golightly intoned, and, going forward on to his knees, he reached out to Timmins. With the aid of Golightly and the pallbearers, Timmins clambered out of the grave.

Bungay, overcome by mirth, slapped his thighs as the vicar emerged, dishevelled and streaked with mud, from the hole in the ground. "I say, Golightly, you're supposed to put people in the ground, not take 'em out!" roared Bungay, tears streaming down his face.

Glaring at the solicitor, Timmins rubbed his rear end – he would be unable to sit in comfort for some time, of that he was sure. Could today get any worse?

"Oh, no! Mr Bungay! You are most disrespectful!" Lavinia shook her head at the solicitor who, red in the face, took no notice of her but continued chortling with amusement at his own joke.

"Vicar! You poor dear!" puffed Edna Dobson, who had reappeared at the graveside without her canine charge. "I'm so sorry!" She patted his arm. "Miss Gore-Hatherley has taken him home with her. She's more used to dogs than I am. Oh but look at the state of you! You're covered in muck!" She beat him with her hands, from top to bottom, spinning him round as she did so and brushing the dirt from his clothing.

Timmins blushed; she should not be laying her hands upon him in such a personal manner. "Oh, dear, Mrs Dobson, please do not trouble yourself!" he cried. "Desist, I beg of you. You will make yourself dirty. I am quite all right, I assure you."

"Don't be silly, Vicar. Let me get that mud off your face." To Timmins' horror, she took her pocket handkerchief out, spat on it, took hold of his chin with one hand and dabbed at his face with the wet cloth.

"Ugh!" He recoiled. "Please don't trouble yourself, Mrs Dobson. Please!"

"Now, now, Vicar! It's just a lick and a promise." She wagged a playful finger at him. "You're worse than my little grandson."

A squeal of brakes announced the arrival of Arnold Bubb on his rusty old bicycle. Dismounting, and leaning the bicycle against a lichen-covered gravestone, he lumbered towards the vicar. "Here, you!" His voice was loud, and he was waving his fist. "Reverend! I've got a bone to pick with you! What the devil do you mean by making off with my little girl's scooter? Crying fit to burst, she is. You should be ashamed of yourself!"

Timmins freed himself from Edna's grasp. "I'm sorry?" he said, wiping his face with the hem of his surplice. "I know nothing of any little girl." He paled and backed away as Bubb lumbered towards him.

"Well, it's my Ethel's, so what've you got to say about it, eh? An' what've you done with the scooter? Eh? Eh?"

"I ... er, I..." Timmins quailed.

"Arnold Bubb, leave the vicar alone!" Lavinia stepped forward and grabbed Ethel's father by the arm. "If anyone should be ashamed, it is you, shouting at the Vicar in that loutish fashion and threatening him. You must know he would not have borrowed the scooter unless he was in desperate need, and he

55

would have brought it back. You are making a spectacle of yourself. Now, kindly leave. You will find the scooter at the entrance to the cemetery."

Arnold Bubb seemed about to protest, but Lavinia, maintaining her grip on his elbow, propelled him some way along the path. He glared over his shoulder once more at Timmins, then lumbered away.

"I say, old girl,' Bungay boomed when Lavinia returned. 'I never knew you had it in you. Bravo!"

Lavinia shrugged. "The man is a bully. He needs to learn some manners."

"Well, that was without doubt the most lively sending off I've ever been to!" Bungay said. "Most entertaining. Like a lift home to the Vicarage, Timmins? Daresay you won't want to walk back through Quillington like that; you look as if you've been dragged through a bush backwards, as my old Ma used to say. Come along, let's get you home. I think a large whisky and soda is in order, don't you?"

Timmins nodded. He most definitely did.

CHAPTER SEVEN

GOOD NEWS - AND BAD

Dorothy Manifold was renowned in Quillington Parva for her superb baking and today, thought Timmins, she had excelled herself. The windows of The Fat Rascal were a spectacle to behold. Elegant china plates piled high with fruit scones and flaky vanilla slices took pride of place at the front of the display, while behind them, fluted glass stands displayed the mouthwatering choice of larger offerings - a Victoria sandwich dusted with sugar and filled with jewel-bright jam, two plump swiss rolls; a coffee and walnut sponge smothered in coffee icing, a glistening lemon drizzle and one of the dark, spicy fruitcakes which Timmins loved.

He licked his lips. "I really deserve a treat after what I have suffered!" For a split second he was back in Mrs Prout's grave. He shivered. How humiliating! On his return to the Vicarage, he had downed a rather large whisky and taken a bath, then decided that he needed some fresh air, but the walk through the village had done nothing to lighten his mood. Everyone he passed seemed to laugh at him. A cup of tea and a morsel of something tasty would calm his nerves.

Timmins' favourite table – next to the inglenook fireplace and hidden behind an enormous parlour palm - was unoccupied. He lowered himself into the comfortable Windsor chair and studied the menu. Swiss roll or coffee and walnut? His stomach rumbled loudly, and his mouth watered as he decided first on one, then the other, and then changed his mind again. At last, inspiration struck. "Fat Rascal!" he said aloud.

"You talking to me?"

That voice! It was all too familiar! Timmins groaned. Arnold

Bubb, of all people, was sitting with his wife at a nearby table, his thinning black hair slicked down and his belly straining the buttons of a very shiny suit. Cissie Bubb put out a hand to restrain her husband, but he brushed it away, heaved himself out of his chair, fixed Timmins with an angry glare and approached with a heavy tread.

"I said, were you talking to me? Calling me fat? Flamin' cheek. I'm sitting here, quiet as you like, enjoying a birthday tea with my wife and you come in an' start insulting me. I should've given you a fourpenny one at the cemetery!" He loomed over Timmins.

"Er, no!" squeaked Timmins, pointing to the menu which trembled in his hand. "Fat Rascal... it's a scone."

"Wot?" Bubb shifted forward slightly. Timmins shrank in his seat, but Bubb simply snatched the menu and glared at it. "Humph!" he said, throwing it back down on the table. "I'll let you off - this time!" and with a last, angry glare, he turned and plodded back to his wife. A brief exchange between the couple ensued, Bubb pointing to the menu and Cissie Bubb dissolving into fits of laughter. To Timmins' relief, they got up to pay their bill and with a final scowl, Bubb followed his wife out of the tearoom.

That was close, thought Timmins, making a mental note to avoid Bubb henceforth - the fellow was clearly deranged! He studied the menu once more - fear had increased his hunger and his belly rumbled. Where was the waitress?

Finally, Dorothy Manifold herself appeared, flour-dusted as usual and armed with a crumb tray and brush. "Sorry for the delay, Vicar," she said, reaching across the table in front of him and brushing it vigorously. She gave off a faint aroma of violets and sweat. "There, all shipshape and Bristol fashion now, Vicar. Oh!" Her hand on the small of her back, she stretched. "Me back's giving me gyp something rotten," she said. "And me legs! Got terrible veins, I have, like purple mountain ranges all the way up.

You should see 'em Vicar!"

Timmins shuddered as, with one swift movement, she twisted round, took hold of the hem of her overall and lifted it up high. "Just there!" She pointed to the pattern of blue and mauve running down behind her knees. "See?"

Timmins glanced at the offending leg. "Oh, er, yes," he mumbled, feeling suddenly rather warm. This visit to the Fat Rascal was becoming rather too ... physical. "A peril of your occupation, I imagine? You have my sympathies. Can you not take time to enjoy a brief rest?"

"Bless you, dearie," she said and then, to Timmins' surprise, she pulled out a chair, sat down beside him and patted his hand. "It's kind of you to think of me, Reverend," she said. "I could do with taking the weight off for a little while."

Oh no, thought Timmins. He loved the Fat Rascal. It was, next to the Vicarage, his favourite place on earth. The one disadvantage of the tearoom, however, was Dorothy's tendency to talk. A lot. When the place was busy he could avoid her attentions by dint of shuffling a few papers about on the table and wielding a pen, but this afternoon he would have to wait for his tea while she chatted.

"Yes," Dorothy continued. "I'm a martyr to these legs, you know. My doctor says I should have them treated. They can do all sorts with injections, and they can even strip the veins right out!" She shook her head, disgust on her face. "Can you imagine it? Must look like great skinny snakes when they're out. Ugh. I wouldn't be a surgeon for all the tea in China, would you? Rummaging about people's insides? No, thank you very much. And besides," She took on a more confidential tone. "I'm not too keen on doctors, after what they did when I 'ad..." Dorothy cast a quick glance round, to make sure that nobody could overhear, then mouthed the word 'Piles'. "Couldn't walk for a week after that little procedure!" She paused, tapped Timmins on the back of his hand and pushed back her chair. "You are naughty, Vicar, keeping me chattering like this!" Little clouds of flour whirled into the air as she smoothed her apron. "Now, what can I get you? Your usual, is it? Pot of Lapsang Souchong and a slice of my fruit cake? Oh, and a Fat Rascal too? Right you are then. Shan't be a jiffy!"

Timmins put on his spectacles and picked up a copy of The Quillington Courier from the pile of papers and magazines in the corner. "Gives people something to linger over," Dorothy always said, "and the longer they linger, the more tea they'll take." Flicking through it, he came to the Obituaries page. A grainy photograph of Mrs Prout headed the column, and there was a short entry beneath the picture.

"Mrs Daphne Aurelia Prout, only daughter of the wealthy banker, Sir Ambrose Cumberbatch and his wife Honoria, third daughter of the Earl of Quillinghampton, has died, aged 85. Educated at Cheltenham Ladies' College, Daphne then attended finishing school at Brilliantmont in Lausanne, Switzerland. On her marriage to the Honourable Magnus Prout, the couple lived at Prout Court, Worcestershire until the death of Magnus Prout in 1881 at the early age of 41. Fighting in the First Boer War, at the battle of Majuba, he had received a shot in the buttocks which later became infected.
Following her husband's unfortunate demise, Mrs Prout moved to Tall Trees, a large Arts and Crafts house in the village of Quillington Parva, where she lived until her own death last Tuesday. Mrs Prout was a generous benefactor of several local charities and left a large fortune. There are no descendants."

Hmm, thought Timmins. That promised well for him. The fewer claims upon her large fortune, the better for Saint Uncumber's. How wonderful it would be if she bequeathed enough to restore the bells! He might even be able to install heating in the draughty old building. That would keep the Bishop happy. Besides, if the church was warmer then the congregation might increase and then there would certainly be no question of moving him to some ghastly parish in the city.

Dorothy Manifold hummed into view, bearing a large wooden tray. "Here we are, Vicar!" she sang. "This will perk you up - just what the doctor ordered!" She deposited the tea things on the table with the instruction to "Shout if you need anything."

Timmins' mouth watered. The grandfather clock ticked, and the aromas of beeswax and baking filled the air. There was nothing else he needed. Afternoon tea in The Fat Rascal was balm for the soul. He knew that Dorothy Manifold would allow him to linger in this favourite spot for as long as he chose, and he intended to remain there for a good long while, to purge all thoughts of the funeral and that blasted dog. "For what we are about to receive," he muttered, "may the Lord make us truly thankful!"

Which delicacy to eat first? The Fat Rascal, perhaps, bursting with fruit and topped with glistening red cherries and three toasted almonds. He made short work of it. Delicious! He poured pale, smoky tea into the dainty, bone-china cup and when the pot was empty, he yawned, resting his feet on the stretcher of the little oak table. Bliss!

The sounds of the shop doorbell and Dorothy roaring with laughter woke him. His mouth was dry and a thin trickle of drool was making its way down his chin. Dear Lord, how undignified! Had he been snoring? He sat up straight in the Windsor chair, wiping his mouth on the napkin, and picked up his fork but as he did so he noticed familiar voices and, peering through the fronds of the parlour palm, he saw, seated at a little table under the window, Lavinia, deep in conversation with Edna Dobson.

He could not face them again just yet... The thought of Edna Dobson brushing mud off his clothing, and that dreadful spit-wash, made him shudder - horrible! The two women, however, showed no signs of being ready to leave. Were they talking about him? Laughing, perhaps, at the spectacle he had presented in the graveyard? He leaned forward not, he told himself, to eavesdrop on what they were saying. No, that would be wrong. It was simply that his back was playing him up. Stretching it would do it a power of good. Resting his elbow on the table, he cupped his hand round his ear and caught the words "Mrs Prout."

"Tell me, Lavinia, who d'you reckon will end up with all her money? Has that rogue Bungay dropped any hints?" Edna Dobson had a reputation for tactlessness.

"No. He has said nothing. That would be most unprofessional. We must wait and see. I am sorry for the poor woman - I know how lonely it is to be without family, since my poor cousin died. I still miss dear Papa too."

Edna took a big bite of Victoria sandwich and munched it. "Hmm. Wonder who will get it?"

So, he was not the object of their gossip. He should stop listening...But his back really was enjoying this nice, long stretch.

"Are you certain there was no family, Edna? You worked for her for years - you would know?"

"No, dearie. No relations and no friends either, unless you count the Vicar. I think she thought of him as a friend. Popped in on the odd occasion, he did, and she was always glad to see him. She said the dog liked him too. Judging from what happened at the cemetery this morning, though, it's clear Poffley likes the Vicar more than the Vicar likes him!"

Timmins snorted.

There was a short silence and then Mrs Dobson continued, "Wonder what will happen to the poor creature now? Mr Bungay told me that Mrs Prout had planned for him to go to a new home. He's paying me to look after the dog until the new owner takes charge of him. More tea, dear?"

A rattle of teacups ensued before she continued. 'If you ask me, Vicar was a saint to call on her at all. When I first went to work for her, oh, about thirty years ago now, she weren't so bad." She gulped her tea. "But she'd become a right old misery guts. Dunno if it was just her age, but some days there was no pleasing her. I never put up with none of her nonsense though. Told her straight, I did. 'There are plenty of other jobs I said, so don't you be playing lady of the manor with me, madam, if you please.'"

"Didn't that make her angry?"

"Angry? No. Between you and me, Lavinia, she quite liked it when I stood up to her. She'd always had her own way, and once I showed her I would not allow her to push me around, she stopped trying. And it paid off because she told me she'd left me something in her will – enough to keep me comfortable."

"So, if she told you that...I mean, didn't she say who was to..."

"Get the rest of her money? Well, all she said was that she had set up some kind of trust fund to support a very dear friend. Gawd knows who that might be, but he - or she – is a lucky so-and-so and no mistake. You finished your tea, dearie? I must take that bloomin' dog out for a walk."

Behind the palm, Timmins' heart missed a beat. He was Mrs Prout's only friend – Edna had just said so. The trust fund must be for him - or rather, for the church! Marvellous! Wonderful! To celebrate, he would have another pot of tea and, yes, another Fat Rascal. Why not?

Three days later, a large white envelope bearing the crest of Bungay and Biggs, Solicitors, plopped through the Vicarage letterbox. Timmins tore it open and unfolded the single sheet of headed notepaper. It invited him to attend, at his convenience, the office of Mr Harold Bungay where he would learn "information to his advantage." He resisted the urge to whoop with delight. "This is it," he said, adjusting the hat at a jaunty angle and stepping back to admire the effect. A broad smile lit up his round, pink face, and his blue eyes twinkled. "No time like the present. 'At your own convenience,' the letter said. Well, this is a very convenient time for me, very convenient indeed."

The pale spring sunshine gladdened his heart and a cool breeze caressed his cheek. "Good Lord, what a bracing day!" he exclaimed. A tune danced into his head and he hummed as he walked, calling out "Good morning!" to everyone he passed, whether he knew them or not. It felt good to be alive.

Messrs Bungay and Biggs had their offices in an imposing, pink-washed Georgian building at the end of the High Street. In less than a quarter of an hour, Timmins was sitting in a comfortable leather chair in Bungay's vast office. He was admiring the confection of stuccoed swags and swirls of the Robert Adam ceiling when the door opened and Bungay shuffled in, puffing.

"Ah, Timmins," he said. "Praying for good news, are you?" With a wheezing laugh he lowered himself into his place at the enormous kneehole desk.

"Er, no! No, Mr Bungay. I was, in fact, admiring the beautiful ceiling and.."

"Ha! Just teasing! Now, let's get down to business, shall we? I'm sure we're both busy men. I've got clients to see, and you've probably got weddings or funerals to conduct. Which reminds me, how are you after your little mishap at the cemetery the other day?"

Timmins flinched.

"Jolly funny, really," Bungay continued. "That great hairy ginger beast knocking you headfirst into the hole! Jolly funny. Ha! Haven't seen anything so amusing in years. Oh, dear!" Gasping and red in the face, he pulled a crumpled white handkerchief from a pocket in the velvet waistcoat which strained across his vast belly and blew his nose with a loud trumpeting sound. "Jolly funny!" he repeated, opening a file on the desk. "But, to business. Dear oh dear! Now, then." He blew his nose again. "I have asked you here, Reverend, in connection with the Last Will and Testament of the late Mrs Daphne Prout." He peered at Timmins over the half-moon glasses perched precariously on the end of his nose, then shrugged his shoulders. "Hmm. Not an easy woman to get along with," he said. "Somehow, you seem to have been in her good books."

Timmins glanced sharply at the solicitor. What was he implying?

"I visited her when I could," Timmins replied, bristling, "in my capacity as her spiritual advisor, although I would be the first to confess that in the weeks prior to her death I had not seen her often - I was, you understand, busy about Parish business. I like to believe, however, that she considered me her friend. She did not have many visitors, and if I was able to offer her some comfort through our discussions and readings of the Good Book, I am glad. Our meetings were always...interesting."

"Ha! I bet they were! Especially with that damned beast, Poffley, interrupting the proceedings. Don't suppose he was at all interested in the Good Book?"

"No, indeed," Timmins replied. "He could be a trifle...testing I will admit, but the dear lady was so fond of him that I felt bound to accept his attendance at our meetings."

"Yes, yes, of course. Well, the long and the short of it is, my dear chap, that your fortitude in the face of suffering, so to speak, has brought some good fortune your way."

Timmins' heart beat a little faster.

"Yes, yes. Quite a sizable fortune, in fact."

Timmins' heart raced.

"As you might expect where such a sum of money is concerned, there are one or two conditions attached to the will... Ah, Miss

Bellamy, thank-you."

Unnoticed by Timmins, the door had opened to admit Lavinia Bellamy, who flitted in, bearing a loaded rosewood tray. "I thought you might both like a little refreshment," she said, the unexpected sound of her voice causing Timmins to jump. "I'm just lending a hand," she said. "Harold's secretary has had a bereavement in the family and I offered to step in."

"And jolly helpful she's been." Bungay said. "You'll have a cup, Vicar? And a fondant fancy? Baked by her own fair hands. Miss Bellamy, besides being an excellent secretary, is also a very good cook, it seems. Knows her way to a man's heart, don't you my dear?"

Lavinia picked up the teapot and poured out two cups, adding milk from a little silver jug. She handed a cup to Timmins, and then poured one for the solicitor, hovering at his side for all the world, Timmins thought, like a little moth fluttering round a light bulb. Was there something going on between them?

"So it would seem." Lavinia said as she left the room.

"Lovely," Bungay commented, his mouth. "Not tempted, Vicar?"

Timmins was not sure whether the solicitor was referring to the cake or to Miss Bellamy, but the thought did not linger long. This delay was torment – just what was in Mrs Prout's will? "Er, no, thank-you, Mr Bungay," he replied. "I have an appointment in a quarter of an hour – I wonder, could we...?"

"What? Oh, yes, the will. You're eager to find out what the old bird left you. I understand. Well, let's see...Ah yes!"

Brushing crumbs from his waistcoat, he peered over the half-moon glasses at Samuel Timmins. "Well, this is the top and bottom of it. Dear Mrs Prout left a legacy of a few hundred pounds to her housekeeper, Mrs Edna Dobson, and a similar sum to the Quillington Hunt, then there are one or two other smaller bequests to various charities and so on. She was a regular supporter of several of them, you understand."

Good Lord! thought Timmins. When would Bungay get to the nub of the matter? "I'm sure," he replied, "but if you could just tell me..."

"Why you are here? Yes, of course you do. Well, Reverend, you are quite the lucky dog in all this, if you will forgive me for saying so." He chuckled then beamed at Timmins, "Quite the lucky dog. Although – ha! - there is another to whom I could apply that epithet."

Timmins frowned. What was the man chuntering on about?

"Just my little joke," said the solicitor. "You – or rather, St Uncumber's Church – will eventually come in for the rest of the old lady's sizable fortune. She stipulates that I, as executor, must sell everything and that the proceeds should go towards the repair of the church bells and any future updating and maintenance of the building."

Dear Mrs Prout! What joy! What a relief! Before Timmins could stop himself, he clapped his hands together, hurriedly transforming the gesture into one of prayer. "Lord bless the dear lady. May she rest in peace."

"Hmm. Yes, of course." Bungay said, a quizzical expression on his face, "That is, eventually."

"I beg your pardon? I do not quite understand..."

"Yes," continued the solicitor, "the church will be the ultimate benefactor, but you have to earn it. She wanted to make sure that Poffley continues to live in the manner to which he has become accustomed. So you won't get full access to the money until I, as her executor, am satisfied that you, as his legal guardian, have fulfilled that condition."

Timmins stared at him. "Legal guardian? Me? Do you mean to tell me that..."

"Yes. If you wish the Church to inherit the old gal's cash, you, and you alone, must afford Poffley – ridiculous name! – a comfortable and pampered existence for the rest of his days – fillet steak for tea, regular visits to the beauty parlour and the vet - that sort of thing. You must walk him twice a day – do you a world of good. Help trim that tummy of yours."

Timmins bristled.

" Now then, let's see. Poffley's birthday is the first of January. The will stipulates that each year, on that date, if he is still hale and hearty, owing to good care provided by you, I may release a fixed amount of loot for the upkeep of the Church. He is now six. When, and if, he reaches the ripe old age of thirteen, I can hand over the rest. Should he die before he reaches that age or should there be any concern on my part that you are failing to do your duty by him, then the money will go to the Canine Defence League." He peered over his half-moons at Timmins. "That clear?"

Timmins bit his lip.

"I say, you're rather pale." Bungay picked up the little silver bell from his desk and rang it. "I'll ask Miss Bellamy for more tea – or would you prefer something stronger?"

"I want no more blasted tea!" Timmins barked. "You mean to tell me that I am expected to take that... beast ...into my home and pander to its every whim?"

"That's about the size of it. I believe Edna Dobson will drop him off at the Vicarage tomorrow." Bungay picked up the decanter. "Fancy a sherry?"

CHAPTER EIGHT

LIFE WITH POFFLEY

Timmins closed "The Amours of Amélie". What an exciting read it had been! Spying for King Louis XIV, Amélie had risked all in search of Guy, Comte de Chalfontaine, a prisoner of the English king, Charles II. The dastardly Duc d'Évergne, impoverished by gambling debts, sought to wed her with or without her consent, and it was only her supreme spirit and resourcefulness that united her with her true love. Their passionate reunion in his dingy cell brought tears to Timmins' eyes. Blossom Madgwick had done it again!

A sense of loss pervaded him, as it always did when finishing a Madgwick novel, and, as always, was accompanied by a final crashing realisation that he was back in his own life, with only himself for company. Not that such would be the case for much longer. Poffley would arrive shortly, to take up residence in the vicarage. The thought did little to lighten his sense of loss, and his low mood was worsened by the memory of the telephone call he had made to the Bishop that morning. He had thought the news of Mrs Prout's bequest would please Archbold.

"It's a start, Timmins!" the Bishop had exclaimed. "But you must not fall back into old habits, you know. Get busy, involve yourself in the community, do things! When's this dog arriving? Today? Well, look after the little blighter, Timmins. It'll do you good to have someone other than yourself to think about. And Timmins - don't muck it up!"

Gloomily, Timmins heaved himself off the sofa, poked his head the door and called, "Mrs Whibley! I'm ready for my tea now, if you would be so good."

Mrs Whibley soon appeared with a laden tea tray and, Timmins noted with interest, three pink-iced buns, each topped with a glistening scarlet cherry. "That blooming animal will be here in half an hour," she said, grimacing. "I'm not happy about it, Vicar, I can tell you. I've got enough to do without having to babysit a dog - so you must make sure you're the one who takes care of him. I've brought you some French fancies. It's odd, I could have sworn there were a dozen in that tin when I went home last night."

Timmins blushed under her steady gaze.

"The Good Lord only knows where they've all gone to - there's only them three left now." She raised an eyebrow.

Timmins, despite himself, could not resist a grin. "Yes, Mrs Whibley, I'm afraid He knows and so, I fear, do you. I am no more keen on adopting Poffley than you are, which is why, I am afraid, greed overtook me. If it is any consolation, I suffered the consequences. I had terrible heartburn for most of the night." He sat up and poured himself a cup of tea, savouring the fragrant smokiness of his favourite Lapsang Souchong.

"Here! You saying my baking made you ill?"

"No, no! Not at all!" Timmins hastened to placate her; Mrs Whibley, scorned, could be terrifying. "On the contrary! In fact, I am quite sure I shall finish these in no time at all!" He picked up one of the little cakes and ate it in two bites. "There, you see?"

She glared at him. "Well, if you ate them like that, it's no wonder you had indigestion and, if you want to know the truth, it's no surprise you've put on weight lately. If you ask me, Vicar, havin' responsibility for this dog might do you some good." She looked pointedly at his rounded stomach. "Dogs need a lot of exercise. You must get out in the fresh air no matter what the weather's like! Now, I'm popping out. I've put your clean laundry on your bed, ready for you to put away."

As he drank his tea and ate the two remaining French fancies,

Timmins could not relax. What on earth was he going to do with a lumbering great dog? There would be hairs on all the soft furnishings, the smell of dog everywhere, and worst of all, he would have to take the creature out for walks. He groaned. The odd stroll in the sunshine he did not mind; having to go out in all weathers, and twice a day, was a different matter. Still, he must put his own desires aside. In the words often used by his late, and not very much lamented, father, Colonel Sir Lionel Timmins, DSO and Bar, he, Samuel Hercules Timmins, would have to "Bite the bullet!"

The thought provoked mixed emotions in Samuel Timmins' mind. Sir Lionel, a burly, overbearing man held trenchant views on every aspect of life, and he considered Samuel to be the least satisfactory of his four offspring, thinking him "A damned cissy!" Claude Augustus, the eldest of the Timmins children, resembled his father in both build and character and delighted in teasing his brother at every opportunity, while Monica and Cecily, his two sisters, took pity on him, including him in their games. Things came to a head one day when their father came home to find the five-year-old Samuel, dressed as a baby in the old family cradle, while Monica sang him a lullaby and Cecily rocked him. "That boy needs toughening up!" Sir Lionel had bellowed. "It's time we found him a damned good school!"

Within weeks, little Samuel Timmins had stood on the doorstep of Grimwade House Preparatory School watching his parents disappear down the driveway, while behind him the wheezing housemaster had clapped a bony hand on his shoulder and urged him to "Stop those tears, young Timmins! We'll make a man of you at Grimwade, you see if we don't!"

The clanging of the doorbell startled him. This was it. Poffley had arrived. He could hear Mrs Dobson telling the dog to, "Sit!" and for a moment he considered pretending that the house was empty. If he did not answer the door, then perhaps both Mrs Dobson and the dog would go away? Again, his father's voice echoed in his head. "Where's your backbone, boy? It's only a dog, and besides, think of the church! Think of the bells!" It was no good. He had to welcome that animal into his life, no matter what disruption the beast caused. "It is a far, far better thing that I do than I have ever done," he murmured, opening the front door.

"Woof!" Poffley hurtled over the threshold and into the hallway where he snuffled about, investigating the hall stand, the stick stand and the neat row of shoes and boots lined up between the two. Edna Dobson followed at some speed, retrieved the dog by his collar and brought him to sit in front of Timmins.

"Oooh, Vicar, I'm that sorry," she said. "He pulled away from me. Got the strength of an 'orse, that one has. You must keep your wits about you with him. Not that he's in any way nasty, you understand - he ain't got a bad bone in his body. He just needs to know who's boss, don't you, Poffley? You must be the iron hand in the velvet glove with him, Vicar, or he'll run rings round you." She patted the dog's head. "Now, shall I give you the low-down on his routine?"

Timmins ushered Mrs Dobson and Poffley into the sitting room. She sat down in the chintz armchair and Poffley sprang on to the sofa where he turned round and round in tight circles, wagging his tail furiously, before flopping down and resting his head on his paws, eyebrows twitching as he watched Timmins edge his way carefully towards the second armchair.

"Now," said Mrs Dobson. "He likes a nice long walk twice a day - once in the morning and once in the evening. Don't let him off the lead for a few weeks, until you've got used to each other, or you'll have the devil's own job getting him back. He likes a bit of chicken now and then, but he puts on weight so don't you listen to him if he tries to tell you he's hungry. And watch he doesn't get into your kitchen when there's food about or – as you have seen - he'll have it."

The list of instructions and advice seemed to go on forever. Timmins' eyes glazed over as Mrs Dobson talked. It wasn't as if he had the slightest interest. What right had Mrs Prout to foist this responsibility on him? "Pah!" he exclaimed.
Poffley sat up.

Mrs Dobson stopped in mid-flow. "I beg your pardon, Vicar?"

"I'm sorry, Mrs Dobson," Timmins said. "Forgive me. Mrs Whibley tempted me with her French fancies just now, and I ate them in rather a hurry. A touch of indigestion, I'm afraid."

Edna Dobson's gaze travelled down from his face to his rotund belly. "Hmm. Well, if you'll forgive me saying so, Vicar, taking on this dog might do you a power of good, what with all the exercise you'll get. Cure your indigestion, that will." She stood up. "And now I must be off. Ta ta, Poffley." She patted the dog's head and made her way towards the door.
Timmins edged his way past the dog on the sofa and followed Mrs Dobson out into the hall.

"Thank you," he said, opening the front door. "And be sure I will take good care of Poffley, in memory of our dear Mrs Prout."

"Hmm, well, that's as maybe," she said, pulling on her gloves. "If I were you, I should start by finding out what he's up to now. He's just gone running up your stairs. Ta-ra."

Timmins closed the door. "Poffley!" he called. "Where are you? Come here!" He hurried back in to the sitting-room. Had Mrs Dobson been mistaken? Was Poffley still curled up contentedly on the sofa? No! The cushions were in a heap on the floor, his tea cup lay on its side and the milk jug had fallen over but there was no sign of Poffley, save for a faint, unpleasant doggy odour. "Oh, dear!" he exclaimed inwardly, his heart sinking. "Poffley!" he shouted again, hurrying up the stairs. "Poffley!" There was no reply. He scurried along the landing towards the one open door - that belonging to his bedroom. Poffley must be in there.

As he drew nearer, he heard a snorting, snuffling sound. What on earth was the animal up to? He burst into the room. "Poffley! What are you...?" The words died on his lips. On his bed was a twisted, rumpled mess of shirts, trousers, socks and underpants and in the middle of the mess lay Poffley, on his back, paws in the air, idly chewing on one of Timmins' favourite Argyle socks.

In the days that followed, Poffley tested the patience of both Vicar and housekeeper. Mrs Whibley's initial response to the incident of the spoiled laundry was to threaten resignation, and it was only by dint of laboriously re-ironing it himself and giving her an extra afternoon off that Timmins could persuade her to stay. "But," she had said, glaring at Timmins, "you got to keep that beast out of my way. I'm a housekeeper, not a blooming zoo keeper, and won't be responsible for my actions if he gets under my feet."

From then on, he and the dog had had scarcely a moment apart. When he sat down in the afternoon to read the Church Times, or, more often, a novel, there was Poffley at his side on the sofa, snoring. When he took a bath, Poffley was there, front paws resting on the edge of the tub, watching his every movement. When Timmins once bolted the door to prevent him from coming in, Poffley howled until Timmins, nerves shredded, heaved himself out of the soapy water and permitted him entry, whereupon he raced in to the room, tail wagging, and leapt in to the bath with a great splash that sent a tidal wave of suds spilling across the linoleum.

Poffley invaded every part of his life - even his bed. On the first night, Timmins shut him in the kitchen, but he howled so long and so loudly that Timmins capitulated, shivering his way down to the kitchen to release him, whereupon the dog raced upstairs, leapt on Timmins' bed and promptly fell asleep. "This is just for tonight," Timmins promised himself, as he tried to make himself comfortable in the remaining space on the mattress, "until he settles down and gets used to living here." Deep down he knew that once having given in to Poffley it committed him to a permanent sharing of his bed, however unpleasant the prospect. Poffley snored.

Poffley's most heinous crime, however, occurred on the first Sunday after his arrival. Snow was falling and Timmins had had no wish to stand around making polite conversation after the service, so he was home earlier than usual, greeted by the delicious aromas of dinner.Mrs Whibley was in the habit of taking the meat out of the oven just before she went home and leaving it under a cover on the kitchen table to rest. His mouth watered at the prospect of juicy roast beef, pillowy Yorkshire pudding, crunchy roast potatoes and plenty of fresh vegetables, accompanied by thick, tasty gravy made from the meat juices and topped off by the burning tang of his favourite creamed horseradish sauce. Breakfast seemed a distant memory, but he thought he would treat himself to a small sherry before lunch, as the apéritif would further enhance his enjoyment of the meal. After lunch, he decided, he would revisit one of Blossom Madgwick's earlier novels, "About Amélie", in which the plucky heiress was first recruited as a spy.

As he sipped his drink, revelling in the prospect of this treat, he heard the sound of breaking china. "Who's there?" He struggled to his feet and made his way into the hallway. "Mrs Whibley?" There was no reply. "Mrs Whibley, is that you?" he cried, louder this time. A faint snuffling came from the kitchen. Memories of his last visit to Tall Trees brought rage bubbling up inside him. Poffley! It had to be! He stepped into the kitchen and there, sure enough, was Poffley, noisily devouring the last remnants of the beef joint. He barked once and returned to gnawing on the bone.

How dare that animal take such liberties? Timmins drew himself up to his full height, threw back his shoulders, levelled the cane at Poffley in the manner of a sword fighter, and roared, "You, sir, are a blackguard! A scoundrel! A thief!! Get down from my table this instant!"

Poffley raised an eyebrow, and Timmins suddenly felt rather foolish. He had no control over the dog and the joint was ruined, anyway. He resigned himself to a meatless meal and resolved to remind Mrs Whibley to shut the kitchen door.

The biggest alteration to Timmins' lifestyle, however, was the daily walks with Poffley. Although the idea had horrified him, he had to admit that increased activity would do him good. "You've got rather tubby," he told himself, surveying his naked figure in the bathroom mirror. He had also to admit to getting puffed out at the slightest exertion. The scooter ride through Quillington Parva on the day of Mrs Prout's funeral had almost been the end of him and since that day the familiar voice in his head had plagued him, telling him "Idleness is only the refuge of weak minds!

Claude Augustus, the apple of their father's eye, had been a keen participant in all the sporting activities that Timmins despised. Much to their father's delight he had excelled at cricket, rugby, swimming, athletics, riding to hounds, shooting - anything, in fact, that required physical effort and a competitive spirit. "You should be more like your brother!" Sir Lionel remarked once to the twelve-year-old Samuel, when Claude Augustus had, for the third year running, scooped the Inter-House Sportsman of the Year trophy. "All this reading and thinking is bad for you - you want to get out there on the sports field, like a real man! Show some mettle, lad!" The result had been that Timmins, knowing he would never match up to expectations, had shrunk even further from such activities, to the detriment of his physique.

The last time he had purchased a pair of trousers from Chetwynd's Men's Outfitters in Quillinghampton, Josiah Chetwynd had informed him, much to his indignation, that he now fell into the category of "Portly Gentleman." He knew he should do something about it, but knowing and doing were two very different things. Prior to Poffley's arrival he had often resolved, and failed, to take more exercise: afterwards, he had no choice.

After their first night together, Timmins fell out of bed at six-thirty, landing with a crash. "Whassup? Eh? Oooh! Ouch!" he grumbled, shocked out of a dream of buttered crumpets. Poffley's hairy face was gazing down at him from above, his tongue lolling to one side. Shivering, Timmins sat up and rubbed his back. He groaned; he had passed most of the night clinging to the edge of the mattress, fighting for his share of the blankets and listening to Poffley's resounding snores. As if that was not bad enough, the ghastly creature had now turfed him out on to the cold, hard linoleum floor! Poffley must have made off with the rug.

The prospect of venturing out at this ungodly hour did not appeal. The weather was unseasonably cold for April, with more snow forecast. For a moment he considered climbing back into bed, but Poffley barked and leaped about, spinning round and round in his excitement so that within seconds the bed was a mess of tumbled sheets, blankets and pillows. With a deep sigh, he made his way to the bathroom and performed his ablutions, while Poffley investigated the lavatory and drank the water.

Finally, wrapped up against the icy wind that whistled round the vicarage and stung his face, Timmins set out on the first of many walks with Poffley at his side. The trees were heavy with snow, their branches lacing the white sky. The breaths of man and dog ghosted in the cold air. There had been a fresh snowfall overnight, and theirs were the first footprints on the virgin landscape. As they walked, the snow crunching beneath them, Timmins felt, to his surprise, a deep sense of pleasure. The pale light of morning, the pristine snow blanketing the world, and the clear air were quite beautiful, he thought, striding through the silent village, his father's favourite thumb stick offering support in a way its original owner never had. Poffley snuffled and panted along beside him. They saw no-one as they walked along the High Street, past the Fat Rascal tearooms and down the path which ran between the offices of Bungay and Biggs and the Toad and Ferret pub to the open fields beyond the village. Here, Poffley strained at the lead, and Timmins gave in and let him loose.

Poffley raced off through the snow. Round and round the field he ran, ears flying, mouth open and tail streaming behind him like a pennant. When the first burst of energy subsided, he pounced on the snow, burying his face in it and then running in zig-zags, stopping to bark at the whirling snowflakes. Finally, he hurled himself to the ground and rolled around, legs in the air, barking in sheer delight.

Timmins, watching this exuberant display, shivered. His toes had gone numb, and he was thinking longingly of the breakfast which Mrs Whibley would prepare for him. Bacon, a sausage perhaps, tomatoes, eggs and mushrooms, all piping hot and served with a thick slice of buttered bread - just what the doctor ordered. His mouth watering at the thought, he called Poffley. "Here, boy! Come along, Poffley!" He jangled the lead.

Poffley, however, had got his second wind and was not keen to give up his freedom just yet. With a glance at Timmins and a loud "Woof!" he sprang to his feet and set off again, tearing across the field to the far corner and disappearing through the hedge.

"Poffley! Come here, boy!" Timmins shouted into the wind, which had got up and was now blowing with some force, slicing across his face and buffeting him so he almost overbalanced. Shivering, he put his hands around his mouth to funnel the sound. "You blasted animal! Come here, sir!" There was no response. The field remained empty, and Timmins realised, with sinking spirits, that he would have to follow the dog by tracking his paw marks in the snow. And every step would take him further from his breakfast. Still, there was nothing for it - if only he had listened to Edna Dobson's advice! He set off across the field, feet sinking into the snow, which crunched and creaked with every step.

As children, he and his siblings had adored the snow. The acres of unblemished whiteness were, to their childish minds, new territory and they the explorers, the first to own it by imprinting it with their footsteps. With a pang he remembered how he and his sisters would race outdoors and jump about, yelling with laughter and claiming various patches of snow-covered ground as their own until they had churned up the entire garden, spoiling its pristine beauty until the next heavy fall. Whilst he had always enjoyed the game as much as his sisters, it had filled the young Samuel Timmins with sadness and a sense of loss to see the ruination of what had been perfect.

Today, as he made his way across the field, he surveyed the beauty of the still, white countryside, heard the rooks cawing in the bare treetops, felt the icy nip of the wind and delighted that he was, temporarily at least, master of all he surveyed. His footsteps and Poffley's tracks were the only disturbance in the acres of clean whiteness. "I am a veritable Adam in this icy world," he thought to himself, as he reached the stile, climbed halfway over and stood for a moment, surveying the wintry landscape. Inhaling the clear, crisp air, it was as if he were born again. He closed his eyes, felt the wind on his cheeks and listened to the silence.

His tummy rumbled. Time to head home. He swung his right leg over the crossbar and disaster struck! The field into which he was now about to venture lay lower than the one which he had just crossed, so there was quite a long step down, and he missed his footing. Down he went, bumping against the wooden structure. "Ow!" he yelled, and then, as he came to rest in the deep drift on the other side, "Oh, I say! Ouch!"

He lay there for a moment, dazed, as soft snow insinuated itself up his nose, into his ears and mouth and down his neck. The cold was intense and stung his skin. "Bother and damnation!" he exclaimed, sitting up and brushing as much snow as he could

79

from his face and clothing, running his finger around his collar. Doing this, however, only made things worse, for there was snow on his glove and much of it fell off as he worked, sliding down between his shirt and his bare skin.

He shivered as he realised the full horror of his situation. Not only was he cold, hungry, wet and injured, but he had also lost Poffley! What would the Bishop say? What if an accident had befallen the dog? True, there were few cars on the roads in this weather, but perhaps a tractor...? "Poffley! Poffley! Where are you? Come here, boy!"

There was no response.

"Get yourself up, lad!" his father's voice intruded into his thoughts. Memories of his father's stories about the First Boer War came drifting into Timmins' head. "Shot in the leg, don't you know, but did I let a trifle like that defeat me? No, sir! I put the pain behind me, remembered all those Timmins men who had brought glory to family and regiment in battles of old, and got myself to safety. Bagged a few of the blighters on the way too."

What was he doing, sitting here and feeling sorry for himself? He had only to get up, fight through the pain and make his way home, where he was sure to find Poffley eating a hearty breakfast. Grabbing hold of the treacherous extra step of the stile, he pulled himself on to his feet. There were no bones broken, but he was winded, bruised, and his right ankle was painful. A searing pain exploded up his leg as he put his foot down. "Oh! Ouch! Damn and blast it!" he yelled, all thoughts of emulating his father vanishing. "Blithering bother and blast! Now what am I to do? I shall have to hop all the way home. In this snow! Oh, Good Lord!"

Thanking his lucky stars he had seen fit to bring it, he retrieved his thumb stick and set off. He would not risk climbing back over the stile; instead, he hobbled along the edge of the field, following the line of the hedge, until he came to the gate which led out into Slugwash Lane. This would lead him back to the village. The wind had increased in intensity and whipped around him. Adding insult to injury, the snow was now falling thick and fast. He slid and slipped, his ankle throbbing more and more with every step, and when, exhausted, he reached the end of Slugwash Lane he did not, at first, hear Lavinia's voice calling him.

"Reverend Timmins! Are you alright? Samuel!"

Lavinia stood before him, coatless, with slippers on her feet. She wore a concerned expression. "You appear to have injured yourself!" she said, hugging herself against the biting wind. "Won't you come in and get warm?"

Timmins' first impulse was to refuse the offer. He had made it this far. As his father had so often said, "Timmins men are strong. They do not surrender in the face of hardship."

"Th-thank-you," he stuttered, "b-b-but there is no need. I sh-sh-shall b-b-be home s-s-soon."

Lavinia Tutted and shook her head. "Oh, no!" she said, "Look at the state of you! You must take shelter in my cottage." Shivering, she pulled her cardigan more around her, and as Timmins made as if to continue with his journey, she burst out, "I must insist, Reverend. I have soup on the hob - that should warm you up, and I baked bread this morning. Do, please, come in."

The thought of soup and fresh bread - perhaps spread with a thick layer of yellow butter - made Timmins' mouth water. After all, he had missed breakfast... Besides, he could not allow Lavinia to stand out in the snow any longer. "Very well, if you insist," he said, and he limped after her as she opened the gate of the little thatched cottage.

CHAPTER NINE

IN LAVINIA'S COTTAGE

An intoxicating cocktail of aromas filled the warm kitchen of Meadowsweet Cottage – clean laundry, beeswax polish, fresh-baked bread and, most inviting of all, the smell of something delicious bubbling away on the hob. His injured ankle temporarily forgotten, he stood sniffing the fragrant air. Lavinia was watching him, a bemused expression on her face. Did she doubt his level of pain? He exhaled, wincing. "Ooooohh! My dear Miss Bellamy! You are most kind to offer me ... agh! ... shelter... oooh!... from the elements. I am sure I ... ow! lack the strength required to complete ... oooh! ... the journey back to the Vicarage. I am quite ... quite ... faint from lack of sustenance and the pain in my ankle. May I ... please ... sit down?"

"Of course!" Lavinia exclaimed.

With her help, he struggled out of his sodden outer garments and hobbled over to the worn old Windsor armchair before the crackling fire. Memories flooded back of the Reverend Ambrose Bellamy, who, in his declining years, had liked to sit in this chair of an evening; in the summer it would be by the sitting-room window so he could admire his garden, and in the winter it would be as it was now, by the fireside where he could toast his feet for, as he often said, he was a "chilly mortal". Timmins had been fond of the old man. In fact, he still missed him.

He settled himself into the chair. His ankle throbbed, and a searing agony made him wince each time he moved.

"We had better see to that ankle, don't you think?" Lavinia said.

"I do." His heart sank. How was he to achieve this manoeuvre without embarrassing himself? Putting on and removing his socks and shoes involved a lot of puffing, panting and grunting.

Pulling in his stomach, he leaned forward to attempt the operation, but Lavinia forestalled him, kneeling at his feet.

"It will be easier if I do it." She unlaced and removed the boot from his uninjured foot. "I am afraid," she said, as she gently lifted the injured foot, "that this might be a little painful. Prepare yourself ..."

Timmins paled. He gripped the arms of the chair as Lavinia tugged at the boot and pain knifed up his leg. "Aaagh! Ow!" he yelled, unable to stop himself. With another tug, the boot was off and as the blood flowed, the pain grew worse, and he sucked air between clenched teeth.

Lavinia stuffed the boots with newspaper and placed them before the fire to dry. She took a bottle of brandy and a glass from a cupboard and poured a generous measure. "Here. This will help. I keep it for emergencies."

Timmins took the glass and swallowed the fiery liquid in one draught, gasping as it burned its way down his throat. "Gah! Goodness! Hah! Hem!" He was not used to spirits. "That ... that certainly ... certainly takes one's mind off.... anything else!" He closed his eyes, enjoying the woozy sensation of his muscles relaxing. "Thank you. If I may, I shall just sit here for a while until I dry out, and then I shall make my way back to the Vicarage."

Lavinia had put away the brandy bottle. She frowned. "Is that wise? Your ankle has swollen. I really think you should rest here for a while and besides," she smiled, "I would welcome the company. It would be quite like old times."

Timmins stiffened. Old times? Yes, they had been very close - but that was a long time ago now. She and that dratted brother of his, Claude Augustus, had hurt him badly - how could she expect him to forget? He swallowed. "I would prefer to go home."

She shook her head. "You were ever your own worst enemy,

Samuel. If you wish to go, I cannot prevent you, but it would be foolish to go out in such inclement weather."

Looking out of the kitchen window, he saw that snow was falling fast, swirled about by a strong wind.

"Besides, you are soaked," she continued. "You will catch your death."

It was true; he was wet from head to toe. There was not an item of clothing that had escaped the snow's icy infiltration and now, in the warmth of the little cottage, steam ghosted from all parts of his body. Water dripped from the hems of his trouser legs and from his socks to form little pools on the red tiles of the kitchen floor. He grimaced, suddenly aware of the unpleasant sensation of cold, damp clothes against his skin. "Well..." He had not forgiven her - not at all - but he was rather uncomfortable. "Yes, perhaps it would, perhaps, be wiser to do as you suggest. Thank you." He sniffed the air and his stomach rumbled again. "Something smells rather delicious."

"It's pea and ham soup," she said. "Father's favourite, especially on days such as, this ... so cold and dark. He believed that there was nothing like it for brightening up a dull day ... Dear Father." There was a little catch in her voice, but she collected herself and continued, "I made it earlier this morning and intend to have some for my lunch later on. You are welcome to have some, but we must get you out of those wet things."

Take off his clothes? Here? In the kitchen of Lavinia's house? He shook his head. "No! I thank you for your concern, but it would not be... seemly."

She handed him a towel. "You must do as I say, Samuel. For your own good."

"I cannot sit here clad only in a towel." He sneezed.

Lavinia laughed. "I shall find you something of Father's to wear."

She disappeared into the hallway and Timmins heard her moving about in the bedroom above, opening and shutting drawers. Finally, she reappeared carrying a pile of neatly ironed clothing. "These belonged to dear Papa," she said. "I am sure you will find something to fit you." She put the pile on the fender - a set of underwear, corduroy trousers, thick woollen socks, a shirt and a lumpy grey cardigan with brown wooden buttons which he recognised as one often worn by Lavinia's father on cold days. "Father was... somewhat shorter," she said, as she moved to pour out the tea, "but in girth he was much the same..."

Surely she was not suggesting that he was anywhere near similar in build to her rather rotund father! He had put on weight over the years, but really! He pulled in his stomach muscles. He was nowhere near as ... solid ... as the Reverend Ambrose Bellamy had been!

"Please, change! This is the warmest room. I shall wait in the sitting room until you are ready."

Timmins groaned. He must do as she said if he was ever to get any soup. His jumper, shirt and vest clung to him in a clammy embrace, and he struggled to remove his socks. He was about to put on the dry shirt when he noticed that the underwear comprised a set of long johns. Hmm. That meant that he would have to remove his nether garments before he could put on any dry clothing. He would be stark naked. What if Lavinia came back into the room before he had time to cover himself? For a moment he contemplated leaving off the long johns altogether, but this might lead to many awkward explanations about why he had done so, and besides, it would seem improper.

With some difficulty, he took off his trousers and underpants, dabbing at his naked form with the towel. Now sopping wet, it was ineffectual, so he toasted his front half before the fire until it took on a rosy glow. His ankle throbbed so much, before he could dry his back, that he picked up the long johns and sat down in the Windsor chair, his damp backside slapping on the seat.

There was a timid knock on the kitchen door, and Timmins froze. She was coming back in! Where had he put the towel?

"Are you all right in there, Samuel?"

"Er, yes. Yes, thank you!" Timmins called, scrabbling round for the towel. "I am not yet decent, however!"

Was that a laugh? No, surely not! There was nothing funny about his predicament.

"Call me when you are ready."

"Yes, yes." He heaved a sigh of relief as he heard her footsteps in the corridor and a door shut somewhere else in the cottage.

It took time to dress himself in the Reverend Bellamy's garments, but Timmins had to admit that it felt good to be wearing dry clothing again, even if the long johns were too short in the body, and to his horror, the trousers fitted a trifle too snugly. "I really must instruct Mrs Whibley not to put so much food on my plate at mealtimes," he thought, "and to cut down on her baking."

The fragrant aromas in the kitchen combined with relief at being warm and dry made him remember how, as a child, he had found sanctuary in the kitchen, thanks to the kindness of Beryl Mouncer - "Mousie" to the Timmins children - who had served the Timmins family for years, and who had a particular fondness for the little Samuel. It was she from whom he had always sought comfort when his father became too demanding, his mother too wrapped up in her own affairs and his brother and sisters too boisterous in the games which, it seemed, always ended in his being the victim. Mousie always made things right, offering a warm embrace, a gentle "There, there," and something delicious to eat or drink.

"There, now drink this tea while it's hot." A voice interrupted his reverie.

"Yes, Mousie," he replied...

"I'm sorry?" Lavinia had re-entered the room, put his own clothes to dry on the clothes horse in front of the fire and was making a pot of tea.

"Er... Nothing. I was thinking aloud. Tea, you say? And Lapsang Souchong. Thank you."

"Yes, well, I had not forgotten... it was always your favourite."

He took another sip. There she went again, referring to their past. What did she mean by it? He stole a glance at her as she drank her tea, and she caught his eye. He flushed. "If I recall correctly," he said, looking away, "your dear Father was also partial to Lapsang Souchong." He took another sip.

Neither of them spoke. Timmins thought back to his time in Quillington Parva as a young curate, and the many errors he had made. Always, the Reverend Ambrose Bellamy had been there to boost his spirits. 'Never mind,' he would say. 'Worse things happen at sea. Why, I was a perfect horror when I was a curate. Did I tell you about the time when ...?' and he would be off on one of his rambling, hilarious stories which never failed to drive out of Timmins' head any feelings of inadequacy at his own shortcomings. Quite unlike his own father, who, Timmins remembered, had never failed to remark upon his failures.

Lavinia was putting the pan of soup on the hob. "Dear Papa," she said. "He spoke of you often in his last days..." A faraway look flitted across her face. "Once, he said he wished we... But what am I thinking? Your ankle needs bandaging!"

She went to a drawer in the dresser, pulling out a little tin from which she took a small roll of bandage, a safety pin and a little white jar. "Arnica," she said in response to Timmins' enquiring glance. "Papa was a firm believer in this stuff, and it may help." Kneeling down in front of Timmins' chair, she put the bandage and pin on the floor and unscrewed the jar. She took his foot in her hands, placing it in her lap.

Why, oh why, hadn't he cut his toenails? They were shamefully long. "Really..." he began, "there is no need..."

"Please, allow me to do this," she said. "Your poor ankle..." She dipped her fingers in the arnica cream, which she then smoothed gently over his swollen foot.

At first Timmins flinched at every touch, but as she worked, rubbing in the cream with deft, light strokes, he floated on a cloud of wellbeing, his whole body relaxing into the sensations engendered by her touch, her quiet breathing and the soft ticking of the clock. The pain in his ankle lessened.

"There,' murmured Lavinia. 'That should help."

Timmins sighed. "Thank you, Lavinia, my dear. You have a healing touch." The tenderness of her expression stirred in him something he had not felt for a long time. The temptation to reach out and stroke her hair overwhelmed him. He lifted his hand but, just in time, came to his senses. What was he thinking? He scratched his knee.

"Good," said Lavinia, picking up the bandage. "I'll just pop this on it, to give it a little support." Working quickly, she bandaged his heel and ankle in a figure of eight movement, fastened it and put his sock for him in one practiced action.

He watched as she worked. How gentle she was - how thoughtful. He must tell her how grateful he was. As she put the second sock on, there was a loud gurgling sound. Timmins clapped his hand to his belly. It rumbled again. "Oh dear! I must apologise!" he exclaimed.

"No need. I'll get you some soup." She put the little pot of arnica back in the dresser drawer, washed her hands, then ladled a large serving of thick, green soup into a china bowl which she placed on the kitchen table. It steamed gently, exuding the most fragrant aroma, and his mouth watered. "Bread?" she enquired, and when Timmins nodded, she took from the green enamel bread crock a large white loaf, cutting a thick slice which she spread with a generous layer of yellow butter.

Timmins took his place at the table where he bowed his head. "For what we are about to receive ..." The soup was thick and delicious. He tore off a piece of bread and dipped it in to the steaming liquid, melting the butter so that a little of it pooled, glistening, on the surface. "Delicious" he said, nodding in appreciation. 'An ambrosial broth. Are you not having any?"

Lavinia shook her head. She seemed preoccupied. "No. I shall have some later. If you will excuse me, Reverend, I have business to attend to in the sitting room. I do not wish to appear rude, but ... would you mind if ...?" Her voice tailed off.
"No, not at all. Please, go ahead." Timmins eyed the pan of soup.

"Help yourself to more." She took the pan from the stove, set it down on an iron trivet on the table, cut another thick slice of bread and put it on Timmins' side plate then, again muttering apologies, disappeared back through the kitchen door.

After another two bowls of soup, Timmins was replete. He leaned back in the chair, patted his stomach and glanced at the clock. Time was getting on and he should, he supposed, brave the elements and try to make the journey back to the Vicarage. He called out, "Lavinia? Are you there? I should make tracks."

There was no reply and no sound of movement anywhere else in the cottage, so he picked up his stick and limped out into the hallway. "Lavinia?" A thin sliver of light gleamed beneath the door opposite, which he took to be the sitting room. "Are you there, Lavinia?" He pushed open the door and there she was, seated at a small occasional table which was littered with sheets of lavender-coloured writing paper. Bathed in the warm glow of light from a pink-shaded standard lamp and engrossed in her task, she did not appear to have heard him, so he coughed.

She started, clasping her right hand to her chest. "Oh! Oh, dear! Samuel!" she exclaimed. "Oh, how you startled me!"

"You appear to have a lot of letters to write." Timmins stepped forward, noting that two sheets of paper had fallen on the floor and drifted underneath Lavinia's chair. "Allow me," he said, stooping to pick them up, but Lavinia was there before him.

"No ... that is, please don't. There's no need," she said, hurriedly snatching up the papers and adding them to the pile on the table. 'There.' She removed her shawl and tossed it on top of the papers. "Silly me - so clumsy!"
Her action puzzled him. Did she not wish him to see the papers? Surely she did not think he would read what she had written? "I came," he said, "to tell you I have recovered from my ordeal. As you are busy, I shall trouble you no further."

"Not at all. I am glad to have been able to help."

The little sitting room was a charming, feminine room with its chintz armchairs and curtains, pretty little ornaments on the mantelpiece, and faded Aubusson rugs. An elegant little Edwardian mahogany bookcase stood against the wall next to the door. Behind its astragal glazing was a set of red Morocco-bound books, their spines gilt-tooled with a name he recognised. 'Blossom Madgwick!' he exclaimed.

Lavinia, tidying her papers, looked up. "I'm sorry?"

"You have the complete works of Blossom Madgwick! And such beautiful editions." So she was a fellow devotee after all!

Lavinia nodded. "I am familiar with the novels."

"Oh, then we are kindred spirits," Timmins enthused. "I recognise that I am a rather unlikely fan, being a man, and an educated one at that... " Unaware of the frown that shadowed Lavinia's face, he continued, 'and I would not like people to think I do not also read works of far greater literary significance, but at the end of a long and taxing day, I do very much enjoy the opportunity of a little escapism.'

There was a moment of silence and then she shrugged her shoulders. "Your secret is safe with me, Reverend. Now, back to the kitchen.'

Timmins hobbled back to the warmth of the kitchen, followed by Lavinia. Glad to sit down again in the Windsor chair, he put his foot up on the fender. His ankle, which had seemed less painful, now throbbed again. "Oh dear," he said, "I fear I underestimated the damage I have done to my ankle. I shall have to trespass upon your hospitality for a while longer. I am not sure I could walk back home. Oh dear, what a to-do!"

Lavinia put Timmins' dirty dishes in the sink, then picked up the soup pan. It was empty. "Hmm, I believe I will just have a sandwich for my lunch." She put the pan in the sink and cut two thin slices of bread. "I am sure that if we telephone Mr Hedgecock, in whose fields you were walking, he will come out in his tractor and get you back to the Vicarage. I wonder, why were you out walking at such an early hour, and in these conditions? It was never your usual habit to do so."

"Ha! You are quite right. I would far rather have stayed at home in the warmth and comfort of my own home, given the choice. It was the dog, you see. He left me in no doubt he wished to go for a walk, no matter that it was snowing and cold."

"Poffley?" She put down her sandwich. "You were walking Poffley?"

"Yes. The silly creature has me out in all weathers. You would not believe the energy that animal has! I tell you, it has been a real strain looking after..."

"Where is the poor animal now?" There was an edge to her voice.

Timmins frowned. "I feel sure he has returned to the Vicarage," he said. "He has done it before. The last time I was at Tall Trees he escaped from Mrs Dobson and returned home alone. He ate all the sandwiches which we..."

"Why didn't you say he was missing? You should have telephoned the Vicarage - he may have gone there. Really, Samuel, have you no sense?" Lavinia disappeared into the hallway, casting a disparaging look in his direction. He heard the murmur of voices as she placed the call. When she returned, she was wearing her coat, scarf and hat. "He is not at home," she said, retrieving her boots from the little shoe cupboard near the front door. "I shall go out and search for him. He could be anywhere by now and he will be cold and frightened." She tutted loudly and sighed an angry sigh, then snapped, "Didn't Edna Dobson tell you to keep him on the lead?"

Timmins had never heard her speak like this. "I ... I... believe that she may ... that is, she might ... have mentioned something of the kind," he stuttered, "but ... well, the dog tugged so, and seemed so eager to have a little fun, that I thought to..."

Lavinia pursed her lips. "I shall find him," she said, opening the front door. A little flurry of snowflakes blew in on a blast of cold air. She hesitated for a moment. She was angry but... was there something else? "You must realise what this might mean? If harm has come to him - if you have lost him then... the consequences... oh dear!" She left, shutting the door behind her.

The consequences? He clapped his hands to his forehead. "Oh, no!" he groaned. "You fool, Timmins! You fool!" He should never have let Poffley off the lead! What had he been thinking? It was clear, from Poffley's behaviour at home, that the animal had no self-control. He, Timmins, should have been more responsible. He could imagine Harold Bungay's reactions when news of the lost dog reached him. "Ha, so you bungled it. Well, that puts the tin hat on your getting hold of old Mrs Prout's cash, you know. Jolly bad show, - and what will you do about those bells now?" Bungay would suck in air in that irritating way he had and shake his head in mock sorrow. "Suppose we'll be bidding you farewell as you toddle off with a heavy heart for pastures new?"

The prospect terrified Timmins. Where on earth would Bishop Archbold send him? Quillinghampton, perhaps, with its traffic and noise and bustle? There were some undesirable parishes in that city... Or would he be sent even further afield? As if that were not bad enough, Archbold would also expect him to work like some kind of newly ordained curate, supervised by another vicar. How humiliating that would be... Timmins shook his head to rid himself of such thoughts. She would bring back the dog... wouldn't she? Heaving himself to his feet, he grabbed his stick and made his way to the sink. He would do the washing up and have a cup of tea ready to warm her on her return.

Lavinia was gone for over an hour, during which Timmins was on tenterhooks. Had his ankle not been troubling him, he told himself, he would have gone to help with the search; as it was, he made a pot of tea, found some sticky gingerbread in the pantry and made a stack of cheese sandwiches. He had just finished eating his third sandwich when he heard panting and scuffling outside, the front door opened, and in flew Poffley. He leapt up at Timmins, barking, then raced around the kitchen, stopping to shake the snow from his coat. "Poffley! Steady on!" Timmins exclaimed. "My dear Lavinia, how can I ever thank you? Where did you find him?"

Lavinia stamped the snow from her boots. "Phew!" she exclaimed, removing her coat. "It is freezing out there." She sat at the kitchen table. "But at least I met with success... Poffley is quite well."

Poffley did seem unfazed by recent events. Having shaken himself, spraying the room with droplets of melted snow, he made straight for the fire, circled round and round for a few moments and then flopped down, his tail curled around his face.

Timmins poured two cups of tea and put one on the table in front of her. "He is. My dear Lavinia, how can I ever thank you?

But I repeat, where did you find him?"

Lavinia sipped her tea. "Well, in fact, he found me," she said. "I retraced your steps, calling him all the while, but there was no sign, and then I thought, perhaps he has gone home. And he had."

"He went back to the Vicarage?"

"Oh, no. When I say home, I refer to his home. The place he knows best..."

"You mean he went back to Tall Trees?"

"Yes. There he was, sitting on the doorstep. The house is empty now... and he, poor thing, was so forlorn. He misses her, I think." Her gaze flicked from the dog to Timmins. "Although he has a nice new home now... does he not?"

Was it his imagination, or was there just the hint of doubt in her voice? Guilt assailed him and he did not like the feeling. Her steady grey gaze made him feel as if she could see into his mind and knew how much he had resented the dog's intrusion into his life. He nodded. "I... I have to admit that I have, perhaps, not taken Poffley's needs into account as much as I might. He has suffered the loss of a doting mistress, and perhaps I should confess that since he arrived at the Vicarage, I have thought only of how much of a nuisance he has been. If I had shown him more affection, perhaps he would not have been so eager to escape from me this morning." He hesitated and bit his lip. "I have learned a lesson today."

"Good." Lavinia said. "Another cup of tea, perhaps, Samuel?" she said, her voice softer now. "And something to eat? I did not finish my lunch, and those sandwiches look tempting."

"Yes, they were... they do, I mean." A daring thought distracted him. In a rush of bravado, he blurted it out. "Lavinia," he said, "you might know I was...lucky enough to win first prize in the raffle at Miss Gore-Hatherley's musical soirée. I have two tickets to see HMS Pinafore in Quillinghampton next week, and for dinner afterwards with Miss Evangeline Honeybell. I had decided that I would not go, but...I wonder...as a thank-you for your help today..would you...would you care to go with me?" He could feel the colour rising in his face. The kitchen suddenly seemed far too hot, and he ran his finger round the inside of his collar. His heart was, for some peculiar reason, beating inordinately fast. Was she shocked? Horrified? He could not tell. " Of c-course, if you are, um, b-busy I shall, er, quite ... quite understand...or perhaps ... you do not care to..."

"Thank you. I would love to come. And now, we had better telephone Mr Hedgecock and see about that tractor ride home?"

CHAPTER TEN

BEETLE!

"Timmins! What in the blue blazes have you been up to?" Bishop Archbold erupted into the sitting room of the Vicarage. "Good Lord, man, you have been through the wars!"

Timmins, ensconced in his favourite armchair with his injured foot resting on an ancient gout stool, shuddered at the sudden disturbance and put down his book. He had been enjoying an indulgent afternoon with a glass of sherry and a bowl of walnuts within easy reach on the coffee table. "They need eating up, Vicar!" Mrs Whibley had said, and he was doing his best to oblige. He was just at a thrilling point in "Amélie and Alphonse" where Amélie had disguised herself as a stable boy and was about to escape the Château d'Évergne on Diablo, the Duc's black stallion.

"Good afternoon, Bishop," he said, grunting as he heaved himself more upright in his chair. "Please, take a seat and pray forgive me for not rising. I am indisposed." It had been several days now since his unfortunate outing with Poffley and although his ankle was not troubling him overmuch, he rather felt he ought to rest it as much as possible.

"Dear oh dear!" his visitor exclaimed, at the sight of Timmins' bandaged foot. "You are a poorly soldier, aren't you?" He threw himself down on to the sofa, rearranging and plumping the cushions. When all was to his liking, he leaned forward, legs akimbo, and grasped his knees so his elbows jutted out sideways. "Tell the Bishop all about it!"

Timmins frowned. Was the Bishop teasing him? Why speak to him in that fashion? He was not a child! He described the adventures of the previous day. "The weather was atrocious, and when I fell and injured my ankle it was all I could do to struggle through the deep snow and the cold to Miss Bellamy's cottage. I was in such agony. The pain was excruciating."

"Quite. And what of the dog?"

"He ran away. I was at my wits' end with worry, but there was little I could do..."

"Hmm. Yes." The Bishop's brow furrowed, and his bushy ginger eyebrows twitched. He scrutinised Timmins for a moment, biting his lip, before he continued. "I met Miss Bellamy just now, in the church."

Timmins gulped. Oh, dear! What had she said? Did the Bishop know that he had allowed Poffley off the lead, despite warnings not to do so, and had then forgotten all about him? Was he aware that he had remained in the cosy kitchen while Lavinia braved the storm? Was that why he was staring?

"I cannot tell you how fervently I prayed for dear Poffley...and Miss Bellamy, who insisted on going to look for him. I suffered such terrors while I waited..." He stopped, suddenly aware that he was gabbling.

"I can imagine." Bishop Archbold said. "It must have been awful for you." He leaned back against the cushions. "It beggars belief."

There was a pause which seemed to last for an eternity, and during which Timmins shifted under the Bishop's scrutiny. Finally, he had to break the silence. "I was at fault. I should not have allowed the dog to run off - I knew that he should have remained on the lead until I had learned to control him. If I had not been so remiss there would have been no need for Miss Bellamy to go out in that awful weather."

Bishop Archbold nodded. "Still, no harm befell the lady, or the errant beast. Now, are you going to offer me some tea?" He sprang to his feet. "I could do with wetting my whistle. Shall I give your good lady - Mrs Wobbley? - a shout?"

"Mrs Whibley," Timmins said, relieved at the sudden lightening of the atmosphere.

The Bishop leapt up, strode to the door, threw it open and bellowed down the corridor. "Mrs Wob... Whibley! Tea, if you please! Cake too, if you have any!" He sat down with an energy that made the old sofa creak. "Missed my lunch," he said. "Tummy's been protesting all afternoon. You're a lucky chap, Timmins, to have a housekeeper who can cook. I'm condemned to the most awful rot, I'm afraid! Inherited dear old Mrs Grice from the previous Bish, and don't have the heart to get rid of her, but between you, me and the gatepost she's getting past it. Burns everything. I shall have to let her go soon though, or I'll starve to death!"

Timmins relaxed. He was just about to offer words of sympathy when the Bishop clapped his hands and wagged a finger in Timmins' direction. "Still, enough about me! Got those bells sorted yet?" He stroked his bushy beard.

Timmins quailed. What? Already? Bishop Archbold had a reputation for efficiency, but surely he could not expect him to have raised all that money yet? He had thrown down the gauntlet only a few weeks ago, in February, and it was only now the start of April. "Er, well..."

"Just teasing!" the Bishop said, a broad grin on his face. "Ha! Had you there! You should see your expression! Don't worry, Timmins! I gave you six months, and six months you shall have." He leaned forward and patted Timmins hard on the knee. "I'm sure there's no cause for concern on my part - in fact, I hear that you've made a start, at least, with a rather swanky musical evening?"

He was on safe ground now - the musical evening had been a tremendous success. Millicent Gore-Hatherley had reported only the other day that the total sum raised had superseded all of their expectations. "Yes," he said. "I believe that we have boosted the coffers considerably, and it was a very... enjoyable evening, on the whole. We also have several other events planned."

This was more like it! The Bishop was smiling. "I am confident," Timmins continued, "that, with the support of my parishioners, I shall be able to raise the money for the repair of the bells - possibly before the end of the year."

'I'm jolly glad to hear that!' chuckled the Bishop. "And here is more good news. Mrs Whibley l has arrived with the tea. Allow me!' He wrested the tray from the housekeeper who had shuffled in. Pushing aside the bowl of walnuts to make room for it, he put the tray down on the coffee table. "Macaroons! Just what the doctor ordered, eh? Timmins? Thank you, Mrs Whibley, you are a perfect angel."

She dropped a deep curtsey, muttered, "Don't mention it, Your Honour," and withdrew to the kitchen, her slippers slapping on the tiled floor.

Bishop Archbold served Timmins and himself with tea. "I gather that one of those events is due to take place this evening? A Beetle Drive, I understand?"

Timmins groaned. He was sorely tempted to cry off the Beetle Drive, leaving it in the capable hands of Millicent and Lavinia. "Er, yes, your Grace," he muttered, wiping crumbs from his mouth. "To tell the truth, I am not convinced that I have recovered enough... my ankle is still rather painful..." A sudden horrifying thought struck him. "Are you... intending to join us, Your Grace?"

The Bishop gave a rueful sigh. "No can do," he said, pouring himself a second cup of tea. " Duty calls, don't you know? I have a meeting with the Archdeacon this evening, and I can't wriggle out of it, even if I wanted to." Timmins flushed under the Bishop's steady gaze. The rebuke, subtle though it was, had hit home. "Shame, though," he continued, "it sounds like a lot of fun. You must tell me all about it when next we meet."

There was an ear-splitting scream, the door flew open and in rushed Mrs Whibley, panting and red-faced. "That animal!" she puffed. "That dratted dog! He's brought in a creature!"

Something small and grey scampered into the room, closely pursued by Poffley.

"A squirrel! Oooh, I can't abide the things. Catch it, Vicar!"

The room became a maelstrom of noisy activity. The squirrel raced up the curtains, leapt on to the bookcase, flew across the room and landed on the sofa, darting hither and thither to escape Poffley who bounded about, barking and thrashing his tail while Mrs Whibley huffed and puffed after them both. Bishop Archbold joined in the chase, but his size hindered him, and the squirrel easily escaped his grasp. The din was deafening and Timmins, afraid something would get broken, leapt to his feet. "Poffley! Poffley!" he called. "Stop this! I say, stop this!"

Poffley took no notice. As the dog passed him in a flying leap over the sofa, Timmins, forgetting his injury, lunged, crashing into Mrs Whibley. She stumbled backwards and fell with a loud, "Oh! Oh, my sainted aunt!"

"Poffley! Naughty dog!" Timmins cried, chasing after Poffley as he raced round and round the sofa. Suddenly, he found his feet flying from under him. Poffley had upset the coffee table and with it the bowl of walnuts. Nuts rolled everywhere, like so many ball bearings. "Aaagh!" he cried, as he staggered and fell backwards, landing on something warm, lumpy and soft.

"Eeek! Vicar! Gerroff!" squealed Mrs Whibley.

The Bishop guffawed.

Timmins, horrified, leapt to his feet. "Mrs Whibley, I'm so sorry..." he began.

"Never mind that," she said, sitting up and pushing her hair back under its net. "You need to catch that creature! There he is!"

The squirrel sat on the curtain rail, observing them and cracking open a walnut.

"Little blighter!" growled the Bishop, seizing an antimacassar and throwing it in one swift movement over the squirrel. "Got you!" Reaching up, he grabbed it, wrapped it up in the antimacassar and stalked over to the window which he threw open. "Off you go now," he bellowed, shaking the squirrel out of the cloth and watching it scamper away across the lawn. He closed the window.

"Seems as if your ankle is better than you thought, Timmins!" He raised a bushy ginger eyebrow. "So you will grace the Beetle Drive with your presence, I presume?"

Timmins nodded, shamefaced. "Er, yes, your Grace," he replied. He glanced at Poffley. The blasted animal was smirking! "Mrs Whibley," he said, "kindly remove this creature and bring us more tea." He glanced at the Bishop. Was he laughing too? "I find, to my surprise, that I can put weight on my foot." He hobbled back to his armchair and sat down. For a moment he contemplated putting his foot up on the stool but caught the Bishop's knowing stare and thought better of it. "You know how it is, Bishop; when one has an injury, it makes one wary of doing further damage by attempting too much too soon. I am delighted that I shall be able to attend tonight's function. Delighted."

"Hmm." Bishop Archbold frowned. "Now, see here, Timmins. I understand it is difficult to accept change, and you have had a pretty cushy time of it here for the best part of thirty years. It's difficult to change the habits of a lifetime."

"Well, I ... "

"Allow me to continue, there's a good chap. I believe the more you put into the parish, the more the parish will give back to you. Do not disappoint me, Timmins - you have it in you to make changes here. As for tonight, just stir your stumps, get off your backside, go to the blithering Beetle Drive and have a blistering good time. What d'you say, eh?" He stood, legs apart, hands clasped behind his back, in front of the window, and his expression left Timmins in no doubt he meant business.

"Yes, you are right, Bishop," he murmured, hot with embarrassment. "I shall do my very best."

"Good chap!" The Bishop clapped his hands once, loudly, as he spoke. "Marvellous! I know you can do it! And now, if you will excuse me, I must scurry away for the Archdeacon expects me." He took out his watch. "Good Lord! I shall be late, and the Archdeacon is not a man to keep waiting. Cheerio!" Clapping Timmins on the shoulder, he left the room, whistling as he went.

By seven o'clock that evening, the Church Hall was thronging with villagers eager for an evening's fun. Lavinia, Millicent and several other ladies were serving cups of tea; there was a buzz of conversation and cheery laughter, and the air was thick with the smell of damp clothing, for it had been raining all evening. Timmins, much against his will, had arrived an hour early and Millicent had set him to work retrieving tables and chairs from the dark, cobwebby store cupboard under the stage. Sweat beaded his brow and trickled down his back, and his shirt and dog collar clung to him most unpleasantly. He was not in a good mood. His ankle hurt.

"Ah, there you are, Vicar!" exclaimed Millicent as he emerged from the cloakroom where he had been sprucing himself up. "I wondered where you'd taken yourself off to! Come along, old sport, and greet your guests. The place is heaving."

The Beetle Drive had proved so popular there were to be two games, each with nine rounds, "That way," Millicent had said, "we can give lots of people a go, and raise as much jolly old loot as possible." There was also a tombola, and a raffle for an enormous fruit cake donated by Dorothy Manifold. Timmins had purchased several strips of raffle tickets.

"I wondered where you'd taken yourself off to!" Millicent continued. 'Thought you might have popped off home - these things really aren't your cup of tea, after all, and I wouldn't have put it past you!"

Timmins was indignant. As if he would leave them in the lurch! He was about to issue a curt reply when Bungay dug him in the ribs.

"I should get this thing started, if I were you. Otherwise we'll be here all night."

"Thank you, Mr Bungay," Timmins said. "I was about to do just that. Ladies and gentlemen...!" There was no response in the room. He cleared his throat and spoke again, more loudly this time. "Ladies and gentlemen! If you would be so kind...!"

"They're not listening," chortled Bungay. "Here, try this. Found it behind the stage curtain." He handed Timmins a megaphone. "That might get their attention."

Timmins glared at Bungay. The man was insufferable. He seemed to delight in the discomfiture of others. He reminded Timmins of Vosper, the most intimidating of all the boys at his prep school. Like Bungay, Vosper, known as Waspy to the boys, had been beefy and red-faced, and, again like Bungay, had seemed to take delight in humiliating the young Timmins. On one occasion, the annual prize-giving day, he was to recite Matthew Arnold's poem, "Self-Dependence", before the entire assembly of pupils, staff and parents. He had been waiting in the classroom set aside for the performers, muttering the poem over and again to himself, terrified that he would forget it. He had stumbled on his first two attempts and had just begun his third -

'Weary of myself, and sick of asking

What I am and what I ought to be,"

when Vosper had grabbed hold of him and tipped white powder down his shorts. "There you are, Timmins, you little squirt!" he cried, and raced off to tell his pals what he had done.

At first, Timmins did not understand what had just taken place, but as he began the poem a fourth time, he noticed an intense discomfort. "Ow!" he squeaked, wriggling. The other would-be performers watched, and then, as Timmins squirmed and hopped about, one of them shouted, "Itching powder! Old Waspy's put itching powder down Timmins' pants! What a lark!"

There had been no time to change. Timmins had mounted the stage, aware of countless pairs of eyes upon him. The itching grew worse - he could not stand still but he could not scratch, so he performed the entire recitation gyrating and twitching in a manner which generated much sniggering amongst the assembled boys, perplexed frowns amongst the parents and fury in the Headmaster.

Timmins flinched as he recalled the beating he had received afterwards in the Headmaster's panelled study. Vosper and the other boys had thought it a "total hoot". For weeks afterwards they derived huge delight from standing up in class and performing the "Timmins shuffle" whenever a master turned his back. When, as often happened, that master sought to find the source of the resulting snorts of laughter, they would cry "Timmins, Sir! It's his fault!" and he would receive further rebuke for the disruption.

Vosper and his tribe had had the upper hand then, but he was in charge here. Grabbing the megaphone he said, at the top of his voice, "Ladies and gentlemen!" Several people standing nearby clapped their hands to their ears with cries of "Oh, I say!" and "Well, really!" He had their attention now. He was just about to issue instructions for beginning the Beetle Drive when an elderly lady in a worn tweed suit and a soft, battered felt hat poked him in the ribs and regarded him with a milky stare through the thick lenses of her round tortoiseshell spectacles.

"'Ere,' she said, in a reedy, shrill voice. "There you are, you dirty stop-out! Don't think I don't know what you've been up to! You ought to be ashamed of yourself, and you needn't think I'm taking you back this time!" She prodded him again with a thin, bony finger.

A hush fell over the room. Someone tittered.

"I beg your pardon, Madam?" Timmins drew himself up to his full height. "I think you must have mistaken me for someone else."

"Don't you Madam me!" the old lady shrieked. "Lor' love a duck! My old Dad warned me about you! I should have listened to him an' then I never would've married you, you useless lump of... "

Before the old lady could finish her sentence, Edna Dobson rushed forward and grabbed her by the arm. "Aunty Vi!" she exclaimed. "Quiet now! This isn't Uncle Alf, it's the Vicar! You've got all muddled up again. Oh, dear, Vicar," she continued, ushering her aunt to a nearby chair and sitting her down, "I'm so sorry! Auntie's fuddled these days but means no harm. I brought her along this evening for a change - she doesn't get out of Twilight House much these days, you know, and I thought a nice game of Beetle would cheer her up - she used to love it so."

"My dear Mrs Dobson, there is no need to apologise"' He composed his face in a benign smile. To his horror, Aunty Vi blew him a kiss.

Bungay could not suppress his amusement. "She seems to have forgiven you!"

Timmins scowled at the solicitor. "Ladies and gentlemen, would the first teams to play kindly take their places at the tables." He watched the scramble for seats and then continued. "We shall play nine rounds of Beetle before the interval, and another nine rounds with the second group of players. The winner of each round will take home a cash prize of ten shillings." A cheer went up.

"Now, for those of you who are not familiar with the game, I shall explain the rules. Each player has a piece of paper and a pencil, and the aim of the game is to be the first player to draw a complete beetle. Each of the Beetle's body parts has a number, as follows; 6 for the body, and each beetle has only one of those; 5 for the head; 4 for each of the two wings; 3 for each of the 6 legs; 2 for each of two antennae and 1 for each eye. There will be two eyes for each beetle. Players take turns to roll a die and, depending on the number thrown, can add the corresponding body part to their beetle. They must, however, throw a 6 and draw the body before they can add any other part. Players may only add the correct number of body parts to their beetle. For instance, only 2 wings, a further throw of number 4 resulting in no addition and the die being passed on. Is that clear?"

"Yes, get on with it!" a voice called from the back of the room. "The pub shuts at ten!"

Timmins continued. "The first person in each team to draw a complete beetle shouts "Beetle!" and at that point play ceases, players tot up their points, as already described, and the person with the highest total on each table moves on to the table to their left. At the end of the game, when all nine rounds are over, the person with the highest total will win. Now then, pencils and dice at the ready? Go!"

At once, a concentrated hush fell as the players, heads bent, frantically shook and threw their dice, and then came the noise: shouts of "Six! Aha, I get a head!" and "Five! Oh blast! I will never get started!", the skittering of dice across tables and on to the floor and the frantic scraping of chairs as the players retrieved them. After a short while, the triumphant cry of "Beetle!" rang out, and a red-faced man in a spotted neckerchief waved his paper aloft. Timmins threaded his way through the tables to check it.

"Yes, that's complete," he affirmed. "Now, tot up your points, and winners move to the table on the left. Ready? Go!" As the game resumed, Timmins felt a glow of pride. This was all going so well! Who would have thought a Beetle Drive would engender such a competitive spirit?

"Beetle!" cried a shrill voice, after a surprisingly short time had elapsed. Aunty Vi waved her paper aloft, beaming. Timmins crossed the room to check the paper, but Edna Dobson beat him to it. "No, Aunty. You've only got two legs and one feeler. You need six legs and two feelers. Sorry, Vicar!"

The game recommenced. Dice rattled and rolled, players cheered or groaned, and beetles took shape. Glancing at Bungay's paper, Timmins was not best pleased to note that the solicitor's beetle wore a dog collar and bore a remarkable resemblance to himself.

"Beetle!" cried Aunty Vi, after another five minutes. Timmins glanced at Edna Dobson, who shook her head.

"Continue playing!" he cried, and the game went on, with the same intensity as before, until they had played all nine rounds and Dorothy Manifold was victorious.

"Now, we shall have an interval of half an hour," called Timmins, "during which we hope you will all treat yourselves to a slice of cake and a cup of tea. We shall draw the raffle before we begin the next round, so if you have not already bought your tickets, now is the time to do so. There are still some lovely prizes on the tombola. Remember, all proceeds go to the repair of the church bells, so dig deep! I shall start the proceedings by ordering a cup of tea and a slice of that delicious chocolate sponge, please, Miss Bellamy!"

Timmins spent the tea break chatting to as many people as he could. In the normal run of things, he did not find it easy to make small talk, especially with people whom he did not know well, but this evening something had changed and to his surprise he found that he was enjoying himself. The only fly in the ointment was Aunty Vi. Wherever Timmins was, there she was too, and each time he caught her eye she either winked at him, blew him a kiss, or, on one occasion, slowly lifted the hem of her skirt on one side, revealing a skinny leg encased in a thick, wrinkled beige stocking and the elasticated hem of her pink flannelette bloomers. To his great relief, Edna Dobson had swooped on her aunt before the skirt had gone far above the knee, and hurried her off to sit in the kitchen, out of harm's way.

When the half hour was up, Timmins announced that it was time to draw the raffle. "And I would like to ask Miss Bellamy, who has worked so hard organising the lovely refreshments, to please come and draw the first ticket."

Wiping her hands on a tea towel, Lavinia emerged from the kitchen, reached into the box of tickets and drew one out. Unfolding it, she read out the number. "Green, 235." Timmins waited.

Nobody came forward.

"Green, 235!" he called. "Come along, somebody must have it? Somebody here has won this superb prize, baked by our own Dorothy Manifold, of the Fat Rascal Tearoom, and we all know how delicious her cakes are."

"You certainly do!" a voice called from the other side of the room, much to everyone's amusement.

Timmins blushed. Was his sweet tooth so well-known to the villagers? Making a mental resolve to limit future visits to the Fat Rascal, he called once more. "Number 235, green ticket."

Still nobody came forward and then Mrs Whibley, who was sitting with her brother and his wife, called out, "Have you checked your own tickets, Reverend?"

No, he hadn't. He felt in his pocket for the strip of tickets, took them out and glanced at them. There it was. Number 235. Green.

"Oh dear, seems as if I have won," he said, beaming.

'I say! You lucky devil!' called Bungay, pushing his way through the crowd towards them. 'You seem to have rather a habit of winning raffle tickets, doesn't he, Millicent?' He slapped Timmins on the back, causing him to stumble into a rather portly, red-faced man with a handlebar moustache, who spilled his tea. The man glared at him and dabbed at his waistcoat with a spotted handkerchief.

Millicent nodded. "He does. First the raffle at my little musical evening, and now this - you seem to be very lucky, Reverend Timmins!"

Timmins was not so sure. A cake was one thing, but an evening in the company of Evangeline Honeybell was quite another. He had, in fact, considered donating his earlier prize to this raffle, but had decided that to do so might appear a little ungallant. "Yes," he said. "I am sure I do not deserve both."

"Ha! Most noble of you to say so!' Bungay cried. 'Hear that, everyone? Reverend Timmins says he does not deserve the first prize. So you won't mind if we chuck it back in the pot, eh? Draw another ticket for it and let some other lucky blighter win?"

"What?" Timmins squeaked.

"Good lad!" cried Bungay, slapping him on the back again and winding him. "That's the spirit! Noblesse oblige and all that!"

"But...but...I..." Timmins began, but there was no getting out of it. A round of applause greeted the solicitor's announcement. "Don't mention it,' he grimaced, dipping his hand into the tub of raffle tickets and withdrawing another ticket. "Pink. Number 96."

There was a moment's silence as people checked their tickets, and then Edna Dobson cried, "You've got it, Aunty! You've won! Isn't that nice? Off you go to collect it, dear!" She put the ticket into her aunt's hand and gave her a gentle shove. "Get your prize!"

Aunty Vi fixed Timmins with a gleeful stare and tottered across the hall towards him, waving her ticket. She cackled gleefully and, much to the amusement of the assembled crowd, took hold of Timmins, pulled him towards her with a strength surprising in such a little, thin old woman, and kissed him full on the lips. When she had finished, she let him go, wiped her mouth on the back of her hand, picked up her prize and tottered back to her niece.

Timmins shuddered and took his handkerchief from his pocket. Feigning a loud sneeze, he wiped all trace of the old woman's very wet kiss from his lips. Blast Harold Bungay! How dare he interfere? The familiar feeling of shame made him squirm, while the ghost of an itch troubled his nether regions.

"Reverend Timmins?" A voice interrupted his reverie, and he shook himself. Lavinia was gazing up at him. "Should we not begin the second round of the game? It is getting rather late."

Timmins agreed. He clapped his hands, and to his immense surprise, silence fell over the room. A little thrill of pride ran through him, and he glanced at the megaphone which lay on a nearby table. No need to use that now - he had the crowd in the palm of his hand. Ha! So much for Bungay's snide comments about his lack of presence! "Ladies and Gentlemen," he said, "I am sure we would all like to thank the ladies who have provided us with such delightful refreshments, and all those generous souls who provided the prizes for the raffle." A vision of the lost fruit cake flashed in his head as the ripple of applause rose, then died. "And now, let us continue with the second half of our evening's entertainment. It looks such fun! I intend to join in, so I shall ask Miss Gore-Hatherley to superintend proceedings this time, if she will be so kind."

"Delighted, Reverend!" She picked up the megaphone, switched it on and put it to her lips. "LADIES AND GENTLEMEN! PLEASE

TAKE YOUR PLACES AT THE TABLES. THAT'S IT! COME ALONG NOW, PLENTY OF SPACE FOR EVERYONE!"

Those near her ducked away, covering their ears as her already loud voice resounded through the room, but she was not about to give up the symbol of authority. "NOW, ARE WE SET? DICE AT THE READY? PENCILS POISED?"

Timmins found himself at a table with Dorothy Manifold, a frizzy-haired woman whom he did not recognise and, to his dismay, Harold Bungay. He picked up the little cup containing the die, intending, out of politeness, to offer it first to one of the women. Instead, a sudden feverish desire to win overtook him, and when Millicent boomed "GO!", the rest of the room faded, he bit his lip and, willing with every fibre of his being it should throw up a six, he cast the die. His skin prickled with eager anticipation as the little wooden cube danced across the table and came to land just at the edge, in front of Bungay. It must be a six! He picked up his pencil, ready to draw the head of his beetle.

"Ha! Four!" cried Bungay. "No good, old thing."

Gloomily, he passed the cup to Dorothy Manifold. He had felt in his bones he would throw a six. He tapped his fingers on the table as each of the other players did what he had failed to do. When, at long last, it was his turn again, the die spun round and round on one corner for a few seconds before coming to a halt. "Three!" cried Bungay, scooping it up. "No luck there!" Winking at Timmins, he passed the cup again to Dorothy Manifold.

His companions had almost finished their beetles while he had yet to begin, and they were being very creative. The frizzy woman had decorated her beetle's head with curly hair and some very elegant antennae complete with little stars on the ends; Dorothy Manifold's beetle was fat-faced with an enormous belly and wore a waistcoat with straining buttons, while Bungay's was, this time, female, sporting six very shapely legs. Finally, Timmins threw a six. He gave a delighted whoop and had just picked up his pencil to draw the beetle's head when Dorothy Manifold cried "Beetle!"

A collective sigh went up around the room, and Timmins threw his pencil down in disgust.

"Hard cheese!" Bungay said, his jowls wobbling.

Millicent strode over to their table to check that Dorothy Manifold's beetle had all of its constituent parts. "JOLLY GOOD MRS MANIFOLD! YOUR BEETLE LOOKS AS IF HE'S EATEN A GOOD FEW OF YOUR DELICIOUS CAKES," she bellowed through the megaphone. "HE'S A NICE CHUBBY CHAPPY, ISN'T HE? HA! WHAT FUN!" She burst forth in loud, appreciative laughter, still with the megaphone clamped to her mouth, and the noise was deafening. Timmins wondered if he should say something to her, but she soon recovered. "YOU WIN THIS ROUND, DOROTHY DEAR. TOT UP YOUR POINTS EVERYONE! NOW, THE WINNER FROM EACH TABLE SHOULD HOP OVER TO THE TABLE ON THEIR LEFT AND WE'LL BEGIN ROUND TWO."

The next two rounds proceeded in much the same vein until, in the fourth round, Timmins struck lucky. Each throw of the die seemed to bring him the number he needed. Finally, with the last throw, the last leg sketched in, he threw down his pencil in a burst of excitement and he leapt to his feet exclaiming, "BEETLE! Beetle! Oh, I say! Beetle!"

A ripple of laughter ran round the room. "Steady on!" someone shouted, and Timmins sat down again, aware that all were watching him. His heart was pounding, and his face burned. "You fool!" a scornful little voice in his head reprimanded him. "What an exhibition, and over a childish game!" Subdued, Timmins submitted his paper to Millicent for inspection, then gathered up his pencil and paper. He got up and moved to the next table where Dorothy Manifold was sitting with the frizzy-haired woman from the first round and, to Timmins' dismay, Edna Dobson's Aunty Vi. He sat down, blushing. "Sorry about that," he muttered. "Got rather carried away. I'll try to behave myself better this time round."

Dorothy Manifold, who had failed to repeat her earlier success, patted his arm. "Don't worry, Vicar. It's nice to see you show enthusiasm for a change. You always seem to have the troubles of the world on your shoulders if you don't mind me saying so. You let yourself go - enjoy yourself. That's what this is all about. Isn't that right, Auntie Vi?"

Auntie Vi was arranging and rearranging a small collection of fountain pens which, Dorothy Manifold explained, had belonged to her late husband, a schoolmaster, and which she always carried with her. She frowned at Timmins, as if trying to place him and, as recognition dawned, she leered at him. "'Allo, Arthur, me duck," she said, blowing him a kiss.

'Oh, I say, Reverend!' said Dorothy Manifold. 'I think you've got an admirer! Don't worry,' she continued, seeing the panicked expression on Timmins' face, 'Edna will be back in a tick. She's just gone to spend a penny and then she'll help Auntie.' She grimaced. 'That woman will deafen us all again. I'd like to know what silly fool gave her that megaphone, I really would. She's a menace.'

Millicent gave the command as loudly as before, and the next round began. Once again, Timmins found himself gripped by the desire to win as first Dorothy Manifold scored four and then he threw a three. The frizzy-haired woman scored a six, much to her delight, and then it was Aunty Vi's go.

'What's this?' she said, mystified, as she peered into the cup. She reached in with bony fingers and took out the die. 'Ooooh!' she exclaimed, showing it round the table with the air of one who had just discovered a rare and precious jewel.

'Yes, dear, it's a die,' said Dorothy Manifold. 'Put it back in the cup, dear, and see if you can throw a six.'

Aunty Vi put the die back in the cup and swirled it round and round. At the other tables, people were shaking cups, rolling dice, shouting out their numbers in delight or disappointment. Somewhere in that room, thought Timmins, one player was edging ever nearer to victory, while still Aunty Vi rattled the die in the cup. He clenched his fists. Finally, Aunty Vi threw a six.

'That's it, dear!' cried Dorothy Manifold. 'Now draw the beetle's head.'

Aunty Vi surveyed her row of pens. She picked up a blue one, carefully unscrewed the cap then put both cap and pen down and blew another kiss at Timmins.

'You've got to draw the beetle's head!' he said, pointing to her piece of paper. She picked up a mottled green pen and unscrewed its cap, before attempting to screw it on to the blue pen. She carried out the whole operation with deliberation, and when she then picked up the cap of the blue pen and appeared to be about to attach it to a pencil, Timmins lost patience. What was the silly creature doing? Didn't she realise this was a competition?

Finally, he could no longer stand it. "Here, let me draw it for you!" He snatched up her piece of paper, drew the beetle's head and hurled it down in front of her. "There!"

As he grabbed the little cup and threw the die into it, he glanced up at the other occupants of the table. Aunty Vi was gazing at her paper with a puzzled expression on her face, and both the frizzy woman and Dorothy Manifold frowned at him. Oh dear, what a shameful display! Not behaviour fitting a man of the cloth. He steadied himself and prepared to throw.

Just then, to the sound of raucous laughter, the hall door burst open. The room fell silent as three men barrelled in. Leading the trio was the burly figure of Arnold Bubb, cloth cap awry, beer bottle in hand, swaying from side to side. "Pub's shut!" he announced, waving the bottle. "So we've come to drive some beetlesh! Beetley-weetley beetlesh. Wha's goin' on?" He took a long swig from the bottle, then staggered over to one table. He peered over the shoulder of one player, snatched up their paper and cried, "'Ere, Nobby, this beetle's the dead spit of you!" He waved the paper at one of his mates. "Bloomin' ugly blighter!"

Nobby, a gangling, red-headed man with slack lips and a livid scar on his brow, frowned. "You wanna watch yer mouth, Arnold Bubb!" he said, taking a step forward. "Just watch it, d'you 'ear me?"

The room prickled with tension. Timmins' heart sank. How dare these drunken louts spoil the evening? Somebody needed to step up and sort them out. He looked around the hall. Nobody moved.

'Nah, only jokin', Nobby!' Bubb, somewhat deflated, drained his bottle of beer, dropped the empty on to the floor, where it splintered into jagged shards, and took another from his pocket. 'Ere, have a pull on this!' He proffered the bottle to his companion. Nobby took it, bit off the cap and took a long draught. He wiped his lips and with a mocking glance at Bubb, passed the bottle to the third man, a lean, well-muscled individual with heavy black eyebrows and thin lips. 'Go on, Reg, have a drink on Bubb! He doesn't mind, do you Bubby-boy?'

Arnold Bubb seemed to shrink slightly as Reg drank. "Don't drink it all, Reggie!" he said, subdued. "Tha's my last one!"

Reggie turned the bottle upside down. It was empty. "Too late, old fella!" he said. 'What you going to do about it? Me an' Nobby reckon it was your round anyhow." He leered at Bubb, revealing discoloured, uneven teeth. "Not a problem is it, mate?" There was menace in his tone.

Bubb hesitated.

'Thought not,' said Reg, and laughed. 'You're all mouth, Arnie-boy!'

Bubb bristled.

Oh, Lord! thought Timmins. This situation threatened to become nasty. Panic bubbled up inside him as it always had at the merest hint of violence. Where was Millicent Gore-Hatherley with her megaphone? Or Harold Bungay, who was never backward in coming forwards? Why was nobody challenging these louts and asking them to leave?

Nobby staggered up to Arnold Bubb and ruffled his thinning hair. "Take no notice of Reggie!" he said. "Come on, I'm still thirsty... Let's 'ave a nice cuppa." He lurched past Bubb, knocking into the tables as he went, and disappeared into the kitchen where, to judge from the noise, he was rummaging through cupboards and drawers. "Where are the biscuits?"

Bubb and Reggie, bellowing with drunken laughter, followed him into the kitchen. There came the sound of crockery breaking.

'You need to do something about this, Vicar,' a voice whispered in Timmins' ear. Lavinia had materialised by his side.

'M... me?' squeaked Timmins. 'What can I do about it?' The thought of confronting these three drunken reprobates filled him with terror. Throughout his entire life he had hated violence, taking the motto 'Turn the other cheek' as his watchword. It had earned him the disdain of his father, who regarded him as a 'dashed cissy!' and of his schoolmates, who had nicknamed him as Trembler Timmins.

'You are in charge here, Samuel,' Lavinia whispered. 'For goodness' sake, do something before this gets nasty.'

Timmins got unsteadily to his feet. He opened his mouth to speak, but no words came. He swallowed hard and tried again. "You chaps! Come on now, don't spoil things."

Nobby poked his head out of the kitchen door. "Somebody say something?" he snarled.

Arnold Bubb appeared in the kitchen doorway. "The Vicar says we're spoiling things, Nobby, when all we want is a nice game of Beetle and a cup of tea, ain't it?" He staggered up to Timmins and stood over him with his arms folded. "Spoiling things, are we? That's not a very nice thing to say, is it? An' you a vicar an'? all. 'Ow are we spoilin' things, may I ask?"

Timmins gulped. His heart thudded and sweat prickled his brow.

'Show him who's boss!' a voice called from across the room. Bungay was enjoying the situation. 'Come on, Timmins. Sort them out so we can get back to our game.'

Seeing the amused expression on Bungay's shiny red face, Timmins felt a burst of anger. Why was he always the butt of the solicitor's jokes? The man was no better than Vosper and the ghastly boys at Grimwade College. As for Bubb and his loutish mates, how dare they spoil the fun? He glanced round the hall. White, worried faces stared back at him. He understood just how they felt at the bullying behaviour of the three interlopers. All his life he had been on the receiving end of such conduct. No longer. He could not allow Bubb, Nobby and Reggie to intimidate the crowd. He would show them all.

In a sudden burst of energy and resolve, he leapt to his feet, causing Bubb to stagger backwards.

'Take care, Samuel!' Lavinia cried.

Timmins rolled up his sleeves.

The Beetle players watched.

Bubb growled. Nobby and Reg came to stand beside him.

Timmins stepped forward. "Gentlemen!" he cried. "Welcome, Mr Bubb, and welcome to your friends. We are so pleased that you have come to join us..." He held out his hand, first to Bubb and then to his companions. Taken aback by the unexpected turn of events, they all shook it. "Allow me to introduce myself. I am Samuel Timmins, the vicar of this parish. If you would both take your seats at this table with Mr Bubb, we shall be glad to have you join in our fun and games. Miss Gore-Hatherley, perhaps you would be so kind as to explain the rules of the game while we rustle you up a fresh cup of tea and some biscuits. I am sure the rest of us do not mind waiting for a few minutes, do we, ladies and gentlemen?"

A murmur of surprise ran round the hall as the men went back to their seats and listened to Millicent's explanation of the game. Soon the competition continued, Nobby, Reg and Arnold Bubb joining in with surprising fervour.

Timmins, resuming his seat, felt that this had been a job well done. He, Samuel Hercules Timmins, had triumphed. He had vanquished the enemy and without having to raise his voice, let alone resort to fisticuffs. It might not have been the show of physical strength that his father would have admired, but it had been enough. Bungay was watching him, open-mouthed.

The rest of the evening passed without incident. When the time came for everyone to leave, there was general agreement that the event had been fun, and that the Vicar was "a jolly good sort." Donations to the church fund filled the little biscuit tin which Lavinia had placed by the door, and Arnold Bubb, Reg and Nobby each threw in a coin or two as they left with a muttered, "Night, Vicar. Thanks - and sorry about earlier."

Finally, when everyone had gone, Timmins surveyed the empty hall with its mess of chairs and tables. He collected up the dice and their cups, putting them into the cardboard box ready for storage under the stage. It would take ages to clear the room, but it had, he thought, been worth it. They had raised money, created goodwill and, best of all, he had triumphed in the face of adversity.

'Well done, Samuel.' A voice behind him startled him. There was

Lavinia, smiling. 'You did well tonight. Father would have been proud of you. I am proud of you.'

Timmins felt a pang, remembering how things had once been between them before she and Claude Augustus had betrayed him, leaving him feeling heartbroken and worthless. He turned away, busying himself with pushing the chairs neatly under the tables while he struggled to contain his emotions. What right had she to be proud of him?

The two years after his arrival in Quillington Parva had been years in which his feelings for her had deepened. He had wanted to marry her. For weeks he agonised about declaring his feelings, hesitating because he did not know what to say. He pictured the moment of declaration so many times, rehearsing different proposals. "Marry me, dearest," seemed either desperate or dictatorial, depending on how you looked at it, while "Lavinia! Darling! I adore you! Let us be together forever!" was a trifle too histrionic. How did one declare one's love? Girls were a mystery to him - there had been no females of his own age at school or at his theological college. The only girls he had ever had anything to do with were his sisters, Monica and Cecily, neither of whom had had any experience of relationships with the opposite sex, and each of whom would have squealed with laughter at the notion of their "baby brother" as a romantic lover.

From the moment they met, Lavinia's kindness, calm demeanour and thoughtful, dark-lashed grey eyes struck the young Timmins but each time he was in her capable, quiet presence he blushed and stammered. "She will never love you!" he told his reflection in the bathroom mirror each morning. "You cannot even speak to her without making a fool of yourself!"

One day, however, she found him reading in the study. He had picked up a copy of the rather racy "Red Hair" by Elinor Glyn, which lay on the desk, and, engrossed, he had not noticed her entering the room. He almost jumped out of his skin when she spoke.

'Good morning, Reverend Timmins! Have you seen my book? I cannot remember where I ... Oh! I see you have it. I do so admire Elinor Glyn! Her works are rather shocking but oh, such fun, do you not agree?'

Timmins, in a moment of abandon, agreed. "Oh, I do! They take one out of oneself. One cannot regard them as having much literary merit, but for sheer escapism they..." He stopped and the two of them burst out laughing. "I sound like a pompous fool! Literary merit be damned! I enjoy them! There, I confess! I like to read romantic fiction!"

From this point on the relationship had grown closer; they took long walks together, discussing their shared love of books, spent evenings reading aloud to each other and, as his shyness had faded, he realised that he was falling in love.

And then Claude Augustus arrived for a visit, handsome, self-assured and silver-tongued. "Just a few days," he said, blowing a cloud of smoke from his Turkish cigarette into Timmins' face. "Had a spot of bother with a lady, don't you know." He tapped the side of his nose with a manicured finger. "Need to lie low until her husband has cooled off a little." Breezing into the Vicarage, he installed himself in the guest bedroom and stayed for five weeks.

Claude Augustus was everything Timmins was not - urbane, charming and confident. From the moment he arrived, he monopolised Lavinia. Claude Augustus was a thrill seeker - he would take Lavinia "out for a spin" in his motor car, a gleaming green Spyker, challenge her to energetic games of tennis and flirt with her at every opportunity. He had so much energy and so many exciting tales to tell of his years "biffing about the world" in the Army and then "having a bash" at being a tea planter in Ceylon - how could he, Samuel Timmins, a mere curate in a quiet country parish, compete with such glamour?

Although she seemed happy to spend time with Claude

Augustus, from time to time she cast Timmins the odd concerned glance and sometimes he felt she was appealing to him to intervene, but he felt incapable of asserting himself. Claude Augustus, as was his wont, teased or ignored his brother, and Timmins felt once again that sense of helpless inadequacy that had dogged his childhood and youth. He was no match for Claude Augustus with his tales of adventure in far-flung places, his energy, daring and rugged good looks. How could he ever have thought Lavinia would favour him?

He could not bring himself to talk to her. No, it was better, he decided, to keep out of her way and avoid the risk of further rejection and humiliation. If she loved him, she would come to him - but she did not. Timmins had given up all hope of a future with Lavinia and avoided her company. When, at the end of the five weeks, Claude Augustus packed his bags and announced his imminent departure - "Can't moulder about too long in one place, don't you know?" - Lavinia tried to resume their old relationship, unaware she had offended Timmins, but he could not forgive her.

It had all come to a head one night when an invitation arrived to a ball at Hatherley Court. It was to celebrate the twenty-first birthday of Millicent Gore-Hatherley and would be a very swanky affair. Lavinia, excited at the prospect, made no secret of the fact she expected Timmins to escort her.

'Won't it be wonderful?' she said to him. 'I shall have a new dress and I shall wear mother's pearls! Oh, it will be such fun! And what of you, Samuel, dear? What shall you wear?'

Timmins pondered long and hard before he spoke. He could not forget how she had abandoned him for Claude Augustus. "I shall not be accompanying you and your father," he replied. "I do not approve of such frivolity and intend to spend the evening in study and quiet prayer." He saw the hurt expression on her face, felt the urge to twist the knife further. "What a pity it is that Claude Augustus is no longer here. I am sure that he would have proved a far more exciting companion than I, a mere curate in a dull little village such as this."

Her face fell. Part of him wanted to gather her in his arms and apologise, to shower kisses on that lovely face, but he also felt a cathartic pleasure in inflicting pain.

From then on, their former closeness had disappeared, replaced by a stiff, awkward politeness. Lavinia had devoted herself to caring for her ailing father while Timmins concentrated on his work. Claude Augustus had never again visited, and when Reverend Bellamy had died, Lavinia had moved out of the Vicarage to take up residence in the little cottage on the outskirts of the village which she had recently bought. She had lived there ever since, apart from the few years spent in Wales as a nurse and companion to her ailing cousin.

How long ago all that had been! What a waste of their two lives! And now here they were, two middle-aged people learning to be friends again. He looked around the empty hall and glimpsed his reflection in the window - plump, balding and well into middle age. Life was too short for petty squabbles.

'Thank you,' he said. 'Your father was dear to me. I valued his friendship... as I value yours.' She seemed tired - she had worked hard all evening, and now it was getting late. "We should leave the clearing-up until tomorrow. I am eager to tally up the takings - I feel in my bones we have raised a decent amount of money. Let's close the door on it for now and go home. I think we are both entitled to some rest, don't you?'

"Whatever you say, Samuel," she replied, putting on her coat. "And we shall have our reward next week, shall we not, when we go to see Evangeline Honeybell in concert?"

Oh, Lord! A whole evening in the company of that dreadful woman! Gloom descended upon him at the thought. "Yes," he replied. "What a prospect!"

CHAPTER ELEVEN

OUT FOR THE EVENING

The following Friday evening his little Austin 7 drew up outside Lavinia's cottage and Timmins stepped out, unfurling a large black umbrella. It had been raining all day. He shivered, drew his coat round himself, picked his way up the glistening brick path and rang the bell.

If only he had not won those blithering raffle tickets! He did not enjoy the works of Gilbert and Sullivan and had no desire to meet again with Evangeline. He was also uncertain about spending an entire evening with Lavinia. He had asked her to go with him on the spur of the moment, out of politeness, but a closeness seemed to have developed between them of late and he found it unsettling.

If only Claude Augustus had not insinuated himself into Lavinia's affections all that time ago, perhaps things would be very different. He and Lavinia might have married and, who knows, even had children? He tried to picture what they might have looked like. Would they have inherited her grey eyes with their long, dark lashes, or his blue, sandy-lashed ones? Would they have been slim and graceful like her, or would they, like him, have a tendency to plumpness? In his mind's eye he saw three, two girls and a boy, gathered around the fireplace in the Vicarage, Lavinia writing in her notebook, the children playing on the rug and he reading aloud to them.

"By sorrow of heart the spirit is crushed, Proverbs 15 verse 13," he lectured himself. "Be strong, Samuel." What had possessed him to invite Lavinia and risk stirring all that up again? He could have spent a cosy evening before the fire at home.

Finally, the door opened, and Lavinia stood before him in a pale grey velvet evening coat with a little matching hat trimmed with pearls and white ostrich feathers. "Good evening, Samuel," she said. "So sorry to keep you waiting. Ugh, what awful weather."

Her appearance took him by surprise, used as he was to seeing her clad in skirts and cardigans, home-made and dull. "I hope I am not over-dressed? I have not been to the theatre for such a long time." She took his arm and, as ever, she smelled of Lily of the Valley.

"Your outfit is exactly right, and, may I say, you look utterly charming." Head held high, shoulders back, Timmins sheltered her with his umbrella as they hurried back down the path. When they were both seated in the car, he turned to look at her, nodding in approval. "You will put all the other ladies to shame tonight, and I shall be the envy of all the gentlemen."

He was flirting! Quite a Don Juan, in fact! What was it that Guy, Comte de Chalfontaine had said to Amélie? Something about the moon and the stars? Ah, yes, that was it! "Your beauty," he exclaimed, "is as the silvery moon to the insignificant stars which pinprick the velvet black of the night."

"I beg your pardon?"

"What? Oh! Ha ha! Harrumph!" Timmins blushed. "Oh. Er, I beg your pardon! I don't know what I was thinking! I cannot say why it popped in to my head! I did not intend to offend! I say, are you quite well?"

Lavinia had made a strange, gurgling noise. Withdrawing a lace-edged handkerchief from her reticule, she blew her nose, "Yes, thank you. It surprised me to hear you quote from my ... one of my favourite books. Did not Guy, Comte de Chalfontaine, utter them when he and Amélie..."

"Yes! Yes!" Excitement caused Timmins to squeak. He cleared his throat. "Oh yes! Bravo for recognising them! Do you know, Miss

Bellamy, I can think of no more perfect way to spend an evening than to sit by my fire with a glass of sherry and a Madgwick novel. I'm not one for gallivanting about, nights on the town and so forth." Too late, he realised how she might interpret this. "Not," he hastened to add, "that I shall not enjoy your company this evening!" She did not reply.

Both were glad to exchange the chilly intimacy of the small car for the warmth and hubbub of the ornate red and gold theatre foyer. The air was thick with perfume, cigar smoke and the smell of damp clothing. Timmins escorted Lavinia to the Cloakroom and as Lavinia removed her coat, he felt a peculiar flush of pride. How elegant she looked in her powder-blue silk dress! How beautifully it draped, showing her slender figure and how the diamond clip in her neatly coiffed hair sparkled in the light. Lavinia carried herself with such grace and composure that she was, he thought, the most alluring female present.

"Samuel?" She looked at him quizzically. "Are you alright?"

Her words startled him. What was he thinking of, ogling her in that fashion? "Yes, of course," he said, and handed their coats to the cloakroom attendant. Pocketing the ticket, he turned to Lavinia, thinking to ask if she would like a drink before the show. He found her in conversation with a tall gentleman whose back was towards him. There was something familiar about the man's stance and he realised with a sinking heart who it was. Claude Augustus! What on earth was he doing here?

"Samuel! It's your brother!" Lavinia said. "How delightful! You didn't tell me he would be here."

So, she was pleased to see Claude Augustus, was she? Timmins pursed his lips.

"Ha! That's because he didn't know," said Claude Augustus, clapping Timmins on the shoulder so hard that he staggered. "Sammy and I don't keep in touch, you know! He's a miserable old devil. Keeps himself apart from the family, don't you know.

The dear old Pater was always saying he didn't know what we'd done to upset him. Still, we're here now. How are you, Sammy, old fruit?" He lodged his cigar in the corner of his mouth and thrust out a hand.

"Claude Augustus, what are you doing here?" The old feelings of helpless rage and impotence rose up again in Timmins, and he could not meet Claude Augustus's gaze. His older brother pumped his hand for several seconds, then slapped him still more vigorously on the back.

"Heard that Evangeline Honeybell was performing here and, as I've always been an admirer, I thought I'd pop along. I was in the area anyway - visiting a lady friend of mine in Quillinghampton. Her husband's away for a while, at Her Majesty's Pleasure, and she's lonely, so I offered to keep her company, don't you know? Last thing I expected was to bump into you. Thought you never ventured out at night." He turned to Lavinia. 'Always was a dull old stick, our Sammy. I swear nobody would guess that I'm the older brother - much less that he's ten years younger than me. I've got twice the get up and go that he has."

Before Timmins could reply, Lavinia spoke up. "Would you like a drink? We have time."

"Top-hole!" Claude Augustus exclaimed. "Mine's a whisky - large - and a splash."

Timmins scowled. What right had the fellow impose himself on their evening out? Surely Lavinia could see through his insufferable cockiness? He would like to knock the fellow's block off. He clenched his fists. How good it would feel to biff the stuffing out of Claude Augustus! A vision entered his head of his older brother lying spread-eagled on the ground before him.

Lavinia interrupted his thoughts, laughing at something Claude Augustus had said, sotto voce. "I'd like a small sherry please,' she said, then resumed her conversation with Claude Augustus.

Feeling that they had dismissed him, Timmins returned to the bar and ordered the drinks. The crowd jostled and shoved him as he made his way back with the tray of glasses. A fat man with a shiny bald head turned on him. "I say! Watch where you're going..." The words died on his lips as he noticed Timmins' dog collar. "Sorry, Vicar. Allow me." He stepped aside. Others were less accommodating and by the time Timmins rejoined Lavinia and Claude Augustus, his hands were sticky, the glasses all a little emptier than they should have been, and he was in a bad temper.

"What-ho, young Sammy!" Claude Augustus said, as he handed them their drinks and handed the tray to a passing usher. "No good as a waiter, are you? Half my tipple seems to have disappeared. Or did you snaffle it on the way?" He lifted his glass. "Down the hatch and all that." He quaffed the remaining whisky in one go. "Good stuff! I'd buy another round, but the show's about to kick off. I need to pop to the little boys' room first, so I'll see you later, perhaps?" With that, he bowed to Lavinia and disappeared.

"Well, that was a nice surprise," said Lavinia. "He hasn't changed."

Timmins snorted. Claude Augustus was still the same cocksure, unreliable, self-centred man he had always been, although the years had taken their toll on him. Once lithe and handsome, his figure was now stout and his florid face weather-beaten from his various adventures abroad, big game hunting and working for the Colonial Service, something he had taken up in later years. "I fear," he said, "that my brother will never alter his ways. Now, shall we find our seats? We are in the Royal Box."

"Ooh, how exciting!" To Timmins' surprise, Lavinia took his arm and together they made their way to the box.

The performance was all that Timmins had expected and feared. In her role as Buttercup Evangeline was, he thought, overblown and blowsy. Her voice was powerful enough, but she would keep looking at him!

"Ah, I know too well,

The anguish of a heart that loves but vainly!"

she trilled, gazing at the Royal Box, and in Act 2, clasping her hands over her heart and fluttering her eyelashes she declaimed, scowling at Lavinia,

"Of whom is he thinking? Of some high-born beauty?"

"It may be!" Evangeline continued.

"Who is poor little Buttercup that she should expect his glance to fall on one so lowly? And yet if he knew - if he only knew..."

Timmins shifted in his seat, the plush upholstery prickling through his trousers. She was outrageously forward! What a spectacle she was making of herself. All the time she was singing of love, she was directing her words in his direction.

When, at long last, the operetta finished, to rapturous applause, the door of the Royal Box opened and in came Claude Augustus. "What-ho, old boy!" he greeted his brother. "Fancy a snifter or two? I'm sure the lovely lady could do with a reviver, eh, Lavinia, my dear?" Sidling up to her, he slid his arm around her waist. "Sammy is probably desperate to get home to bed - always was a wet blanket, weren't you? I'll never forget that time when Pa and Ma were entertaining Lord and Lady Plogstead, and you..."

"Miss Bellamy and I have a late supper engagement." Timmins glanced at his wristwatch. "So we will be on our way."

"Oh, yes?" Claude Augustus squeezed Lavinia, who, with a squeal of surprise, prised his arm from her waist. " I say," Claude Augustus stroked his moustache. "Well done, you."

"Lavinia, we should not keep our hostess waiting." Timmins crooked his arm. "We are dining with Miss Evangeline

Honeybell," he said to Claude Augustus. "If you will excuse us, we shall be on our way."

Claude Augustus bowed over Lavinia's hand, kissing it. "Enjoy the rest of your evening, my dear," he said. 'I trust that Sammy is taking you two lovely ladies somewhere nice?"

Lavinia withdrew her hand, wiping it surreptitiously on her dress. "Thank you," she said. "We are meeting Miss Honeybell in the restaurant. She has booked a table for us at L'Amuse-Bouche," she said, glancing at Timmins for confirmation, and to his horror she added, "I am sure you would be most welcome to join us, to make up a four."

"Ha!" Claude Augustus exclaimed. "It would delight me - what say you, Sammy old lad?" He raised one neatly trimmed grey eyebrow. "You wouldn't mind if I tagged along, would you?"

This was appalling! To give his assent would mean having to endure the company of his older brother for far longer than he cared, yet to deny the invitation would be to make him appear churlish at the very least. He glared at Lavinia. "I suppose not, if Miss Bellamy wishes you to join us. I shall retrieve our coats. Miss Honeybell will meet us at the restaurant."

L'Amuse-Bouche was busy. Waiters in black waistcoats and long white aprons bustled hither and thither, laden with tiers of white plates. Tantalising odours of garlic, meaty casseroles, strong cheeses and fresh-baked bread filled the air. Plumes of aromatic tobacco smoke spiralled upwards to create a blue haze in the room, while the music of cutlery on china and clinking glasses punctuated the noise of conversation. Timmins' stomach rumbled. It was so long since he had last eaten.

"Bonsoir, messieurs dames." The maîtred'hôtel slid into view behind a carved mahogany desk. Thin, and brown as a nut, with slicked back black hair and a toothbrush moustache, he inclined his head in a small bow of greeting. "Vous avez une réservation?"

Timmins gave his name.

The maîtred'hôtel frowned and ran his finger over the open pages. "Timmins... Timmins," he muttered, shaking his head. "Non, m'sieur, je suis désolé mais je ne vois pas.... I do not see zis name." He sniffed. "I am afraid, Monsieur," he said, his small mouth curving in a fixed smile, "zat I cannot accommodate you zis evening. As you see, we are vairy busy."

"Ha, Sammy, old lad," Claude Augustus said. "That's a facer! No room at the inn and all that." Frowning at the maître d'hôtel, he cleared his throat. "Now, my man," he said loudly, wagging his finger, "Mon frère here is a man of the cloth - un homme de dieu, voyez-vous. Never told a lie in his life. If he says he's got a reservation, then bien sûr, he has got a reservation. So run your eye over the book again and let's have a little less of an attitude." To Timmins and Lavinia he remarked, "You've got to be firm with these people, you see?"

Themaître d'hôtel flushed, and the smile disappeared. Straightening his back, he met Claude Augustus's gaze. "Monsieur, zere is no booking in ze name of Timmins. You may take my word for it. Now if you will excuse me, I am a leetle busy..." He gave a curt nod, and with a curl of the lip, made as if to leave them.

"But..." Timmins protested. He had been so looking forward to his meal.

"If I may..."Lavinia interrupted. "Monsieur, perhaps you will find a table booked in the name of Miss Evangeline Honeybell. We are guests of that lady."

"Ah! Mais, oui! Mademoiselle 'Oneybell! Zat is a different matter! She 'as booked ze best table in ze 'ouse." He frowned at Timmins. "Why did you not say zis? Suivez-moi s'il vous plaît." Beckoning them to follow, he slid through the restaurant, weaving round the busy waiters and climbing the few stairs that led to a raised dining area at the side of the room. This was where people sat when they wanted to be seen and Timmins, despite himself, found his back straightening with pride as the maître d'hôtel showed them their table right at the front, overlooking the main body of the restaurant.

"Permettez-moi." The maître d'hôtel relieved Lavinia and Timmins of their coats, handing the to a waiter whom he summoned with a snap of the fingers. He pulled out a chair for Lavinia.

Claude Augustus removed his own heavy overcoat and threw it at the waiter, who, reeling from the unexpected impact, folded the coats over his arm and bustled away. Claude Augustus pulled out the chair beside Lavinia, sat down, leaned back and ordered a bottle of champagne. "Quick as you like" he said, snapping his fingers at the maître d'hôtel, who bowed and muttered, through gritted teeth, "Mais oui, monsieur, bien sûr!" glided away to instruct the wine waiter.

"This is just the ticket!" Claude Augustus exclaimed, taking a fat cigar from a silver case and lighting it. "I say, Sammy old thing, I'm jolly glad I bumped into you this evening." He drew on the cigar and blew out a plume of smoke. "This is better than a pint and a pie down the old Fox and Hounds! Oh, and if I'm not mistaken, your lady friend has just arrived."

Something was afoot in the main body of the restaurant. There was a change in the atmosphere - voices stopped chattering, glasses ceased clinking, and in the sudden quiet they could hear a familiar voice trilling.

"I'm called Little Buttercup, dear little Buttercup,
Though I could never tell why,
But still I'm called Buttercup, poor little Buttercup,
Sweet little Buttercup, I!"

Rapturous applause greeted her as Evangeline entered, dressed in a shimmering, elaborately beaded puce and black dress and a sparkling diamond and feather headband. "Darlings!" she cried, blowing extravagant kisses to the diners and waiting staff alike as she followed the maître d'hôtel like an ocean liner following a tug. "How kind! You are too kind!" The two feathers in her headband, one puce and one black, bobbed and waved as she walked, and as she approached their table Timmins caught a strong whiff of the familiar Nuit d'Amour perfume. Good Lord, the woman must bathe in the stuff, he thought, as he rose and stepped forward to greet her.

"There you are, you darling man," she trilled, holding out her hand for him to kiss. He took it, shuddering at its clammy feel, and touched it briefly to his lips. "Miss Honeybell," he said, "I am sure you remember Miss Lavinia Bellamy, who has, as my guest, taken the second ticket which I, er, which I was lucky enough to win."
"Good evening, Miss Honeybell," said Lavinia, smiling. "We are most honoured to be here. We so enjoyed your performance this evening, did we not, Reverend?"

"What? Oh, yes. Yes, it was most, um, entertaining - quite delightful," Timmins replied.

Evangeline glanced at Lavinia. "Why, thank-you," she said. "I am honoured that you should join us, Miss... But who is this?" Her gaze moved to Claude Augustus, who waited for an introduction, twirling his moustache and regarding the singer with an expression that Timmins thought most inappropriate.

"Allow me to introduce my older brother, Claude Augustus Timmins."

Claude Augustus clicked his heels, drew himself up to his full height and saluted the singer. "Major Claude Augustus Timmins at your service, ma'am," he said. "I trust you will forgive my intrusion, but I could not resist the opportunity of meeting the celebrated Miss Evangeline Honeybell, and at the risk of seeming indelicate allow me to say I shall pay my way. May I say," he continued, as Evangeline inclined her head, "that your talent is matched only by your beauty. How could I resist the chance of spending an evening in the company of two such delightful representatives of the fair sex?"

He took Evangeline's hand, kissed it,and blew a little kiss at Lavinia.

Evangeline blushed, fluttering her eyelashes at Claude Augustus. "You are too kind," she simpered.

Timmins shifted in his seat. Claude Augustus was up to his old tricks again. It did not make for pretty viewing.

"I am honoured you should wish to join us," said Evangeline. "It is so much more pleasant to be a party of four, do you not think, Miss... Miss... Billingly? Three is such an awkward number. I have been so thrilled at the prospect of renewing my acquaintance with this darling man and now neither of us need to play gooseberry to the other." She mouthed a little kiss at Timmins.

Claude Augustus chortled, the ends of his moustache dancing as his body shook. "Hear that, Lavinia, old love? We appear to have been brought here under false pretences! Seems we are here only to chaperone these two lovebirds. Ha! Well, well, well, Sammy, you sly old dog! When did you get to be such a ladies' man? Didn't think you had it in you!" He blew a cloud of smoke across the table and picked a shred of tobacco from his teeth.

Timmins felt a rush of anger. How was it that Claude Augustus made him feel so small and stupid? It had always been the same. He opened his mouth to protest, but no words came out. Instead, he uttered a little squeak of surprise, for Evangeline, with that tinkling laugh he found so irritating, had reached out under the table and given his thigh a most painful squeeze. She removed her hand, put her elbows on the table, linked her fingers and rested her chin on her plump hands.

"I think you wrong your brother, Major Timmins," she said, in a voice which she clearly considered seductive. "He is an attractive man. Very attractive, and I am sure he has all the ladies of the parish at his beck and call. Is that not so, Miss Bottomley?"

"Bellamy," replied Lavinia. "My name is Bellamy, but please, call me Lavinia." She picked up a menu and opened it. "Perhaps we should order."

A shadow passed over Evangeline's face. "Oh, my dear, Miss Bellamy, you poor little thing!" she cried. "You are hungry!" She patted Lavinia's hand. "Are you au fait with French cuisine? It can be quite ... daunting when one is confronted by a menu entirely en français. I shall be delighted to help, should you need assistance."

Lavinia regarded the singer levelly for a moment. "Thank-you, Miss Honeybell, but that will not be necessary. My mother was French et je parle couramment le français."

"Oh. Très bon." Evangeline turned to the men. "To my mind la cuisine française is the finest in the world, and "L'Amuse-Bouche" one of its best exponents - exclusive, and so difficult to get a table here! I am a lucky, lucky girl to be on such good terms with dear Fabrice, the owner. He always saves this table for me when I am in Quillinghampton." She sighed. "Alas, my lifestyle means that I rarely dine anywhere else but in the most highly regarded restaurants. I am so accustomed to the best that to me, foie gras is as meat paste to others." She giggled. "As a result, I eat very little. I have been spoiled, you see. Nevertheless, I shall try to force down a mouthful or two - Fabrice employs the best of chefs. I shall begin with the moules marinière - just a few, then a bite or two of the salmon rillettes, and then possibly a small helping of the coq au vin, and if I have room afterwards, the crêpes Suzette."

"Ha ha!" roared Claude Augustus, snapping his fingers to summon a waiter. "Jolly good! Spiffing choice, my dear lady. I shall follow suit. What about you, old lad, and you, Miss

Bellamy? Made your minds up yet? I'm ravenous; my stomach thinks my throat's been cut! By Jove, I could eat a scabby horse!"

Timmins shuddered. Claude Augustus could be so coarse!

The food, and a bottle of champagne, arrived in due course, whereupon Claude Augustus proposed a toast to the evening and drained his glass, refilling and emptying it a second time before the others had drunk more than a few sips. Timmins was aghast at the way both Evangeline and Claude Augustus attacked the first course. Conversation ceased as they got to grips with their mussels, ripping the molluscs out of their shells and making little grunting noises of pleasure as they chewed. Claude Augustus paused only to order a second bottle of champagne.

Timmins glanced at Lavinia, who was eating consommé. Her manners were so far superior to Miss Honeybell's, despite the latter's professed familiarity with all those fine dining establishments. In between bites of toast and chicken liver pâtéhe watched her, noting as if for the first time how elegant she was, and how dainty. Where and when had she gained that air of sophistication? Evangeline might be more worldly wise, but Lavinia was by far the most appealing of the two.

"Penny for them, Sammy, old lad," Claude Augustus interrupted, dipping his great fingers in the finger bowl and wiping first them, and then his mouth, on his stiff white napkin. He drained his wineglass and poured himself another drink, emptying the bottle.

"What? Oh, er, nothing."

"Snap out of it then, there's a lad. Ah, here's the chappy to clear the plates. What say we order a bottle or two of Viognier and then a couple of bottles of claret to go with the entrées? Yes?"

Timmins stared at his brother. Was there no end to the man's desire for physical gratification? He had gobbled his appetiser in the most disgusting manner, drunk greedily of the champagne, and now he proposed to order yet more alcohol. He opened his mouth to protest, but Evangeline spoke first.

"Oh, yes, darling. She dimpled at Claude Augustus. "Why not? Let us ... indulge ourselves." Once again she reached out under the table to find his leg while Timmins attempted to avoid her grasp. "I have an insatiable appetite for all the good things in life." The black and puce feathers in her headband trembled as she spoke.

Claude Augustus let out a bellowing laugh. "And why not? You're a gal after me own heart I must say!" He stroked first one side of his neatly manicured handlebar moustache, and then the other, gazing appreciatively at her. "Cannot abide a thin woman. That Captain Corcoran chappie got it quite right in Pinafore when he called Buttercup a 'plump and pleasing person!' Description suits you to a T, if I may say so without causing offence - you are quite the most delicious, luscious, delectable plump and pleasing person!" He savoured every word, twiddling the end of his moustache as he spoke. Evangeline giggled.

The man was almost salivating. It was most disconcerting. What gave Claude Augustus the confidence to behave like this with women? He had always been the same, never doubting his own masculine appeal. As a young man he had been of athletic build, handsome in a way that Timmins had always thought rather bovine. Married and divorced twice, he was now, in his early sixties, still able to exercise some kind of charm over the opposite sex. Evangeline was putty in his hands, and even Lavinia had been eager to invite the fellow to dine with them.

He watched as his brother and the singer blew kisses to each other across the table, listened as Claude Augustus regaled them with off-colour stories of his time in the army and then, unable to bear it any longer, spoke out. "For the Lord's sake, Claude Augustus! Please, consider the feelings of these ladies and moderate your language. In the words of the Good Book, "Let your speech be always with grace, seasoned with salt, that ye may know how ye ought to answer every man..."

He had spoken more loudly than he intended. A hush fell over the diners at nearby tables and a waiter stumbled in surprise, almost dropping his burden. Timmins felt the blood rush to his face. Feeling suddenly very exposed, he sank down in his chair, slumping his shoulders to shrink from view.

Claude Augustus opened his mouth and Timmins waited for the verbal assault that was sure to follow. Instead, his brother roared with laughter. "Well, I never! That told me, old fellow! Didn't know you had it in you! Ah, here's our next course, by Jove."

As the waiter placed the plates before them, Timmins felt Evangeline's hand on his knee once more. She leaned towards him and said in a theatrical whisper, "You darling man! How sweet of you to defend my honour – so noble of you!" Timmins withdrew his knee from her grasp.

The fish course passed without further incident but as they ate their entrées, Timmins noticed that Evangeline, after several glasses of wine, seemed once more to be edging closer to him and putting her food into her mouth in a manner he could only suppose she believed to be seductive. He tried to concentrate on his meal, but it was no good; he may as well have been eating sawdust. Halfway through his coq au vin, she serenaded him, her face flushed and her words slurred.

"For he loves little Buttercup, dear little Buttercup.

Though I could never tell why;

But still he loves Buttercup, dear little Buttercup,

Sweet little Buttercup, aye!"

Timmins could bear it no longer. He threw down his knife and fork. "Madam," he hissed, as he got to his feet, "I thank you for your hospitality but..."

"Wha's up?" Claude Augustus burst in. "You going to entertain us all with a song now?" He put his fingers in his ears. "I'd recommend you two ladies follow suit. Not much of a singer, our laddie here. Got a voice like a squeaky gate."

Rage bubbled up inside Timmins. What right did his brother have to insult and demean him? He had had just about enough. The Lord knew just how much effort he had put into being polite this evening towards Claude Augustus and this dreadful woman, and they had, between them, done nothing except ridicule and tease him. Enough was enough!

"I am glad, brother," he said, "that you find me so amusing. I cannot, in all honesty, however, say I have found your behaviour, or that of Miss Honeybell, similarly entertaining this evening. I have tried to ignore your excessive drinking and your lewd conduct, but I can tolerate it no longer. As the psalm says, "Your arrows have sunk deep in me, your hand has come down upon me." I shall leave you both to enjoy the rest of the meal together. Miss Bellamy, will you join me? I shall be more than willing to order you a taxi, at my expense, should you wish to finish your meal?"

Lavinia dabbed at her mouth with a napkin, glanced apologetically at Evangeline and Claude Augustus, and stood up. "No, Reverend Timmins. I came as your guest and it is only right I should leave with you. Please excuse us, Miss Honeybell, and thank you for a most interesting evening. Good evening, Claude Augustus."

CHAPTER TWELVE

AN EXCHANGE OF WORDS

Timmins and Lavinia left the restaurant to find it was still raining and blowing a gale. They hurried through the empty streets to the car, Timmins striding ahead of his companion, who half-walked, half-ran to keep up with him, and as he walked, he replayed the events of the evening in his mind.

What a fool he had made of himself! He was used to Claude Augustus ridiculing him and usually managed not to respond, but this evening - in front of all those people - he had allowed his brother to provoke him into making a spectacle of himself. It was galling, particularly as he had had to leave his coq au vin unfinished and had missed out on the dessert course. He sighed at the thought of the bombe néro he had ordered. It was the show-stopping signature dessert, a miraculous concoction of sponge, ice-cream and meringue for which L'Amuse-Bouche was famed; the description on the menu had made his mouth water and now Claude Augustus, that dreadful woman and his own stupidity had conspired to make sure he would not get to enjoy it.

"Reverend Timmins! Samuel! You have gone too far!"

Timmins stopped. Had he heard right? Was Lavinia now going to chastise him? What did she mean, he had gone too far? "What?" he barked.

"You have gone too far," she repeated. "This is our car." She was standing some distance back, next to his little Austin 7. He had been so wrapped up in his thoughts he had stalked past it.

The wind buffeted the little car as they wound their way back to Quillington Parva and the windscreen wiper struggled against the onslaught of the rain. Timmins leaned forward as he drove, clutching the wheel and peering over it to see the way ahead. There was silence apart from the noise of the engine and the rhythmic clonk of the wiper, and then Lavinia said, "Are you going to explain your conduct this evening?"

Timmins could not believe his ears. Explain his conduct? His knuckles whitened. Fury, indignation and misery coursed through him, while a niggling little voice in his head told him he was being unreasonable. Lavinia had invited his brother to dinner, true, but deep in his heart he knew that throughout the meal she had been just as uncomfortable as he. Claude Augustus had been in the wrong. He must have known Lavinia had invited him to join them only in a spirit of politeness. Nevertheless, he, Samuel Hercules Timmins, had once again ended up looking foolish and now, not having the true perpetrators of his humiliation present, he could only vent his spleen on Lavinia.

"I do not see how you need to ask me that question." He bit his lip as he negotiated a tricky bend in the road which, in his heightened state, he had taken too fast. Lavinia gasped and he saw, out of the corner of his eye, that she was gripping the door handle. Irritation at her clear lack of trust in his driving ability compounded his bad mood. "Did you not see the way Claude Augustus behaved?" he snapped, his tone icy. "Were you not aware of his excessive drinking, his revolting table manners, his constant flirting with that dreadful woman, his lewd tales and the continual insults directed towards me? What self-respecting man would put up with all that? I tolerated it for as long as I could, but even a worm will, they say, turn. I am sorry if you feel hard done by, but you did not have to leave the restaurant with me. You seemed perfectly at ease in the company of those two creatures and could have stayed to finish your meal. I did, as I recall, offer to pay for a taxi."

Lavinia was quick to respond. She spoke in a calm, reasoned tone which grated on him. "You did Samuel, but I could not possibly have remained. You understand that. When one attends an event as the guest of another, one's loyalties lie with that person. To have stayed in the restaurant when you were so unhappy would have been to have made an implicit statement that I did not agree with your behaviour and would have given Miss Honeybell and Claude Augustus cause to be even more critical of you. As your friend, I could not behave in that fashion. I had no alternative."

Timmins set his jaw. Friend, she said! Ha! A true friend would have protested against the humiliation they had forced him to endure that evening. Why did nobody ever support him? It had ever been thus.

He drove on through the darkness. The rain was heavier now, crashing against the windscreen. Streams of muddy brown water raced and tumbled along the side of the road, here and there spilling over to flood the road surface itself. A bellowing roar of thunder drowned the engine's noise. Timmins jumped, shock prickling his skin, and momentarily lost control of the car which swerved. Fear gave him the ability to regain control. That was close! A second thunderclap cracked and immediately afterwards a streak of lightning sliced a jagged cut in the sky, illuminating, for a brief second, the twisting road ahead and the trees which overhung it.

"Look out!" Lavinia grasped his wrist.

A large deer had sprung out from between the trees into the road in front of the car. For a fleeting moment it stood there, pale against the black night. Timmins slammed his foot on the brake, clutched the steering wheel and prayed as the car headed straight for the creature. Time seemed to slow down as Timmins awaited the dreadful impact and its terrible consequences. At the last moment, however, the deer jumped back into the safety of the woods. The car skidded and came to a halt where the animal had stood.

"Good Lord!" Timmins exclaimed, although whether the

exclamation was a response to the shock, or because Lavinia was still clutching his arm, he was not sure. The unfamiliar contact with her had disturbed his equilibrium. Nobody ever touched him - unless it was to shake hands. Her gesture was intimate and possessive - caring, even?

At the moment when this thought entered his head, however, she removed her hand, regarded him coolly, and said, "Well? Do you have nothing to say?"

He shuddered. Her words, if not her tone of voice, reminded him of boyhood scoldings, and, just as had happened back then, it robbed him of the power of speech.

They sat in silence for a minute or two as the rain thrummed on the roof and he tried to collect his thoughts. Lavinia's words whirled round in his mind - how should he respond? On the one hand, her assessment of the evening's events was reasonable - she had been his guest, referred to herself as his friend and she had, in leaving the restaurant with him, showed Claude Augustus and Evangeline that her first loyalties were with him. Yet she had said she had had no alternative - did that mean she had, in fact, wished to stay and finish her meal? Was she implying that he had been selfish in putting her in that position?

Without speaking, he put the car into gear and they set off again through the cold, wet darkness of the night. Oh, how he wished he had never come out this evening. At last, when the silence between them had become so thick it was almost tangible, he burst out, "I should have given the raffle prize to you. You could have invited Claude Augustus and the pair of you would have had a much better evening together."

"For goodness' sake, Samuel!" she said, "don't be so disingenuous. Your invitation pleased me, and it delighted me to accept. I enjoy your company far more than that of Claude Augustus - you know full well that he has a way of getting what he wants and once he found out you and I had an engagement with

Evangeline, it was only a matter of time before he got himself invited along." She tutted and shook her head. "Between you, me and the gatepost, and at the risk of offending you, Samuel, I have never liked him but he is your brother and so I feel I must be polite to him. As for that woman - well, I feel sorry for her. She, it seems, still believes herself to possess the charm and allure of youth and cannot stop herself from trying to exercise those charms on any man who is unfortunate enough to catch her attention."

Timmins stared. Never had he heard her speak in such a forthright manner. "But you jilted me in favour of my brother!" he exclaimed. "I was, as you well know, on the verge of proposing to you and then Claude Augustus landed on our doorstep, insinuated himself into your affections and you spurned me. Oh, I know that he was largely to blame, but you deserted me! You rebuffed me in the cruellest fashion while you and Claude Augustus made fun of me behind my back and..."

"I did no such thing!" There was steel in her voice. "I did not understand, Samuel, that you had any intention of proposing marriage. No, do not interrupt! You gave not the slightest sign you had any such idea, although I believe that my fondness for you cannot have gone unnoticed since I always took every opportunity to seek your company."

"Until a better prospect came along and..."

"I found you attractive, Samuel; I loved you. Surely you knew it? You were so vulnerable, yet so determined to learn from Papa and to do your job well; I admired you. When Claude Augustus came to stay that time, hiding from the husband of some woman he'd had an affair with, I could not help but notice the difference between you and ..."

"Ha! You see?"

"...and it increased my affection for you. Here was your older brother who was everything you were not, confident, outgoing, flirtatious, physically strong..."

"Ha again! Now we're getting to it!" Outside Lavinia's cottage, Timmins switched off the engine and yanked up the handbrake.

"... but a liar and a cheat, untrustworthy, rapacious and selfish."

"And yet you spent all your time with him! You ignored me and went off with him!"

"Because he was our guest!" The note of exasperation in her voice cut through him. "You would have nothing to do with him and Father was too busy to entertain him. One cannot have a house-guest and then ignore him - I had no choice but to fulfil the role of hostess, and that is all it was." She gave a little sigh of exasperation. "I don't believe you, Samuel. Do you think so little of me? Do you imagine I would prefer a man like that? That I could be so easily taken in by him? No! I was simply doing my duty by him, and then you seemed to reject me. You would not speak to me." She paused, and there was a catch in her voice when she spoke again. "You hurt me, Samuel, and so I left you alone, hoping that you would, one day, come back to me. I see now I was mistaken in that hope."

Could this be true? Had she never known of his intentions towards her? The thought of two lives being so affected by a misunderstanding was more than he could bear. "Lavinia, I..."

She gathered her bag and her gloves. When she spoke, her tone was terse. "No, say no more. Thank you for this evening. It has been most enlightening. I have business to attend to in London and shall not see you for some time now, which is probably for the best. As Amélie Delacour said to Guy, Comte de Chalfontaine on the occasion of his apparently having been unfaithful to her, 'It is better to live with the golden thought of what might have been, rather than the tainted memory of something that was.'"

Despite a turmoil of emotions, this speech struck Timmins. When had Amélie Delacour ever said that? He did not recall the words and his was, he thought, an extensive knowledge of the works of Blossom Madgwick.

'I see you do not intend to comment Samuel, so I shall say farewell. There is no need to see me to the door. Goodnight.' She got out of the car, letting in a blast of cold air and needle-sharp rain which jolted Timmins out of his thoughts. She hurried up her garden path, head bowed against the wind and rain. A light came on in the cottage.

Rain lashed the car, thunder roared, and a fork of lightning split the sky, illuminating for an instant the outline of the village ahead of him, the church tower standing tall at its centre. Timmins did not move. The black cloud of misery that engulfed him was almost palpable. What had just happened? Somehow, in the space of a few moments, he, not Claude Augustus, had become the villain of the piece! "Oh Lord," he whispered, "what am I to do?"

The only reply was the whistling of the wind as it fingered its way in, groping its way down his neck. He shivered and pulled coat closer around him. He pictured his father's glaring face. "Don't be such a milksop, boy! We Timmins don't feel sorry for ourselves! We pull ourselves up by our bootstraps and soldier on. Get a grip, for goodness' sake!"

At the Vicarage, Mrs Whibley had left the porch light on, as he had requested, but apart from that the house was in darkness and the silence struck him as he let himself in the front door. He had nobody to welcome him home. Nobody to offer comfort after a very trying evening; nobody to take his side and tell him they loved him. A great weight of loneliness and misery settled itself on his shoulders as he removed his coat, hat and shoes and went to sit on the bottom stair, head in his hands. "You fool, Samuel Timmins," he said aloud. "You utter fool."

At his words, a cacophony of barking began. Mrs Whibley had shut Poffley in the kitchen where he had spent the evening snoozing in front of the range, but on hearing Timmins' voice he scraped and hurled himself at the kitchen door.

Timmins did not respond. "What have I done?" he groaned. "Lavinia! Oh, Lavinia!"

"Woof! Woof!" Poffley barked, hurling himself at the door.

"Be quiet, you dratted beast!" shouted Timmins. He was in no mood for the animal's boisterousness. "Leave me to my misery!" Even as he spoke, he knew how ridiculous he sounded, and he blushed. He must pull himself together. He stood up and put his shoulders back. Life must go on. He was, after all, a Timmins.

Just then, Poffley succeeded in forcing open the kitchen door. He came bounding and barking along the corridor and launched himself, tail wagging and tongue lolling, at his master. The sudden impact of the dog's weight sent Timmins reeling. "Down, Poffley!" he cried, shielding his face from the wet, pink tongue. "Get down, you blasted creature!" But Poffley was not listening to instructions; he bounced and leapt and licked and barked until Timmins, overwhelmed, staggered, lost his footing and fell over backwards, landing with a thud on the floor, the dog on top of him.

"Oh, Poffley! You ridiculous animal!" he gasped, attempting to fend off Poffley's kisses. The dog, however, would not give up, and at last Timmins lay back, succumbing to his attentions. When he had finished, Poffley lay down beside his master and gazed at him. Timmins felt the dog's warm breath on his face, and this time he did not resist. There was something comforting about it. He reached out and stroked Poffley's silky ear, and for a time the two of them lay there.

"Good old boy," Timmins murmured, whereupon the dog recommenced licking his face. "Ugh! That's enough!" He pushed Poffley gently away. "I had a bath this morning - I'm clean enough, thank you!" For a few moments the pair of them wrestled on the hall floor, until Timmins sat up. "Come on, you ludicrous beast. I wonder if there are any tasty morsels in the kitchen." He shoved Poffley off his lap and clambered to his feet. He felt rather peckish. "I missed my pudding. I wonder if Mrs Whibley has been baking?"

At the mention of biscuits, Poffley barked again and went tearing off down the hallway to the kitchen, followed by Timmins. "I shall have a splendid bruise in the morning, Poffley," he called, rubbing his back, "thanks to you!" However, he found that he did not mind; Poffley's enthusiasm and energy was, he realised, an effective antidote to the misery of the evening; it was refreshing, and rather enjoyable, to receive such a warm, affectionate greeting." Dear old Poffley!" he said, as he searched through the tins and packets in the larder for something to give the dog. "You're not such a bad lad, are you?"

"Woof," Poffley barked in agreement, and Timmins laughed, tossing the dog a bone-shaped biscuit he had found in a dog-shaped tin.

While Poffley crunched his treat, Timmins cut himself an enormous slice of chocolate sponge he had discovered hidden at the back of the pantry. "It's not quite a bombe néro, Poffley, but if I cannot have that, then this will have to suffice." A thick layer of chocolate butter cream sandwiched the two layers together and covered the top and sides. "I say!" Timmins murmured, wondering if the slice he had taken was big enough.

Mrs Whibley had stoked the fire before she left for the day, and the sitting-room bathed in its cheery red glow. Timmins switched on the standard lamp and sat down on the sofa, sinking into its deep, feather-filled cushions. "Aaah," he sighed, "that's better!"Poffley jumped up beside him on the sofa, turned round and round, nudging and snuffling the cushions, then flopped down.

"A glass of sherry! That's what's missing!" Timmins perched his plate on the coffee table and got up to pour himself a large glass.

As he did so, he noticed, next to the cut crystal decanter, a brown paper package with a little note attached. "This came by the late afternoon post. Do not touch the chocolate cake - it is for your meeting with the Fête Committee tomorrow."

"My book!" he cried. He had ordered it last week by telephone from Gimble's, his favourite bookshop in Quillinghampton. "I say, Poffley, it's the latest Blossom Madgwick! Just what a chap needs after such a trying evening!" Tearing off the brown paper wrapper, he gazed at the front cover, which depicted a raven-haired beauty, her scarlet cloak wrapped around her and blowing against the wind. She gazed up at the lighted window of an imposing château where a man stood gazing out into the night. At the woman's feet was a large, handsome dog with amber eyes. "Amélie and Aristide" was the title of this latest adventure.

"Good gracious! Look at the picture of the dog on this book cover, Poffley. Looks just like you," he said, taking the book and his sherry back to the sofa. Contentment and wellbeing spread through him. This was more like it! Better than gadding about in theatres and fancy restaurants. He took a sip of sherry, opened the book and read. The clock ticked on the mantelpiece, the fire crackled and Poffley snored as Timmins indulged himself in his three favourite things.

This book was, if anything, more enjoyable than any of Madgwick's previous romances. Amélie Delacour, on the eve of marriage to Guy, Comte de Chalfontaine, had been tricked into believing that he had betrayed her with Madame Berthe de la Cochonnière, her cousin. In a heartbreaking scene Amélie wrote a farewell letter to Guy, before fleeing her home accompanied only by her faithful hound, Aristide. The adventurous heroine had determined once again to offer her services, and her life, as a spy for the King. This, she explained in the letter to Guy, was because a marriage between them could never be pure, now he had betrayed her. "It is better," she wrote, "to live with the golden thought of what might have been, rather than the tainted memory of something that was."

Timmins frowned. Lavinia had said the same thing to him! "Am I imagining it, Poffley?" he said. "Did Lavinia really use those words?" He yawned, Yes - she had done so; he could picture the sad expression on her face as she uttered the lines in the car outside her cottage. How strange that she had not cared to discuss the new book with him despite knowing how devoted he was to the works of Blossom Madgwick! "Perhaps, Poffley, she did not wish to spoil my enjoyment," he said, and Poffley made a little growling noise in response. "But surely," Timmins continued, "she would at least have told me that she had read the new book? After all, it is a very exciting event when a new Blossom Madgwick comes out - very exciting! Had I received the book before this evening's outing, I should have mentioned it in conversation."

He yawned again. It was late. "I don't know, Poffley," he said. "Women are very peculiar creatures. I do not pretend at all to understand them." The image of Lavinia disappearing up her garden path came fleetingly into his head, but he shook himself free of it. "We can manage well enough as we are, can we not? Come along, Poffley - time for bed."

CHAPTER THIRTEEN

A FÊTE WORSE THAN...

Over the following three weeks, Timmins suffered, feeling that he had caused Lavinia's departure from Quillington Parva. She had mentioned something about having business elsewhere, but that, surely, was a mere excuse? She had run away because of him. That was the truth of the matter. To forget their quarrel, he immersed himself in his work, all too aware that time was slipping by and that the Bishop would soon check up on his progress.

By far the most important event in the calendar was the village fête, on the twentieth of July. It had taken a lot of organisation; he had lost count of the number of FêteCommittee meetings he had attended, but he knew that if all went well he would see a significant boost to the Church Bell Fund.

The big day dawned bright and clear, and he was up with the lark. He had, at first, attempted to ignore Poffley's efforts to wake him, but it was impossible. Every morning the dog licked his face, pawed at the bedclothes, barked and jumped up and down on him. He had accepted that from now on, since Poffley rose early, so must he and as the mornings grew lighter and the days warmer, he had to admit there was something to say for being up and about in the early hours. Walking with Poffley through the village and out into the surrounding countryside had given him a new appreciation of his surroundings. He took delight in the gentle slopes of the hills around Quillington Parva, marvelled at the variety and beauty of the wild flowers - blue cornflowers and forget-me-nots, spidery ragged-robins, sunshine-yellow dandelions and marsh marigolds - and he was beginning to learn the names of the butterflies flittering amongst them. He filled his lungs with the sweet-smelling morning air and was ready, on his return to the Vicarage, for whatever the day might throw at him.

Today, Timmins decided that he would not eat before their walk; instead, he would drop in at the Fat Rascal and treat himself to one of their famous cooked breakfasts. It would be a busy day; he would need a good meal inside him. "Now then, Poffley," he said, attaching the dog's lead, "hop to it, there's a good lad. Let's get this walk over and done with. If you are a very good dog, I'm sure Dorothy Manifold will find you a tasty treat." Poffley wagged his tail and barked. It was just as if he understood, thought Timmins.

They set off at a brisk pace down the gravelled driveway, out into the High Street. The cottage gardens were in full bloom and a riot of clematis, buddleia, roses, lilies, phlox and jasmine perfumed the air. Skylarks soared, their joyful song filling the blue and cloudless sky, and man and dog strode through the village and out into the open fields beyond. Poffley spent a happy hour snuffling into rabbit-holes and chasing his ball until Timmins gave into the pangs of hunger, called the dog to him, and set off for the Fat Rascal.

Their journey, as it had done each day since their parting, took them past Lavinia's cottage. Perhaps today she had come home, and, spying him from her kitchen window, would give a cheery wave? Each morning, as he approached the cottage, he uttered a quick prayer, but each morning he was disappointed. Today was no exception; there was no Lavinia. The cottage windows were blank.Thank goodness for Poffley! The dog's presence was a support and a comfort. 'Still, never mind. We are a good team without her, aren't we?" he said, as Poffley sniffed around the cottage gate."She will miss the fun of the fête but, well, if that's her choice, then she must live with it." Aware of his own bravado, he tugged on Poffley's lead. "Come along, my lad, let us find our breakfast."

The much-anticipated fête promised to be a great success. There was to be the usual choice of stalls and attractions, a dog show and to top it all, the revival of the St Uncumber's Day parade in which the unmarried girls of the village would march through the village to the church, each sporting a false beard and moustache in honour of Saint Uncumber. With luck, he thought, we should make a tidy sum for the Church Bells fund.

"Morning, Timmins!" There was Harold Bungay waddling along behind him, decked out in a mustard-coloured linen suit and straw hat. Timmins stopped to wait for the solicitor who, red-faced and panting,soon caught up. "Good lord, man!" Bungay puffed. "How can you walk that fast?"

"There are benefits to owning a dog," he said. "I confess, I would never have believed it, but having Poffley has been rather good for me." Poffley barked in agreement. "Was there something you wanted, Mr Bungay?"

"Just to wish you good luck for the fête this afternoon, that's all." Bungay replied, mopping his brow. "Should be a jolly good show, provided all goes to plan." He bent to pat Poffley's head. "This chap entered for the dog show, is he? Stands a good chance of winning, I'd say. Lively little fellow, ain't he? Always was, if I remember right." He straightened up, rubbing the small of his back. "Dear old Daphne Prout liked to watch him give the run-around to her visitors. Livened up her otherwise rather dull life, I suppose. I used to dread those summons to visit her at Tall Trees, if I am honest, because that little blighter would leap about so, and try to knock me off my feet." He laughed. "When she told me she intended to leave him in your care I thought she was, frankly, off her noddle - never believed you'd have it in you to tame the brute. Rather you than me."

Poffley, having spotted a fat tabby cat sunning itself on the windowsill of a nearby cottage, was barking and straining to get to the gate, while the cat yawned and stretched in a lazily superior fashion.

"He can be a little excitable," Timmins replied. "But he's a good-natured beast at heart." Poffley, giving up on the cat, was now chasing his tail.

Bungay nodded. "Hmm, yes," he said, "you seem to have got the measure of him."

"I haven't entered him for the show, but perhaps I might do so. And now, if you will excuse me, breakfast calls. I have a lot to do today." Tipping his hat to Bungay, Timmins set off towards the Fat Rascal where he tied Poffley to the stone bench in front of the building. "You'll be fine here for a little while, Poffley," he said. "There's a bowl of water over there and I expect Dorothy will bring you a sausage."

The Fat Rascal was fragrant with the smell of bacon and toast. Timmins made his way to his favourite table and ordered his breakfast. It surprised him to see so many people in the tearoom, many of whom - strangers to the village - he did not recognise. Amongst them, however, were several villagers, who all greeted him by name. What a change, he thought. There was a time when he could go about his business in the village with no one stopping to speak; now, it seemed, all that had changed. The Sunday School and Mother's Union had proved popular, although numbers at church were still pretty low. Nevertheless, he had, he thought, definitely made more of a connection with the villagers of late, and this afternoon's fun and games should boost his profile yet further.

Dorothy Manifold appeared after a few minutes, with his tea and a huge plate laden with fat, brown sausages, crispy bacon, two fried eggs, mushrooms and tomatoes, and several slices of golden-brown toast dripping with butter. "Get that down you, Vicar. You need to keep your strength up. It'll be a long day, I reckon." She bent to rub her calf. "My legs are already aching something rotten, and it's still early yet. We will be busy today. Funny crowd, though."

Timmins looked around him, noting for the first time an enormous, fat woman, a tiny man only three feet tall, a great moustachioed giant of a man with vast biceps, and a woman with tattoos covering every visible inch of skin. "Good Lord," he thought, "what an exotic crowd."

"Circus folk you know," Dorothy whispered, "from Bassenpoole's Circus over at Abbots' Tump. They have a day off before they move off again, and they've all come over to the fête. They're a rum crowd and no mistake. Still, all good for business, I suppose. Now, if you don't object, I'll just pop out and make a fuss of that dog of yours."

Later that day, Timmins and Poffley headed for the field. It was bustling with activity; stallholders put the last-minute touches to their stalls; the village brass band warmed up in a series of toots and blasts; balloons danced on the light breeze and smell of crushed grass filled the air. In the centre was a roped-off arena where the afternoon's main events were to take place - a dog show, a display of gymnastics by some local schoolchildren, and the parade of the Bearded Ladies. With another half an hour before the Fête was due to open, there were already crowds of people milling about, getting the lie of the land.

"Reverend Timmins, there you are at long last!" Millicent Gore-Hatherley's stentorian tones hit him like a punch in the solar plexus as he approached the arena, although she was nowhere in sight. Where was she? Who in their right mind had given her the megaphone? Once she had hold of it, she would never relinquish it, and it was he, not she, who should make the announcements today. "Come along, Reverend! We need you in the announcer's tent this minute!".

From her seat at a table in front of the tent, Millicent had a commanding view of the field. Spread out before her were sheets and sheets of paper, typed up with, Timmins presumed, a running order, details of the various stalls so that the announcer could promote them, and other information which might be of use. "Ah, there you are at last, Reverend!" she exclaimed as he approached. "Now, we're all set up, but we've had a setback with our celebrity. Dear Evangeline is delayed, and although she intends to come along, she will not be here in time to open the Fête at two o'clock. We have decided, therefore, that you should say a few words to get things going, and when dear Evangeline arrives, she will instead sing us a few songs. We don't want to disappoint her admirers. How does that sound?"

It sounded dreadful! He did not mind saying a few words of welcome - as the Fête was in aid of the church, that should be his privilege. It would also give him the opportunity to suggest that people should come along to morning service the next day. What he did not like, however, was the prospect of another encounter with that appalling woman.

Millicent did not wait for him to speak. "Good. Now, you sit here and think of something brilliant to say, and I will ensure that all is ready. I can see people are arriving already. Things are due to kick off properly at one-thirty, so we have twenty minutes for you to come up with a bon mot or two." With that, she disappeared, taking the megaphone with her, and he could hear her barking orders as she went.

By the time she returned, he had got to grips with the programme for the day, jotted down a few ideas for his speech, and felt ready to open the fête Millicent handed him the megaphone, and he made his way to the podium where the prize-giving would take place. What a huge crowd of people gathered before him! Imagine if he could persuade even a quarter of them to come to church the next day - the place would be full! Lifting the megaphone, he spoke. "Ladies and gentlemen..."

"Where's Evangeline Honeybell?" a voice bellowed. "They told us she would be here. You're not a glamorous songbird like it said on the posters!"

There was a roar of laughter. Timmins, startled by the interruption, hesitated, scanning the crowd to see who had spoken. Arnold Bubb! Of course.

"Er... Miss Honeybell is, unfortunately, delayed, but she will be here later to er... to charm us all with some songs. You shall have Evangeline ... eventually!" Pleased with this small attempt at humour, he beamed at the crowd, but they did not respond and his own smile quickly faded.

"Get on with it, Vicar!" hissed Millicent. "We have a schedule to keep to, you know!"

"Yes, yes," Timmins nodded, then continued his address to the crowd. "Dear friends, in Miss Honeybell's absence, may I welcome you, one and all, to our little Fête, the first in Quillington Parva for several years..."

"And not before time!" Bubb shouted. "You pulled your finger out at last, Reverend!"

Timmins gritted his teeth. He felt a strong urge to quit the stage, but then he remembered how Amélie had responded to an angry crowd in "Amélie Against Adversity." She had not faltered, although her life was in danger. No, she had stood her ground and through the power of her words alone had changed the mood of the baying mob from antagonism to admiration. He would do the same. He would disarm his naysayers! They would not expect him to agree with them, so agree he would. "You are correct, dear Sir," he said. "Too much time has passed since last we gathered together in a spirit of fun..."

"You said it!" Bubb cried, and there were murmurs of agreement. "This village has been dead on its feet for years. Needs livening up!"

"Which is what we intend for today," Timmins continued, determined they should not browbeat him. "And not just for today. You will recall, I am sure, the Beetle Drive which proved such a success and now here we are, all eager to enjoy this fête It will, I assure you, become an annual event and will, I hope, bring unity, pride in our village, and a great deal of money. This year the money raised will go towards the upkeep of the church, but in future years we will be able to support many other good causes."

There was a ripple of applause. His strategy was working! He had silenced Bubb, the heckler! The crowd were on his side. "And, since I mentioned the church, I would just like to say how welcome you would be - all of you - at our morning service tomorrow. Our morning service begins at ten-thirty, and while you're there, we will welcome your little ones in the Church Hall for Sunday School..."

"What's this? A recruitment drive?" Bubb cried. "Come on, Rev, get thisFêteopened - I want to have a go on the Test Your Strength thingy."

"You won't even be able to lift the hammer, Bubby-boy!" Nobby and Reg pushed Bubb from side to side between them, delighting in his discomfiture.

"Come along, Reverend!" Millicent said, "They want to spend their money, and we have a timetable to stick to."
Timmins once again lifted the megaphone. "I declare this Fête open!"

At once, the brass band struck up a jolly tune, as the crowd dispersed to swarm round the stalls and Timmins and Millicent returned to the announcer's tent.

"Jolly good show, Reverend. Thought you'd lost the blighters for a moment or two. Thought we'd have a bally riot when you told them dear old Evangeline had not materialised, but no, you quelled the beast. Well done, you! And now," she added, wresting the megaphone from his grasp, "I'll take over the announcing. You can leave Poffley here with me. Are you going to enter him for the dog show?"

"I had not thought of doing so..."

"I rather think you should. I'll put his name down. Most handsome dog, perhaps? Now, you mingle. Have fun! Have candyfloss!"

Timmins set off to explore. The jolly atmosphere soon worked its magic, and he hummed as he walked. He most definitely would not have any candyfloss, but he might have a go at guessing the weight of that enormous chocolate cake donated by Dorothy Manifold. It was a thing of beauty, dark, glossy and smothered with little iced flowers in pink and white. What a treat it would be to win that - and this time he would make sure he did not carelessly give it away.

"Wotcher, Reverend," a voice hailed him. "Come and 'ave a go at the Test Your Strength. See what you're made of." Arnold Bubb stood before him, red-faced and shining. He took out a large handkerchief that had once been white and mopped his brow. Nobby and Reg stood behind him, grinning.

"See if you can beat 'im, Rev!" Nobby said, jerking his thumb at Bubb. "He's a weed - couldn't get the bell to ring, could you Arnie-boy?"

Bubb shrugged his shoulders. "Yeah, well, I wasn't far off."

Nobby and Reg cackled. "Bet the Rev can beat you. Go on Rev, have a go."

Bubb gave a hollow laugh and steered the reluctant Timmins towards the striker.It was gaily painted in red and yellow with a shiny brass bell at the top. A large mallet stood beside it and a small crowd had gathered, eager to see him try the thing out. Blast Arnold Bubb and his ghastly friends!They had set him up and now he would make a fool of himself in front of all these people.

Reluctantly, he rolled up his sleeves and picked up the mallet.

It was ridiculously heavy. Lifting it above his head, he wobbled a little before crashing it down on the lever. The puck shot upwards but reached only halfway up the indicator before it gave up the ghost and fainted back to the bottom again.

"You've got a way to go before you beat me, Rev!" Bubb cried. " Even my boy Sidney could have done better than that, and he's only ten! Have another go!"

Timmins grimaced as a ripple of laughter ran round the spectators. Why did he inspire such ridicule in others? What should he do? To walk off now would be to invite ridicule, yet there was no way he could make that bell ring. He hesitated, waiting for that little voice that always seemed to goad him at times of failure, but to his surprise, a picture of Lavinia's face flashed into his mind, smiling as if to say, "You can do it."

He would not allow these people to cow him! Fired by this thought, he brought the mallet crashing down - this time it hit the correct spot on the lever and the puck flew upwards to hit the bell with a resounding "Ding!". Timmins stumbled forward, overtaken by the force of his effort. For what seemed an eternity, nobody spoke or moved while Timmins blinked and rubbed his shoulder.

"Well, I never!" exclaimed Arnold Bubb. "If that doesn't take the biscuit! You did it, Rev." He held out his hand. "I take my hat off to you. Well done!"

Timmins shook the proffered hand, wincing. He might have hit the bell, but he had also pulled a muscle in his shoulder. Still, it was worth it, for, to his surprise, a big cheer went up. So, this was how success felt! It was exhilarating! If only his father - and Lavinia - could have seen the manly way in which he had just proved himself! He scanned the sea of faces. There was no sign of her, and the feelings of elation ebbed away as he handed the hammer to Arnold Bubb.

Just then, Millicent's voice boomed across the field. "The dog show is about to begin in the central arena. Entrants should make their way to the arena now."

Filled with new confidence, Timmins decided that there was nothing to lose by entering Poffley. He set off to collect the dog from the announcer's tent, where Millicent announced that she had entered Poffley for two classes - Most Obedient Dog and Dog who resembles his Master. "You shouldn't have any trouble with him, he's been a good boy, haven't you, Poffley?" she said, tickling the dog under the chin. "And as for resembling his master, well, he wasn't too pleased when I told him I had put him in for that class, but he will be a brave fellow and swallow his pride won't you, Poffles?" She let out a loud, snorting guffaw, and when she noticed the frown on Timmins' face, clapped him smartly on the back. "Don't mind my little joke, Reverend!"

"Not at all, Miss Gore-Hatherley, not at all. Poffley is a handsome animal. I am flattered that you even make the comparison between us. Come along, Poffley." He bent to pat the dog's head. Poffley leapt up at him excitedly, licked his face, and ran in a frenzied circle, wrapping his lead round Timmins' legs. When he had disentangled himself, Timmins grasped the lead, issued a warning to Poffley to "Behave!" and made his way to the ring for the Obedience Class.

The contest required that the dog should be able to sit still and come when called. What could go wrong? He had been teaching Poffley the skill on their morning walks through the fields around Quillington Parva, and if he was honest, he was very proud of the animal's progress. Expecting nothing but success, he gave the order for Poffley to sit, and awaited further instructions. What Timmins had not taken into account was that there would be quite a few other dogs in the ring at the same time. Poffley was used to meeting other dogs but had never been in the presence of more than one or two at a time; here there were dogs of all shapes and sizes. "Lots of new friends for you eh, Poffley my boy," Timmins said as they paraded round the show ring. You must be on your best behaviour, there's a dear chap. You can say hello to some of them later. Now," he continued, as they came to a halt in the line of twelve canine competitors and their owners, "sit, there's a good fellow."

Poffley, to Timmins' surprise, sat. For thirty seconds he sat, his tail beating a tattoo on the ground. "Good boy!" whispered Timmins, patting Poffley's head and flashing an understanding smile at the little girl next to him whose charge - a shaggy hound of indeterminate origin - was tugging at its lead and snarling at all and sundry. "You know how to behave, don't you? How do you feel about entering more classes? Why, if we win all our classes, we could even take the prize for Supreme Champion."

He would, he thought, dedicate the prize to the memory of Mrs Daphne Prout. It would be a touching gesture and one which would, he was sure, go down well with the crowd. How they would cheer as he accepted the huge silver cup from ... oh, horrors!... Evangeline Honeybell, for it was she who was to present the prizes! Oh, dear! That woman! Those puffy white hands, ghastly perfume, and worst of all, that terrible coquettish, flirtatious manner – he did not relish the prospect of seeing her again. "Horrible woman!" Too late he realised that he had spoken aloud.

"I beg your pardon?"

Timmins blinked. A large, bespectacled woman in a vividly patterned, too-tight floral dress and an enormous straw hat stood before him, an outraged expression on her shiny red face. She clutched a red leather lead at the end of which was a fat little Yorkshire terrier, its hair done up in a topknot of the same floral material as its mistress's dress. The dog growled, and Timmins quailed.

"Oh, er, forgive me," he said, backing away from the dog. "I was merely... that is, I... What a delightful little dog you have. May I say how very charming you and your little companion are, in your matching outfits?" He bent to pat the terrier but withdrew his hand quickly as the dog once again drew back its lips.

"Well, thank you, Vicar." The woman fluttered her eyelashes. "Little Bruno is a dear, sweet boy. He loves to dress like his mama, don't you, my little darling?" She bent, dress straining at the seams, and picked up Bruno who licked her face enthusiastically, at the same time giving a sideways glance at Timmins. "He is such a well-behaved little darling, aren't you, my pet? Not like that horrible creature over there." She glanced over Timmins' shoulder. "That dog should be on a lead!"

Horrified, Timmins saw that over the far side of the show ring Poffley, ears flying and tail wagging, was in hot pursuit of Snowdrop, the small, white Pomeranian bitch belonging to the Headmistress of the local school. He had slipped his lead again! Timmins set off after him and by the time he caught up, Poffley had introduced himself to Snowdrop in the usual canine fashion and was clearly intent on showing his ardour. "No, Poffley! Stop that at once, Sir!" Timmins cried to the amusement of the onlookers. He reached the dogs just in time.

"Reverend Timmins, your dog is not ready yet for the obedience class," Millicent's voice bellowed across the arena. "I suggest that you leave the ring and make your way over to the marquee. The Women's Institute competitions await your judgement."

What a disaster! Things had seemed to be going so well. He should never have allowed Millicent to enter Poffley. "You are an infuriating creature," he hissed as they made their way through the crowds to the marquee. "I trust you will behave yourself for the rest of the afternoon or you can forget any thought of that lovely, juicy bone that Mrs Whibley brought for you this morning."

Together they entered the marquee which was full of trestle tables. The W.I. had been busy. There were plates of pillowy scones, towering Victoria sponges glistening with sugar, dark chocolate cakes, lemon drizzle loaves damp with sweet-sour syrup and bosomy buns iced in all shades of pastel colours. "Oh, my goodness!" exclaimed Timmins. "I shall have my work cut out here, Poffley. Now, just you lay down quietly in the corner while I get on with the judging. I don't want to hear another sound from you, do you hear?"

Poffley wagged his tail and sat down. Timmins set about the Victoria sponges, examining each one for its rise, evenness of bake and taste and consistency of the jam. This was more like it! In the warmth of the great tent, the smell of baking mingled with the smell of crushed grass, and outside the brass band played a jolly tune. Humming, he moved along the tables. This was something at which he excelled! He was the man for the job.

It was as he made his final decision, awarding the first prize for the best scones to Edna Dobson, that he noticed a snuffling, slurping kind of noise. It sounded horribly familiar. No, please God, no! He turned, and there, on a table on the other side of the marquee, stood Poffley, snuffling around the ruins of what had been a glorious display. "Poffley!" he cried. Panic engulfed him – his heart raced, and he felt sick. The dog's face was liberally decorated with crumbs, and a dab of white icing ornamented the tip of his nose. "Oh, Poffley!" Timmins cried, as the dog fixed him with a quizzical stare. "What on earth have you done? Get down this instant, you wicked animal!" Hurrying over to the table, Timmins grabbed Poffley's collar and pulled him away from the scene of his crime.

Just at that moment in strode Millicent, followed by the ladies of the W.I. "Vicar, are you ready for us? We are on tenterhooks to find out..." Her voice tailed away as she and the other ladies took in the devastation that faced them and observed the guilt on Timmins' face.

Finally, Millicent spoke. "Well, really, Vicar. When I invited you to judge, I really thought you would understand the requirements of that task. It was not at all necessary for you to devour the entries in that greedy fashion, and neither, I am sure, did any of us expect you to make quite such a mess!"

A murmur of disapproving agreement greeted her comments.

Timmins, blushing furiously, shook his head. "No, no! You do not understand... It was not I... Poffley here was the one. He ..."

Millicent broke in, "Whether it was yourself or that animal who caused this desecration, it should not have happened. If, as you say, that beast was the one responsible, then it is evidence, if we needed more evidence, that you need to exercise greater control over the animal."

"I...I..." Timmins stammered. She was quite right. The angry stares of the Women's Institute members bore into him, and he could not speak.

There was a commotion at the back of the group and a familiar voice trilled his name. "Reverend! Oh, Reverend dear, I have arrived! Your Evangeline has arrived!" Pushing her way through the members of the Women's Institute, the singer shimmied towards him, hands on hips, and blew him a kiss.

The singer's arrival threw Timmins into a state of greater emotional turmoil. His first instinct was to thank the Lord,for all the ladies had forgotten their earlier indignation with him and were now fluttering around her, excited by the presence of celebrity, but he could not help but remember the indignities to which she had subjected him. He did not know whether to greet her or to give into a very strong urge to escape by lifting the wall of the marquee and crawling out. He bent and picked up Poffley's lead. "Come on, Sir," he whispered, and edged a few steps backwards. Poffley barked and Timmins' heart sank.

"Well, Vicar," boomed Millicent. "Dear Evangeline here requires your presence on stage when she gives her little concert. I suggest that we leave these good ladies to retrieve such baked goods as are still edible, and that we introduce our celebrated guest to the crowd. Come along, now."

She took Evangeline by the arm and marched out of the marquee. Timmins and Poffley followed. When they reached the stage, Millicent Gore-Hatherley mounted the steps and picked up the megaphone. "Ladies and gentlemen, your attention please. Our vicar, Reverend Timmins, has an exciting announcement to make. Come along, Vicar!" Timmins clambered up the steps and on to the stage. Pushing the megaphone into his hands, Millicent whispered fiercely, "Introduce Miss Honeybell, Vicar, and remind people to make donations. And do not mess this up!"

Timmins lifted the megaphone. "Ladies and gentlemen," he said, "our honoured guest has arrived! Without further ado, allow me to introduce to you all that celebrated songstress, the - er, the ... charming and er, talented Miss Evangeline Honeybell..." He glanced at Evangeline, who mouthed "Hello" in a very suggestive manner. He shuddered. "Miss Honeybell has graciously consented to entertain us this afternoon, to support the Church Bells fund. So please, put your hands in your pockets..."

"Put yer hands together, don't you mean?" called a voice from the crowd. Arnold Bubb again! Timmins grimaced.

"I mean," said Timmins, " that you should give Miss Honeybell a resounding reception, but please do also remember to dig deep into your pockets and drop any spare change into the collection box... And now, please welcome Miss Evangeline Honeybell!"

Evangeline shimmied to centre stage and curtseyed to the crowd. Her silver and gold outfit sparkled in the sunshine as she planted a wet kiss on Timmins' cheek. He fought the urge to wipe his face as she curtseyed and blew kisses to the crowd. "Dear friends," she called, "I thank you for this very kind welcome. I am delighted to be here, and to be on stage with this darling man, Reverend Timmins." She blew another kiss at

Timmins, who had sidled towards the steps, intending to leave the stage as soon as possible. "Dear Reverend," she continued. "Are you trying to escape? We cannot have that, can we, ladies and gentlemen? Oh, no. You will sing with me, dear man. You would like that, wouldn't you, ladies and gentlemen?"

To Timmins' horror, she ran to him in dainty little tiptoe steps, took him by the hand and drew him back to centre stage. "Let's 'ear your dulcet tones, Vicar!" Bubb and his mates cried. "Sing for us!"

Timmins wished for the ground to open beneath his feet and swallow him. He could not sing! Even in church, he relied on the verger to lead the hymns.

"Together we shall sing, If We're Weak Enough to Tarry, from Iolanthe. I am sure you know it well, Reverend, but in case you do not, I have here the lyrics and music."

Rage and indignation coursed through Timmins' veins. He could not - would not - sing. He had suffered enough embarrassment already today. "My dear Miss Honeybell," he said, as firmly as he could. "These people have come here today to hear you, not me. They do not wish my, ah, my ... tuneless warblings... to ruin your melodic performance."

Evangeline pouted. "Oh, come now, Vicar! Do not be coy! I am sure it would disappoint them if you refused, wouldn't it, ladies and gentlemen?"

There was a roar of agreement. "Sing, Vicar!" called Arnold Bubb. "Let's 'ear what you can do." He muttered something and there was a shout of laughter from those standing near him. "Give us a treat!"

There was no getting out of it. He felt sick. Evangeline nodded at the pianist. As she simpered and fluttered at him, he began, reluctantly, to mouth the words of the song which, as luck would have it, he knew well.

"If we're weak enough to tarry
Ere we marry,
You and I,"

"Give it some welly!" Arnold Bubb shouted. "You ain't goin' to win the lady's affections if you mumble!"

The crowd roared with laughter; Timmins felt little beads of sweat prickle his forehead. How dare that man treat him so? For an instant he was back in the music room at Grimwade Academy, faced with fifteen mocking classmates and the frowning music master as he attempted to sing in tune. He recalled the contempt with which the music master had dismissed his efforts, and how his classmates had later teased him, braying like donkeys. He would not let them all win!
He sang louder,

"Of the feeling I inspire,
You may tire,
By and by..."

"Blimey, Vicar!" cried a different voice in the crowd - Nobby? Reg? - "That's done the job!" for Evangeline had approached him, was leaning against his chest, her face tilted up at his as she trilled her response.

"If we're weak enough to tarry
Ere we marry,
You and I,
With a more attractive maiden..."

"That shouldn't be difficult!" cried Arnold Bubb, to general laughter.

Timmins backed away from Evangeline, attempting to remove her puffy white hand from his face, but she was not to be outdone. She stepped closer to him with a pleading expression that reminded him of Poffley when he had committed a misdemeanour.

If by chance we should be parted,
Broken-hearted
I should die -
So I think we will not tarry
Ere we marry,
You and I"

Evangeline pulled Timmins closer to her and kissed him on the lips, to the great amusement of the crowd and Arnold Bubb in particular. As the song continued, she continued to flirt with him while the audience clapped along. Finally, to Timmins' great relief it was all over, and as the last note died away, Evangeline grasped him by the ears and planted another great kiss on his mouth. Loud applause greeted them as Timmins pulled his handkerchief from his pocket and, under the guise of blowing his nose, wiped away all traces of the kiss.

"Sing us another one, Vicar!" Arnold Bubb shouted, but Timmins had had enough. He bowed to Evangeline and addressed the crowd. "I thank you," he said, "for your enthusiasm, but it is Miss Honeybell whom you have come to hear. Other duties call me, so I shall leave you in her capable hands, but first, please allow me to remind you to donate generously to our fund, and to remind you that next month sees the first of a series of planned church outings, this time to Winkleton-on-Sea. Should you be interested in joining us, there are still spaces, and you can sign up in the Village Hall or after church on Sundays. And now I hand you over to Miss EvangelineHoneybell." With that, he headed for the steps, eager to leave the stage.

Evangeline's voice followed him. "A trip to the seaside - how delightful! I shall join you, Vicar, if you will have me."

"He'll have you, don't you worry," cried Arnold Bubb, and there was more raucous laughter as Timmins escaped the stage.

He retrieved Poffley and together they headed for the Vicarage, a cup of tea and a piece of Mrs Whibley's restorative gingerbread.

They had almost made it to the gate when Millicent's booming voice heralded him. "Vicar! There you are! Where do you think you are going? It's time for the parade of the bearded lady - you cannot have forgotten?!"

CHAPTER FOURTEEN

CHIN-CHIN

Timmins groaned. Blast it! "No, I had not forgotten! Poffley and I were just stretching our legs." He offered a quick prayer for forgiveness of this lie.

"Come along then, Vicar. We have a timetable to keep to, you know!" She set off back towards the main show-ring.
Timmins, following behind, chided himself. "Shame on you, Samuel! It was your idea to reinstate the whole Choosing of the Beard thing!"

In the ring, the young girls and women, all in their Sunday best, were a riot of colours, and each sported a beard. There were long, whiskery beards, great bushy full beards, neck beards, pointed goatees, forked beards and neat Van Dykes - beards in every shape and size. There were beards made from sheep's wool pulled from the hedgerows, some knitted, some made of rope brushed out into its individual fibres... The girls strutted and preened excitedly as they waited for the procession to the church and the final judging to take place.

Millicent Gore-Hatherley deafened bystanders with a thunderous announcement, and Timmins made a mental note to hide the megaphone before the next village event. "Ladies and Gentlemen," she cried. "It is time for the highlight of the day. Most of you will know about the Bearded Lady, but..."

"Never heard of her! She a relative of yours, was she?"

"Saint Uncumber was a young Christian noblewoman whose father had pledged her in marriage to a man who did not share her faith. To escape this union, she prayed that God would make her unattractive and in the morning, she awoke to find that she had grown a full beard..."

"So, she got out of it by the hair of her chinny-chin-chin!"

Millicent was undeterred. "She did, but it enraged her father. He had her crucified and thus she achieved her sainthood. Her statue stands in our church, and her beard is rather moth-eaten now, having been in place for several years..."

"Thought that was a statue of my old lady!" cried Arnold Bubb. A roar of laughter greeted the remark and Bubb's wife, Cissie, elbowed him sharply in the ribs.

"It was a long-held custom in the village that each year, on St Uncumber's day, which is today, the twentieth of July - all the maidens in the village should wear a beard in honour of the saint and that the vicar would choose the best among them to adorn the saint's statue for the next year. That tradition fell by the wayside some years ago..."

Timmins blushed. He had allowed the custom to slip; it was true. He recalled how Reverend Ambrose Bellamy had explained it to him over afternoon tea. "It really is fun and a real honour to have one's beard selected for our dear Saint Uncumber to wear." He had reached for the last Eccles cake. "I can see, young man, that you are sceptical, but, you know, these traditions connect people to their village and to their history. They ground people, don't you know, in their community. Woe betide you if you do not grasp that."

Timmins had been unconvinced. In his first year as vicar he had abandoned the tradition, thinking it rather foolish. There had been grumblings of discontent, but he had had his way. Now, however, Timmins saw how excited the little girls were, how proud their parents and how their older, unmarried sisters, more dignified but no less eager, revelled in the admiration of the young men.

"You fool," he thought. "How ridiculous you have been! Who were you to deny them their fun?" Besides, he reflected, this little tradition linked the villagers to their Church, and surely that would please the Bishop. He held out his hand for the megaphone. "May I?"

"Be quick!" she hissed. "I shall need it before long.We dohave a schedule you know."

"Dear friends," Timmins said, "in my youth and ignorance I ended this tradition, considering it disrespectful. Things were ever thus; what we, the elders in society, hold to be of importance is so often deemed unworthy of note by the younger generations. As the saying goes, with age comes wisdom and I, somewhat older now than that callow youth who ..."

"Put a sock in it, Reverend!" Bubb shouted. "The beards will all have gone white with age at this rate..."

Millicent snatched the megaphone. "Allow me, Vicar!' she barked, frowning at Timmins. 'The Vicar is trying to say that he is sorry. Is that correct, Vicar?"

Timmins nodded and she continued her announcement.

"And so, without further ado, let us proceed. You see before you some wonderful beards. It thrills us to see this tradition revived and to know that our dear Saint will have a glorious new facial ornament. Now, musicians, strike up! Off we go! Licketty-spit!"

She took Timmins' arm and propelled him as they set off on the march to the church. Poffley bounding along beside them. The band struck up a jolly tune and the party set off. Timmins' spirits lifted as they went, thanks to the jollity of the procession and the beauty of the day. He hummed along to the band, marking time with his index finger, while Poffley capered about.

"Look! Vicar'th dog ith dancing!" lisped a tiny girl in a primrose-yellow frock, her face all but hidden behind a bushy, green and orange woollen beard fashioned from the odds and ends of her mother's knitting wool. He recognised her as Ethel Bubb, Arnold's daughter, whose scooter he had borrowed on the day of

172

Daphne Prout's funeral. She skipped along beside Poffley.

"You behave yourself, Ethel!" her mother hissed. "And have a care, or you'll go flying. You know how accident-prone you are!"

"Worry not, Mrs Bubb," Timmins cried, and he took the little girl's hand in his. "I shall not let her fall!"

Ethel laughed as Timmins sang along with the band. "Tra-la-la-la-la-la, pom-de-pom! Diddle-diddle-de, pom-de-pom!" What a wonderful day this was, filled with sunshine, laughter, good company, and community spirit. If only Lavinia was here! He might never see her again! Here he was, surrounded by crowds of people, yet to them he was simply the Vicar, a figurehead. Only Lavinia - and Poffley, come to that - showed any real affection for him and now one had disappeared and the other was a dog. He let go of Ethel's hand.

In the churchyard, Timmins took up his position in the church porch and Poffley curled up in a sunny spot close by as the bearded girls formed an excited semi-circle. Two little girls were playing chase, weaving in and out of the others and ignoring their mothers' instructions to "Stop it, this instant!" while a toddler with a fluffy white beard cried, overawed by the noise.

Timmins noticed a rowdy group of spectators gathered under the spreading yew tree, sprawling on the table-top tombs, or leaning against gravestones and swigging beer. Arnold Bubb and his friends! Surely they had not come to cause trouble again?

Close by them stood the tall, moustachioed strong man whom Timmins recognised from the Fat Rascal earlier that day. On the giant's shoulders, blowing kisses to the ladies, sat the tiny man who had been his companion, while the very corpulent female leaned heavily against a gravestone, fanning herself. There was no sign of the tattooed lady who had also been in the tea-room. Instead, the fat woman was chatting to the thinnest, palest man that Timmins had ever seen.

Millicent sniffed. "They're from Bassenpoole's Circus," she said, her voice clipped. "What possessed them to follow the procession I cannot think, unless the beer tent has run dry."

"My dear Millicent," he said, "I am surprised at you. They do not appear to be doing any harm."

She sniffed again. "Not yet, but that tall person is a Bubb and as far as I understand it there are several members of the Bubb family in the circus. Need I say more?" She nodded towards the crowd under the yew tree and Timmins saw that Arnold Bubb was now dancing a jig on the biggest of the table-top tombs, beer bottle in hand.

"Yes, well, we must hope they do not follow his example," he said. "Now, we should proceed with the choosing. The little ones appear to be getting over-excited, and I am looking forward to my tea."

Millicent took up the megaphone and called the contestants to order. A hush fell over the crowd as Timmins began his inspection, brow furrowed. He had a particular idea of what might suit the statue and wanted nothing too garish, too crudely constructed or too comical in style. That ruled out many of those on offer here, which ranged from dapper little goatees to chinstraps to doorknocker beards as sported by certain famous Victorian novelists, and on to great, bushy full beards of all lengths. Timmins examined each one.

The tension in the churchyard mounted, even amongst Bubb and his cronies, who had ceased their drinking and were craning their necks to see over the heads of the crowd. Nobody spoke. The only sounds were the breeze, the song of the birds and the distant music from the fête. A bead of sweat prickled out of his brow and crept down the side of his face. Which beard to pick? So many families in the village had a daughter or a sister representing them - it would be so easy to upset them.

He glanced at little Ethel Bubb again - her father had been a thorn in his side ever since Mrs Prout's funeral, and now he and many of his relatives were not only present but also rather the worse for beer. They were quiet for the moment, but choosing little Ethel's beard would avoid any chance of nastiness and might cause Bubb to view him with a kindlier eye. For an instant he felt himself tempted to make that choice, but just then Ethel, feeling warm under the great woollen beard, yanked at it and it began to unravel.

Just then, the crowd parted and there it was - the perfect beard to adorn the statue of Saint Uncumber, neither too bushy nor too straggling, not garish nor, on first sight, too flimsy. This beard was perfect! His spirits lifted. Why had he not noticed it and its wearer before?

She was standing a little way behind the other girls and women, a small, plump person in a pink floral dress and wearing a wide-brimmed pink straw sunhat pulled down low on her head. Where the other contestants were preening and lifting their chins to display their beards, she stood still, head lowered, drawing no attention to herself, or to the luxuriant, silky auburn confection which adorned her chin. This, Timmins thought, was the one! What a marvel!

"I have made my choice!" he announced as he pushed his way through the crowd and took the woman by the hand to lead her forward. Why was she so resistant? Why should she pull back? It made no sense to Timmins - why had she gone to the trouble of making a beard if she did not wish to win? "Come along, dear madam!" he cried. "This marvellous beard shall adorn our dear Saint Uncumber!" He pulled the beard. It did not come off. Instead, the woman gave a little yelp.

"Ow!" she cried.

"Oh dear! You must have used a stronger glue than was, perhaps, advisable, that is all. Not to worry - I am sure we can solve that

175

problem."

He tugged harder; the beard did not budge.

"Leave me alone, you nasty piece!" the woman snapped, and hit him over the head with her handbag.

"Ow!" Timmins yelped. How dare she strike him? "If you did not wish to donate your beard, why are you here?"
The woman shrieked, the crowd muttered, and there came a thunderous shout.

"'Ere, you leave her alone!" Arnold Bubb was approaching at speed. "You all right, Aunty Mo?" he said, putting his arms around her. She wailed again.

"You ought to be ashamed of yourself!" He raised a fist at Timmins. "Making fun of my aunty in that way! For two pins I'd knock your block off!"

Timmins took a step back. "What? In what way have I offended? I did not intend to upset your... er... Aunty Mo.... And I was unaware you were in any way related..."

"That's beside the point!" snapped Arnold Bubb, stepping forward and standing legs apart, fists clenched and resting on his hips. "You tried to pull her beard orf!"

"But, my dear man, of course I did! She has the best, most realistic beard of all the ladies here..."

"Yes, you fool!" snapped Arnold Bubb. "And it looks that way for a reason. It is real!"

Timmins felt the colour drain from his face.

"Ain't you never heard of Maureen Bubb, the famous Bearded Lady from Bassenpoole's Circus? That's my Aunty Mo! She's come here for a day out and you insult her in front of all these people! I ought to sock you in the kisser!"

Timmins felt sick. Everyone was looking at him. How should

he put things right? He opened his mouth, but no words came out. The sun beat down upon the back of his neck; perspiration trickled down his temples and a pair of jackdaws chuckled on the roof of the church porch.

Just then, a slight movement to his right caught his attention. There, standing at the edge of the crowd, was Lavinia. She gave a little wave. She was back! How lovely she was, in her buttercup-yellow frock and straw bonnet. Oh, how wonderful to see her again! His heart lifted; he knew what he must do.

"My dear Madam," he said, bowing to her. "Pray, forgive me. I cannot apologise enough for causing you distress. I am afraid the sheer beauty of your beard quite carried me away." He took her hand and kissed it. "Madam, I can think of no better way of making amends than to ask you if you would do us the honour of judging our little competition? Or, if you would prefer, I invite you to go to the Vicarage where Mrs Whibley will give you refreshments and where you may relax away from the public gaze until you are recovered."

"I should bloomin' well think so," said Bubb, his tone less belligerent than before. "What do you reckon, Aunty Mo?"

Aunty Mo stroked her beard. "I think," she said, "that the Vicar ought to do the judging. I could do with a cuppa and a bite to eat. I accept your apology, Vicar."

"Thank-you," he replied. He beckoned Lavinia, who threaded her way through the crowd to join them. "How good to see you again, Miss Bellamy," he said, beaming at her. "I wonder, would you be so kind as to take Mr and Miss Bubb to the Vicarage and instruct Mrs Whibley to give them tea? And yourself, of course. I shall join you all when I have finished here."

Lavinia nodded but did not, he noticed, say a word, and together she and the Bubbs departed while Timmins continued his judging.

When the ceremony was over and Saint Uncumber suitably adorned with new and resplendent facial hair, the crowds dispersed and Timmins called to Poffley who woke from his slumbers, yawned, and stretched. Together they made their way back to the Vicarage. Timmins' stomach rumbled. It had been a long time since his breakfast in the Fat Rascal; he had eaten no lunch, and he knew that Mrs Whibley had prepared him a sumptuous tea. There would be cucumber and tinned salmon sandwiches, pork pie and salad, scones with cream and a tangy lemon drizzle cake. He was definitely looking forward to it... but not, he realised, as much as he was looking forward to once again seeing Miss Lavinia. She had come back. All was well.

He let himself in and hung his panama hat on the hook while Poffley skittered across the tiled hallway and nosed open the kitchen door in search of his bowl of dog biscuits. Good old Poffley! The dog could be rather a nuisance, but he was a dear. He anticipated his own delicious tea in the comfortable sitting room of his beloved home, in the company of the woman he loved. Hopefully, those ghastly Bubbs were not still there!

A burst of laughter stopped him in his tracks. That was not a woman's laugh, nor did it sound like Arnold Bubb. No. Oh heavens! It was Bishop Archbold! The thought of seeing him again made Timmins quail. He sounded jolly enough, but how would he react when he heard about that afternoon's embarrassments? Oh, dear!

Bishop Archbold and Lavinia were sitting on the sofa, their backs to the door, chatting. On the sofa table lay the remains of what had been a substantial tea, now reduced to one or two curled-up sandwiches and a single scone. The Bubbs had feasted well before leaving.

He was about to announce his presence when the Bishop spoke. "Oh yes, he is not a character one warms to. I find his behaviour truly appalling - he has no morals and no scruples either. He thinks of nothing but his own desires and cares not a jot about the feelings of others."

'That is so true, Bishop,' Lavinia agreed. 'I have tried to make him less selfish and heartless, but, well, In all honesty, I find I have no control over him. He goes his own way and appears not to care who he offends. It is very tiresome.'

Timmins stood stock still. They were talking about him! Their words hit him like a punch. Dear God, so this was how they viewed him. Every trace of his earlier happiness vanished. He might have known it would not last. "Good afternoon," he said, his voice clipped as he entered the room. Moving to the armchair, he sat down, knees together and hands clasped across his stomach. "I trust you have enjoyed your tea. I apologise for keeping you waiting. Your Grace, I was unaware of your intention to call this afternoon. Had I known, I would have been able to warn you I should be busy."

"Hey ho! Not to worry," the Bishop said. "Been having a lovely little chat with your guests. Mr Bubb and his charming aunt had to leave; the lure of the beer tent was stronger than their desire to await their Vicar's presence, I believe. Ha!" He slapped his leg. "Never mind. No need to take offence. Who can blame them, really? Why sit around drinking tea in the company of two dull clerics when there's beer to be had?"

"Quite," muttered Timmins. "I am not sorry they have left. I am quite exhausted. I have been very busy today and would welcome my own company." He felt satisfaction in being rude.

Lavinia, who had been sipping her tea while this exchange took place, frowned, and put down her cup and saucer. When she spoke, her displeasure was clear. "I can see, Reverend Timmins, that you are not in the mood for entertaining, and as the Bishop has business to discuss with you, I will leave the two of you alone. If you will excuse me." She picked up her hat. "No need to see me out, Reverend. Good afternoon, Bishop. I have so enjoyed our little chat." With that, she left the room.

Bishop Archbold stared at Timmins for a moment or two, his brow knitted, before he, too, stood up. "I think you have just offended the good lady. Not well done, Timmins my boy, not well done." He moved across to the window and stood with his hands clasped behind his back, gazing out at the garden. "However, I understand that you are tired, and I have to admit that I have been hearing good things about Quillington Parva. You appear to have pulled your socks up. I hear the fête is a rip-roaring success and that you are getting involved with things - even singing on stage today! Jolly good show! That's the ticket!"

"Thank you, Your Grace." The hypocrisy of the man, to tell him off for insulting Miss Bellamy when he and that lady had been heaping insults on him!

"And you have the summer outing coming up next week? A fine chance for you to recruit some new lambs into the flock. Excellent! Well now, Timmins. I popped in to fix a date when we can review the situation in more detail. I know you're busy with the outing on Saturday, but why don't I pop along to the service on Sunday morning, and we can have a chat afterwards? I'll run my eye over the books too - see how the finances stack up now you've been getting your act together more. What say you? Good idea? Right-oh. I'll be off. Mind if I take that last scone?"

Before Timmins could reply, the Bishop lunged for the scone, picked it up and took a large bite. "Delicious!" He strode out of the room, calling over his shoulder as he left. "Cheerio, old boy!"

Timmins flinched as first the sitting-room door and then the front door slammed. Well, that put the tin hat on it. The Bishop would call him to account next Sunday, which meant that he would have to spend a good deal of time over the coming days chasing up those who had raised money at the fête and then making sure that the books were in order. Heaven knew how many people would be in church on Sunday! With a sigh, he stood and collected up the used cups and saucers, stacking them on the big wooden tray. In the kitchen, where Poffley lay snoozing in his basket by the range, Timmins washed up the crockery and, tummy growling, opened the pantry door.

CHAPTER FIFTEEN

A TRIP TO THE SEASIDE

The day of the outing to Winkleton-on-Sea dawned bright and warm. Timmins was ready in good time. Armed with pen and clipboard, he checked off names as the excited day-trippers clambered aboard the coach. None of the fathers had signed up for the trip since it was a working day and the women wrestled with picnic hampers and blankets, handbags and hats, while their children were armed with buckets and spades, fishing nets and beach balls.

Poffley had caught their excitement. Timmins issued repeated commands to "Sit!" but although he appeared to humour his master, his rear end just hovered over the ground for a few seconds and then he was up again, spinning round in circles, bouncing up and down and barking cheery greetings. The children banged on the coach windows, waving, and laughing at Poffley which only egged him on further.

Timmins had had enough. "Stay with Mrs Whibley today, Poffley," he said, snatching up the dog's lead. "If you cannot behave, then you will have to face the consequences, and I shall have to make it up to her somehow. You really are most exasperating!" He was about to take Poffley back into the Vicarage when Lavinia arrived.

"I'm so sorry I'm late!" she puffed as Poffley strained on the lead, jumping and barking a greeting. "Mr Bungay waylaid me - he wishes me to do a few days' work for him this week. Poffley! Sit!"

Poffley sat and remained seated.

"I had intended to be here early," Lavinia continued. "Are we all present and correct?"

Timmins nodded assent. How very attractive she was in her pretty pink sprigged cotton dress and matching straw hat, trimmed with a pink ribbon, but then he recalled the words he had heard her say to the Bishop at their last meeting. "I have managed, as you see." He paused and then added, "I trust that I have not offended by 'going my own way'?"

Lavinia frowned. "I'm sorry?"

"I would not like you to feel that you had no control..." There was bitterness in his voice as he spat out the words which had wounded him but which she seemed not to recognise.

Just then a familiar voice sang out. "Cooo-eeee! Do not go without me, dear man! I have arrived! Better late than never!" and Evangeline hove into view, clad in flapping wide orange pyjama pants and a matching sleeveless top spotted with black polka dots. On her head was an enormous, wide-brimmed straw hat, its brim pinned up in front with a rosette of orange silk. She carried a large carpet bag and was very out of breath. "Darling man!" she cried, planting a loud wet kiss on his cheek. "Now, we can set off on our little trip! How exciting!" Casting a quick glance at Lavinia, she said, "How do you do, Miss... er... What a charming little frock."

She handed her carpet bag to Timmins, who wiped his cheek with his sleeve. "Are we to sit together, darling man? Shall we cosy up on the front seats?" Giggling, she blew him a kiss and headed towards the coach in a cloud of Nuit d'Amour perfume. Poffley leapt to his feet and growled.
"Quiet, Poffley!" Timmins said. He glanced at Lavinia.

"Shall we board, Miss Bellamy?"

Lavinia did not move. "Reverend Timmins," she began, "what did you mean just then?" but Timmins was attending to the dog. She shrugged her shoulders and said, "Shall I take Poffley with me? The children will love to have him ride with them."

She and Poffley climbed aboard, heading towards the rear, while Timmins took up the last vacant seat next to Evangeline.

The coach threaded its way through the rolling green countryside, along winding roads and through villages of thatched, honey-coloured cottages. Evangeline flirted for all she was worth, giggling each time the coach, rounding a corner, threw them together. Each time her soft bulk pressed against him she squealed while he tried to occupy the smallest space possible. The road to Winkleton-on-Sea was full of twists and turns.

It was an uncomfortable journey, made worse by the loud renditions of "Daisy Bell," "Don't Bring Lulu" and other inane ditties, and by the time the coach juddered to a halt in front of Winkleton pier his head throbbed, and he longed for fresh air. How children could make such a din was beyond belief. A certain level of excitement was forgivable - they had been looking forward to this outing for months now, and the beautiful August weather enhanced their happiness – but there were limits!

"Please, children! I wish to explain the rules for today." Timmins called.

The noise continued.

"Children!" Timmins raised his voice. "Quieten down!"

"Get on with it then!" someone yelled. "It's blooming boiling on this bus.'

A piercing whistle sliced across the chatter. "They are listening now," Lavinia said, as Timmins stared in astonishment. She smiled. "Just one of my hidden talents."

Evangeline sniffed. 'How common!' she said, taking a powder compact from her carpetbag and inspecting her face for shine.

Timmins, collecting himself, issued his instructions.

'Righto, Captain!' one of the women cried when he had finished.

"Whatever you say! Let's get off this bus!"

The trippers spilled out of the coach in a chaos of bags, balls, buckets and nets while Timmins had a word with the driver. Lavinia took Poffley's lead and the two of them descended the steps. He watched as they went to join the rest of the party. How unlike the rest of the women she was, he thought. She had always had an air of calm about her, a quiet confidence he found somehow restful; it would be lovely to spend the day with her. The thought had no sooner entered his head, however, than he remembered the conversation he had overheard between her and the Bishop.

"Penny for them, Reverend." Evangeline's voice cut across his thoughts. She had not moved from her seat, but sat there, simpering at him. Now what was she up to? "Oh, Reverend," she cooed, beckoning him and patting the seat beside her. "Before we set off on our merry way, I have a little something for you. Won't you come and see?"

"We should join the others."

The singer's voice took on a petulant tone. "Oh, but I have made you a little gift," she said. "You will not disappoint me?"

With a barely suppressed sigh, Timmins sat beside her. "A gift? You should not' Oh, I say!" She was waving something at him - woollen swimming trunks with a bright yellow knitted belt! "I knitted them myself!" she squealed, waving something soft and purple. 'Do you like them?'

Timmins gulped. What an abomination the garment was! Oh, Lord! He had had no intention of going anywhere near the water! No, his plan had been to find a deckchair and spend the day snoozing and reading 'Amélie Alone' in which the heroine, abducted by agents of the wicked Alphonse, Duc Évergne, found herself abandoned on a remote tropical island. He had got to a thrilling part of the novel where, after some weeks battling the elements and the local wildlife, Amélie's hopes of rescue had

185

been first raised by the arrival of a ship, and then dashed by the revelation that Alphonse himself captained that vessel. The Duc had just offered to rescue Amélie with the proviso she become his mistress. What would she do? Timmins was longing to find out.

"I shall, perhaps, have a brief swim, although I must confess that I..."

"Oh, goody!" Evangeline squealed. "I brought my costume!" and she pulled from her bag a vast, frilly, floral item in shades of pink, purple and green. "We shall immerse ourselves in the briny deep, breasting the waves together."

Her unfortunate choice of verb, together with the mental image of her large frame clad only in that hideous garment, made Timmins feel weak at the knees. Dear Lord, what a frightful picture - the two of them together ... It did not bear thinking about. "Er...the others are waiting for us," he squeaked.

"'You have gone all shy!" cried Evangeline. "What a bashful boy you are!" Heaving herself up from her seat, she pinched his cheek. "Anyone would think you were harbouring thoughts of an ... indelicate nature! Naughty boy!" She collected her belongings and made her way out of the coach.

"She's a caution, ain't she?" The coach driver said with a knowing look. "A proper handful, in more ways than one!"

Timmins ignored him. He stepped out of the coach, and they set off at a brisk pace to find an empty beach at the quieter end of the promenade, near the rocks. Here the wide pavement ended at the cliffs, and beneath them a large outcrop of rocks jutted out into the sea like a protecting arm curled round the little bay of Winklestone. The beach he chose was part shingle, giving way to firm yellow sand, and empty of people.

"Here we are!" he announced, raising his arm to beckon the stragglers. "Come along!"

Evangeline joined him. Her face was now shiny and pink. "Goodness me!" she cried, "That was quite a route march!" She mopped her brow. "I cannot wait to get out of these clothes!"

Timmins shuddered.

"I think I might have a little nap," she said, fanning herself with her hand.

Thank goodness for that, thought Timmins. With luck, she would keep out of his way for a good long while. "Come along, ladies," he said, leading them down the painted wooden steps on to the beach. "Well, this is a nice change of scenery," Timmins announced as they crossed the pebbles which rolled and slipped beneath their feet. Soon they reached the firm yellow sand where Timmins stopped, filling his lungs with sea air. "Smell that ozone! How fortunate we are to have such a glorious day for our annual picnic."

"Annual?" one mother said, struggling along behind him with an armful of bags. (Was it Mrs Snell? Mrs Spinks? No, Mrs Bubb. Yes, definitely, Mrs Bubb. "This is the first one we've ever bloomin' well had!"

Timmins blushed. "Ah, er – well, yes, it is our first one, Mrs Bubb. What I meant was that it will become an annual event. Now I – that is to say, we – have got the show on the road, so to speak, we shall repeat the exercise!"

"Huh!" the woman sniffed. "Let's see how this one goes first, shall we? We've only just got here – bit early to be talking about it being a success! You ain't seen what my kids are capable of!"

Timmins looked about him. "This is the perfect spot." He put down his bag. "I shall mind your belongings – let the children have a good go in the sea, and then we shall enjoy our luncheon." In no time at all, the women had set up camp and their children were soon splashing in the waves. Evangeline erected a green and red striped windbreak, disappeared behind it with a wave at Timmins, and soon, to the amusement of the other women, a loud snore issued from behind it.

Timmins lowered himself into his deckchair, tipping his hat over his face. He wanted to relax in the sunshine.

Lavinia, however, interrupted his peace. "Reverend," she said, "will you not join the children for a swim?"

Timmins sat up, pushing his hat back on to the top of his head. "Oh, no!" he protested. "Perhaps a paddle, later on. I really am no swimmer."

"Oh, go on, Reverend!" said Mrs Bubb. "Have a splash about with the kids. Get to know 'em." She glanced round at the others. "Do you good to let yourself go. And we all know that Honeybell woman knitted you a pair of trunks. She's been telling us all about it."

Timmins shook his head. " No, I am no swimmer. I am afraid I shall have to let you down, ladies," he said. "The children will have to amuse themselves without my help."

Lavinia frowned. "But Reverend Timmins," she said, "surely that is even more reason for you to go swimming today? If Miss Honeybell has taken the trouble to knit...?"

"No excuses now, Vicar!" Mrs Bubb interrupted. "Show us how it's done. No swimming off to France though – you're marrying my Pamela and her Vinnie next month!" The ladies roared with laughter and Mrs Bubb handed him a towel.

And so, beneath the protective towel which was far smaller than he would have liked - he changed. At one point a sudden breeze curled around his bare limbs and threatened to reveal his nakedness. Panicked, he tried to hold it down, to a chorus of ribald laughter and shouts of, "Watch out Vicar!" and "Keep your hand on your ha'penny, Reverend!" This was a nightmare, and all Lavinia's fault!

At last, he stood before them, clad only in the trunks. He had never been this naked in public before - not since he was a child - and the sensation was strange to him. He clasped his arms about his stomach, conscious of the fact it protruded rather too much above the knitted belt. The women gazed at him, and he found their attention to that area of his person very disconcerting. Were they admiring the quality of Evangeline's workmanship... or were simply amused at the sight of their vicar in a state of undress?

"They fit you lovely!" said Mrs Bubb. "Nice and snug."

The trunks certainly were snug and not a trifle irritating. Wool always made him itch when worn against bare skin, and the trunks were no exception. They tickled him in places where it would be too indelicate to scratch. He fidgeted to ease the prickling sensation.

"There," said Lavinia. "That wasn't so bad, was it?"

He frowned. He could swear there was a twinkle in her eye.

"Well go on then, Vicar," Mrs Bubb exclaimed. "Don't just stand there posing - have a splash about! We're all going in, aren't we, girls?"

'We are!' The women changed into their bathing costumes, shrieking with laughter as the occasional gusty breeze caused towels to billow and dance. 'Oh, lawks! Nearly gave away all my secrets there!' cried Mrs Bubb, and Timmins, suddenly aware of being male amongst the group of disrobing females, set off down the beach, Poffley bounding along beside him.

The warming sensation of the sun on his bare flesh was actually pleasant, he thought, and he rather enjoyed feeling the rippled sand beneath his feet. Seagulls screamed and swooped, the waves whooshed and rushed on the shore and the briny scent of the sea was invigorating, but swimming had never been something he enjoyed. As a small child on trips to the beach, he would have contented himself with building sandcastles and collecting shells and seaweed, but his father would not leave him be. 'That fellow's a cissy!' Sir Lionel had said more than once. 'Should be more like his brother and me ' in the water, whatever the weather. Doesn't do to mollycoddle the lad, Prudence. He must at least try to swim.' He recalled the disgust on his father's face as he splashed about. 'Boy's like a drownin' whale!' had been his only comment before he had turned away to watch, with pride, as Claude Augustus cut through the water like a shark.

It was no better at prep school, where he had to endure swimming lessons in the murky pool. He had often almost drowned, either through his own inadequacy as a swimmer or thanks to the antics of the other boys, for whom he was an easy target. And now here he was, standing pale and plump at the water's edge, naked except for the ghastly trunks, and with everyone watching him.

There was nothing for it. He had to go in. "Oh, Lord!" he wailed. He strode forward until he was waist deep. Despite the heat of the day, the water was icy at first and the waves buffeted him. "Ooh! Ahh! Ouch!" He knew that the women, and Lavinia, would expect him to swim. Holding his arms out straight before him, palms together, he launched himself into the waves, his face raised to the sky to keep it out of the water. The cold was painful in those first moments and, once afloat, Timmins, open-mouthed, panted with the shock. "Oh! Ouch! Whoooo!" He thrashed his arms and legs about to get the circulation going, and, as he became accustomed to it, he could breathe normally. Crouching to keep his shoulders submerged, he gave himself up to the pull and push of the sea, rocking back and forth and using his arms, spread wide, to steady himself when necessary.

"This is really rather pleasant," he thought, listening to the hiss and seethe of the waves, the shouts and laughter of children playing on the beach, and the squalling chatter of the herring gulls as they wheeled and circled in the cloudless sky. Why had he not done this long ago? Winkleton was not so very far from Quillington Parva. What a waste! Now he was here, he would jolly well make the most of it!

In a sudden burst of energy he swam, with more enthusiasm than style. He splashed along, chin up, hands pawing at the water and buttocks cresting the waves. Poffley, who had been running in and out of the water, came swimming towards him, and for a little while they paddled along together. Timmins moved through the waves, enjoying the rush of the water, and listening to Poffley's panting breaths, the distant laughter of the children on the sand and the piercing cries of the seagulls. "Good show, Samuel," he thought. "If your Papa could see you now."

A heavy blow struck him between the shoulder blades, sending him lurching forwards, mouth open in a shocked gasp. "Pllgghh!" He sank under the water, taking in a mouthful of salty brine. Arms flailing, he struggled, spluttering, to find his feet and stand upright. "Wh..what?" he coughed, nose and eyes salt-stung and burning. "What was that?" For an instant, rage and impotence suffused his whole being. He had been the victim of so many "sinkings" in the school pool.

"Who did that?" Timmins growled. They should have a piece of his mind, whoever it was!

"It wath me, Thir. Thorry, it wath an acthident."

Blinking, Timmins saw a small boy, freckled and fair, whom he recognised as one of Edna Dobson's grandsons. He was bobbing about in the water, clutching a big red beach ball. "We wath playing Piggy in the Middle an' my brother throwed the ball to me an' I mithed an' it hit you. Thorry!"

"You all right, Vicar?" one woman. "Why don't you join us?"

Recovered now, Timmins felt a glow of pleasure. "I rather think I would like that!" he said. "Shall I be Piggy?"

It was as he jumped for the ball for the first time that he noticed a dragging sensation around his nether regions. The trunks! Forgetting the ball, he reached beneath the water to investigate. Glory be! They were heavier now, and loose. He could not risk jumping out of the water again. "On second thoughts," he said, "I - er - I have a little cramp in my leg. I think I shall call it a day if you don't mind." Grasping the trunks with both hands, he waded towards the beach. He would get changed and read a little before lunch.

Before he had got far, however, a shrill greeting pierced the air. "Yoo-hoo, Reverend! Here I am." It was Evangeline. She looked, he thought, like a collection of large pink balloons - upper arms, thighs and, most disturbing of all, her bosom, billowed out in soft masses from the green, purple and pink frilled costume. A most unflattering flowered bathing cap clung to her scalp. Waving, she blew him a kiss as she reached the water's edge. "Evangeline has come to play!" Dipping her toe, she squealed. "Ooooh! It's so cold! You are brave!" Filling her lungs and pinching her nose, she plunged under the waves, surfacing a few feet away from him. 'Ooh!' she gasped. 'What fun!' She scooped up a handful of water and splashed him.

When he did not respond, other than to wipe his face, she repeated the action, this time sending a far bigger shower of water in his direction. "There!" she said, as the waves gently bounced her up and down. She ran her tongue round her top lip and said, "What are you going to do about that then? Are you not going to play? No? Well, you naughty boy, I shall have to come and get you!" and she waded towards him, using her arms to push away the water as if she were swimming. Each movement of her arm caused her to float up so that her ample bosom appeared above the water, and he remembered what she had said about them breasting the waves together.

"Er, no! Oh Lord, no! I think I shall swim ... Oh heavens!" He set off, but as he swam the trunks slipped further down his legs, the knitted belt failing to keep them in place. "Oh, good grief!"

He tried to pull them up but swallowed a mouthful of seawater. 'Eeugh!' Spluttering, and wiping his eyes, he let go of the trunks which slipped off his legs and floated away like some outlandish jellyfish.

Horrified, he glanced back to see if Evangeline was still after him. What if she discovered his nakedness? Luckily, she had been distracted by Edna Dobson's grandson. He had to retrieve and reinstate his trunks before she resumed her pursuit of him. But how? The water was up to his chest. He could not stand upright, but if he swam, he would risk his bare backside bobbing about in full view.

Rocked by the current, his feet barely touching the seabed, he made a desperate grab for the trunks, but at that moment a powerful wave swept them out of reach, submerging him and sweeping him off his feet. By the time he had righted himself, spluttering, they had disappeared.

"NO! Oh, Good heavens! Come back!" he cried. Treading water, he scanned the sea. There was no sign of them. Should he shout for help? No, that would draw too much attention. "Dear Lord!" he wailed. "What am I to do?"

"Having fun, Vicar?" cried Mrs Bubb, who was floating on her back some distance away, a small island of sunburned flesh and bright yellow costume.

"I'm having a lovely time, Mrs Bubb. What a glorious day!"

"It must be about lunch time now," Mrs Bubb shouted. "Yes - Miss Bellamy is beckoning us all in." She rolled over and began swimming towards the shore.

"I think I'll stay in a little while longer," Timmins said, but she did not hear him. He was alone in the water. The sun beat down upon his naked shoulders and the waves lapped gently against his skin. His stomach rumbled. In the various picnic baskets, he knew, were sandwiches of all kinds - creamy egg with the inevitable crunch of peppery cress; salty pink ham and home-made chutney, and tangy cheddar with juicy, sweet tomatoes. There were golden brown pork pies, boiled eggs and crisp, fresh salad vegetables and packets of crunchy potato crisps with their little blue bags of salt. Dorothy Manifold had insisted on donating a sticky, spicy gingerbread, a great fruit loaf replete with sultanas, currants and glace cherries, and a huge chocolate sponge, thickly layered and topped with chocolate buttercream. "The kids'll like that one," she'd said.

His stomach gurgled - he was hungry! Why had no-one noticed his absence? Surely they would wish him to say Grace? Lavinia would not contemplate eating a meal without it being said - why had she not come in search of him? Squinting in the sunlight, he scanned the beach - there she was, still towelling dry some smaller children.
He must get out of this mess! The tide was retreating and to maintain his dignity he would have to retreat with it, which meant moving further and further away from the happy gathering on the beach - and further away from his clothes. Oh, how he longed to feel the reassuring hug of his dog collar, the snug protection of his trousers and shirt!

Surely Lavinia would notice he had not joined them? He lifted both arms out of the water and waved them in a criss-cross motion over his head. "Yoo-hoo! There was no response. What was he to do? "I say there! Help!" he shouted, as loudly as he could, waving his arms.

The beach party did not notice and his voice, affected by the chill, had come out as a squeak rather than a shout. He redoubled his efforts. "I say, there! Help!" An unknown child, flattening a sandcastle with a red spade, stuck out his tongue.

What was he to do? He could not stride up the beach in a state of nature. Neither could he remain in the water. Why would Lavinia not look up?

An idea came to him. He had chosen a beach near the rock pools so that the children could clamber about and search for crabs, sea anemones and tiny fish. On those rocks and in those pools would be seaweed - perhaps he could find enough to conceal his nakedness? Hope flooded back as he pushed his way through the water, feeling his feet sink into the sand as he went. Wavelets slapped against his chest, sending sprays of salty drops up into his face.

The going was hard, but finally he reached the rocks, thankful for their thick covering of bubbled bladderwrack. Grabbing hold of a large handful, he pulled. Nothing. The plant was stronger than he thought. He tried and failed again, this time falling backwards with a loud splash and sinking into a fizz of bubbles as the water closed over his head.

Blast the stuff! What was he to do if he could not gather enough seaweed? He had no other plan. Visions of himself, rising like Botticelli's Venus from the waves, without the benefit of that lady's golden tresses, made him shudder. He would be a laughingstock. Regaining his feet, he surfaced and drew a lungful of air, ready to try again.

"Coo-ee! Reverend!" Lavinia! There she was, in her bright blue bathing suit, standing at the water's edge and waving something at him while Poffley barked and jumped at her side. Timmins' heart leapt at the sight. She had his trunks! Thank the Lord for that! Dear old Lavinia! She had come to his rescue.

Waving, he offered a silent prayer of thanks and pushed his way as fast as he could towards the shore. As he walked, the water level dropped, uncovering first his chest, then his belly, then...

"Samuel!" Lavinia called. "Be careful!"

Timmins stopped.

"Wait for Poffley!" Lavinia shouted, and she bent and whispered something to the dog before giving him the trunks. "Call him!"

she continued. "He will bring them to you."

Timmins' heart filled with affection. "Poffley! Dear old thing! Come here, there's a good doggie!" he called.

Poffley hesitated for an instant then, with a leap and a bound, he was in the water, swimming towards him with the trunks in his mouth.

"Good old Poffley!" Timmins exclaimed as he retrieved the trunks and put them on, struggling against the pull and push of the water. Finally, he was decent again. Thank the Lord for that! "You clever dog, you. Oh, you clever boy!" Poffley swam in circles around him. "You shall have the biggest bone the butcher can find as soon as we get home, but now, let us have lunch. I am hungry." He was also rather cold by now, his skin popping up in goosebumps. "Brrrr!" he shivered, staggering out of the water.

Lavinia handed him a large, fluffy towel. How warm and soft it felt! He patted himself all over and then reached for her hand, which he kissed. "Dear Lavinia - I cannot thank you enough! You saved my reputation and my honour. I owe you a debt of gratitude."

"That's a little dramatic, Samuel! I am only sorry that I did not notice your predicament far sooner. I only realised what must have happened when Poffley deposited that... garment at my feet."

The tide must have swept them on to the beach and Poffley, recognising his master's scent, had retrieved them.

"Luckily," continued Lavinia, "everyone else was busy eating by that time so your ordeal remains our secret." She glanced down at her hand, still clasped in his, and he followed her gaze.

The silence between them grew almost palpable. Timmins opened his mouth, feeling he must say something and half afraid of what it might be. He remembered the words spoken by Guy de Chalfontaine to Amélie Delacour. "My darling, I love you so! You are my saviour and my soulmate. Be mine, and we shall be as one throughout all eternity!" But he did not speak.

"Are you alright?" Lavinia peered at him. "You seem preoccupied."

Timmins blinked. Those might have been the words of Guy de Chalfontaine, but they expressed what he felt. I love her, he thought, and in a sudden rush of emotion he kissed her on the cheek. "You are my saviour!" he said.

She pulled away from him.

"I'm sorry," he exclaimed. "Forgive... How can I apologise? Oh, dear, oh dear, oh dear! It shall not, I assure you, happen again."

Lavinia shook her head. "Don't apologise! I was glad to be of assistance. Those frightful trunks! I cannot think Miss Honeybell counts knitting as one of her talents! Still, it was a generous gesture on her part."

Timmins nodded. It was like Lavinia always to see the good in other people. "It was a generous gift, and it is just a shame the trunks themselves ended up being rather too extraordinarily generous!" He laughed, amused at his own joke. "Never mind. Shall we see if there are any sandwiches left?"

CHAPTER SIXTEEN

ON THE ROCKS

Timmins ate an enormous lunch. To his great disappointment, the children had polished off the chocolate cake - the evidence was there on their faces, but he consoled himself with gingerbread. By the time he had finished, he could barely move and when Mrs Bubb said that the children were clamouring to go to the funfair, he declined her offer to join them. He had eaten far too much to risk being thrown about, and the thought of the noisy, brash fairground with its accompanying smells of fried onions and candy floss made him feel queasy. It was easy to insist that they go without him.

"Sounds like you want to get rid of us, Vicar!" said Mrs Bubb, in mock indignation. "Perhaps you want to be alone with a certain someone?" She indicated the windbreak, some feet away, behind which Evangeline had earlier disappeared. "What do you think, ladies?" Ribald laughter answered her question.

Timmins frowned. "I am afraid I do not understand..."

"Oh, come along, Reverend - you know what I'm talking about. A certain someone who has been, shall we say, singing your praises, if you catch my drift. Singing them loud and clear. Come on, Vicar, don't deny it! You know as well as we do that she's keen on you!"

"Keen as mustard!" one of the other women agreed.

Timmins felt his face flush. "Miss Honeybell?" he exclaimed. "What can you mean? That lady and I have nothing -"

There was a movement behind the screen and Evangeline's head appeared above it. "Did I hear a certain someone call my name?" she purred and broke into song. Timmins recognised it at once

- The Indian Love Call. She emerged from behind the screen, slinking her way across the beach.

Heaven help us! Timmins thought, noting, with a mixture of fascination and horror, how the flesh wobbled as she walked. That costume!! Not only did it not leave a great deal to the imagination, but the lurid colours quite clashed with the redness of her skin! She would regret that in the morning. He made a mental note to roll down his shirt sleeves and trouser legs in case he should fall asleep, which was likely, he thought, given the size of the lunch he had just eaten.

"What's afoot?" Evangeline said, removing her tortoiseshell sunglasses and surveying the little group. There was a ripple of barely suppressed laughter, for although the rest of her face was bright scarlet, the area round her eyes, protected by the glasses, had remained white. She was, Timmins thought, rather like a species of panda. Evangeline frowned. "Is there something wrong?"

Somebody ought to tell her. "You've got..." he began.

"Er, no. No - not at all. Nothing that would amuse you, I'm sure." Lavinia said, shaking her head at Timmins. The gesture was slight, but enough for him to understand that she thought it unwise to say anything, and on reflection he realised she was correct. Evangeline would make a song and dance about it, he was sure, if she thought she presented a less than perfect appearance.

Evangeline shrugged. "Did you miss me? I have been having the most delicious dreams, darling." She let out a trill of laughter and shuddered in ecstasy. "Deeelicious."

Mrs Bubb gave a loud and disapproving snort. "We were trying to persuade the Vicar here to come with us to the funfair, he isn't keen. Don't suppose you want to come with us?" She paused and then added, "You look as if you've had enough lying in the sun."

Evangeline bridled, but before she could speak Lavinia said, "Dear Miss Honeybell, I have had quite enough of this strong sunshine and have decided to see the show at the end of the pier. Will you come with me? I am sure that your presence would create quite a stir."

Evangeline hesitated, and Timmins crossed his fingers behind his back. Surely she would not stay? Please God, no!

"Dear Reverend Timmins, would you mind so very much if I abandoned you for a little while? I cannot resist the lure of the theatre, however humble, and I cannot allow dear Miss Bellamy to spend the afternoon alone. I know my presence might cause excitement amongst the audience of that little theatre, and Miss Bellamy will enjoy the opportunity of seeing what it is like to be famous. Life in a little village such as Quillington Parva cannot furnish you with much excitement."

Lavinia raised an eyebrow and turned to Timmins. "You won't mind if we leave you?" she enquired, with the ghost of a grin, and he was quick to reassure her.

"Please, enjoy the show! I shall occupy myself with guarding all of your belongings and catching up with some... some important reading." He pointed to the copy of The Church Times poking out from his bag. It concealed his copy of "Amélie Alone". How he longed to rejoin Amélie on her island, and to find out whether she could outwit the evil Duc d'Évergne. "Please, enjoy yourselves, everyone."

The funfair party set off while those who preferred the beach sprinted off to a clear patch of sand to build "the biggest sandcastle ever". Evangeline vanished behind her windbreak, emerging fully dressed a short while later, and she and Lavinia disappeared towards the pier.

Poffley curled up beneath the deckchair while Timmins reached for his book, withdrew the bookmark - an Order of Service for some long-forgotten funeral - and lost himself in Amélie's struggles. The screaming seagulls, the children's laughter and the regular swoosh of the waves all receded into the distance as he read. The sun played on his skin and a sensuous, warm breeze caressed him, lulling him still further into a state of total relaxation. This was the life ...

Smack! Something hard and wet landed on his belly. "Wha..? What's that? Eeugh!" He woke with a start, spluttering and struggling to sit upright in the sagging deckchair. Pushing his hat back on to the top of his head, he squinted in the sudden brightness of the sunshine. "What on earth?!!"

"Thorry, thir! It wath my ball again!" The same small, fair, freckled boy stood before him, thumb in his mouth and red beach ball at Timmins' feet where it had landed. This was intolerable! Timmins was about to issue a reprimand when he saw the boy's frightened look. He frowned. The child bit his lip and took the tiniest step backward.

Good grief! Could it be that the boy was afraid of him! A jolt of recognition hit him with a thud in the chest, the sensation as strong and as real as if someone had punched him - this must be how he had appeared to his childhood tormentors. Oh, dear Lord, how frightful! The poor child had not intended to disturb him. He smiled. "Never mind, little fellow," he said, his voice as gentle as he could make it. "These things happen. Here, take this threepenny piece and ask your mother if you can buy an ice-cream."

The little boy hesitated for the merest fraction of a second before snatching the coin with a quick, "Thank-you, Thir!" Scooping up the ball, he raced back to his mother. She looked up at Timmins, beaming, while the little boy raced off towards the ice-cream kiosk on the promenade, just a little way off.

Timmins made himself comfortable once again, tipping his hat over his face. The child would enjoy his ice-cream - dear little chap. Later, perhaps, he would buy one. "Would you like an ice, Poffley my boy?" he murmured, and from beneath the deckchair Poffley gave a little grunt.

Before long he was dreaming. At first, the dreams were pleasant, but then he noticed something menacing, something chasing him. Who, or what was it? He thought he heard it muttering as it thundered along behind him... Whatever it was, it seemed to speak in a medley of strangely familiar voices; "A Timmins never runs! Where's your backbone, lad?", "Come here, Timmins, you little squirt! I've got itching powder!", "Timmins! What about the bells? The bells, Timmins - the bells!", "Run, Sammy, old lad! Run!" and then a woman's voice, "Yoo-hoo! Darling man! Yoo-hoo!"

This last utterance came from somewhere so close he shrank from it. "No, no, no!" he protested, shaking his head, and trying to fend off his attacker with flailing arms. "Let me alone!"

"Reverend Timmins! Samuel!" The voice was gentler now.

He opened his eyes, but all was darkness. "I cannot see!" he wailed. He clutched at his face; it felt strange, rough, and puffed-up, as if it did not belong to him. "Aagh!" he wailed. "Help me!"

And then someone whisked away his hat, the sun's brilliance hit him, and he squinted in the bright light. There was a throaty, theatrical laugh, and a voice sang words he recognised from somewhere,

"When you get some repose in the form of a doze,
With hot eyeballs and head ever aching,
Your slumbering teems with such horrible dreams
That you'd very much better be waking..."

"Darling man, you were having a bad dream, but your Evangeline is here now! Wakey-wakey, dearest!"
Sure enough, there she was, fanning her sunburnt face with his hat, the white circles round her eyes giving her a startled

appearance. Who else would sing Gilbert and Sullivan? Good Lord - if he never heard another syllable or note of comic opera, it would be too soon!

"There, that's better!" she cooed as he struggled to sit up. "Nothing to worry about now!"

He was not so sure. She had called him "dearest". How persistent she was. He must make it clear that he had no romantic interest in her. "I am quite alright, I assure you," he said, struggling to get out of the deckchair and ignoring the hand she offered. "May I have my hat?"

She giggled and held it out to him, but when he tried to take it, she snatched it away with a coquettish giggle and hid it behind her back. "Come and get it," she whispered, thrusting her capacious bosom forward. "If you dare!"

Just then, to his great relief, Lavinia joined them. "Reverend, it is almost five," she said.

"Goodness! I must have slept for longer than I intended. Thank you for reminding me." he said. "My hat, if you please, Miss Honeybell."

Evangeline pouted and handed the hat back to him. "Spoilsport!" she mouthed and flounced off to retrieve her belongings from behind the windbreak.

"I am rather afraid that she is too used to having her own way," Lavinia said. "And she intends to have her own way with you."

"Hmm," Timmins replied. "I don't know why she should think I am interested in her."

"Are you not?"

"Of course not!' Timmins exclaimed. 'Nor shall I ever be! Surely you cannot think...?"

There was a mischievous twinkle in her eye. Lavinia was teasing him! He studied her face, remembering how she had looked when he first met her. She now had a few lines and her hair had silvered, but the years had, he thought, been kind to her. What a contrast there was between her and that awful Evangeline! There was something restful about Lavinia - restful, gentle, and trustworthy. His lip trembled. "My dear Lavinia," he began, but a shout interrupted him.

"Ethel! Where are you?" Mrs Bubb was scanning the beach.

"Is there a problem, Mrs Bubb?" Timmins made his way across the sand towards her. The tide, he noted, was fast coming in, and they would need to move their things.

"It's my Eth - all the other kids are back but Ethel's not with them and nobody seems to know where she is!" Mrs Bubb's voice betrayed her concern.

Fear prickled Timmins' neck. This could not be! It had gone so well until now! For a brief second he imagined the furore that would ensue if anything had happened to the child. He would stand no chance of remaining as Vicar of Quillington Parva if... No! He checked himself. What was he thinking? What did his needs matter when compared to the real desperation of poor Mrs Bubb, and the awful calamity of little Ethel's disappearance? 'Forgive me, Lord,' he thought, in a silent prayer. "We shall find her, Mrs Bubb, I promise you," he said, and there was a note of confidence in his voice that surprised even him.

At that precise moment, Poffley, who had been sitting at Timmins' feet, lifted his head, pricked up his earsthen raced off down the beach.'Poffley! Where are you going? Come here, sir!' cried Timmins, but Poffley took no notice. Instead, he remained at the water's edge, barking.

"What on earth has got into him?" Timmins exclaimed. "Poffley!"

Lavinia ran down the sand to where the dog was standing. "Poffley's found her! She's out there!" she shouted, beckoning

Timmins. "On the rocks!"

The little girl was clinging to the pinnacle of the largest, most jagged rock, while all around her the ever-deepening water crashed and surged.

"Oh, Ethel! My Ethel! Save her, somebody!" wailed Mrs Bubb. "My baby girl!"

Timmins' heart leapt into his mouth. He must save the child. He raced down to the water, his muscles and joints protesting, his chest tight and his throat sore. "Don't worry, little girl! I'm coming to get you!" He stripped off his trousers and shirt, hurled them aside, and plunged into the water. Ignoring the shock of the cold sea, he swam for all he was worth towards the rocks.

It was hard work swimming against the tide; however hard he fought, he seemed to make no headway. Waves smacked him in the face and salt water went up his nose, leaving him spitting and gasping with the pain. The sea roared and crashed against the rocks as seagulls screamed and whirled overhead. Little Ethel's face was white with fear, her whimpering cries mocked by the screeching gulls. Her plight gave Timmins a strength he had never felt before. Ploughing through the water, he prayed as he had never prayed before; "Let me save the child, that is all I ask. Help me, Lord!"

At last, he reached the rock where Ethel was sitting, "Thank you, Lord!" he muttered. "Now grant me strength to save her." With a last gasp of effort, he grasped hold of a sharp, craggy projection. Drained of all energy, he rested for a moment while the waves buffeted him. His hands hurt, his skin was being cut and grazed against the barnacle-covered rock and his eyes stung from the salt' Had he been foolish to attempt such a rescue? The little girl perched precariously on a ledge high above him. How could he save her?

"I want my mummy!"

"You m..must t... try to climb down, Ethel my dear." He was shivering so much that it was a struggle to get the words out. "You m... must t..try, dear! Be a b... big, brave girl now!"

But the child cried louder. "Mummy!"

Something brushed against him. "Woof!"

Poffley! Dear old Poffley had swum out to join them! His heart lifted and hope gave him new energy. "Ethel! Look! Poffley is waiting here for you! He wants you to come and say hello to him!" he called, and the child, peering over the rock and seeing the dog bobbing about in the water, stopped her crying, hesitated, then picked her way towards them. It seemed to take an eternity, and Timmins' heart beat loudly as he watched the little feet testing out the footholds, but at last, she was at the level of the water.

"Now dear," said Timmins. "Be very careful, but if you jump to where Poffley is, you will not hit any rocks and you can hold on to him. He's a big, strong dog and he will take care of you."

Ethel hesitated. Timmins offered up a prayer. She had to jump - there was no way he could heave himself out of the water to fetch her.

"Woof!" Poffley barked again and the little girl launched herself into the water, disappearing beneath the surface. The fraction of a second until she resurfaced was an agony for Timmins. Was she alright? He scanned the water for a sign of her. Why did she not come up?

Yes! There she was, clinging to the dog. Thank the Lord!He pushed off from the rock and swam towards the pair. Taking the little girl under the chin, he muttered reassurance. "Try not to panic, dear," he said, "or you might frighten Poffley." He could feel her little body shivering with cold and fear. He ploughed his way back to shore, pulling at the water with his free arm. It was exhausting and progress was slow. Several times he swallowed a mouthful of salty water but each time he felt as if he could go no further, Poffley swam close, nudging him and the child as if to say, "Keep going. After what seemed an age, Timmins felt the seabed beneath him. He struggled to his feet, lifting Ethel clear of the water, and staggered on to the blessed warmth of the sand, where a sobbing Mrs Bubb gathered her daughter in her arms.

"Thank you! Oh, thank you!" she cried, wrapping the child in a towel. "You saved my baby! Oh, you darling, darling man!" She held out her hand to him, but the shock of her ordeal and her mother's emotional state were too much for Ethel. Sobs racked her little body as the other women crowded round the pair, urging them to "Come and have a nice hot cup of tea".

Timmins, shivering, waved away Mrs Bubb's thanks. "D-d-do as they say, dear lady," he said. "D - do as they say." He watched as they made their way up the beach, the women in little huddles, the children trailing after them, to sit amongst the picnic baskets, where Mrs Bubb rocked little Ethel on her lap and the women gathered their own offspring to them.

A cool breeze had risen. His legs and arms felt heavy, and it was all he could do to remain on his feet.

"Samuel! Oh, Samuel! You look terrible! You need some hot, sweet tea." Lavinia's voice was soothing and calm as she came to stand by him. "Get down, Poffley!"

The dog, who had been desperate to lick his master's face, shook himself, showering them all with tiny droplets of water, then yawned and flopped down on to Timmins' feet. His tail thumped the sand and Timmins bent to stroke him. Thank God for Poffley!

Lavinia held out a towel. "Here, dry yourself off with this and then we will see about getting you a hot drink," she instructed, but he could not move.

"My dear!" Lavinia said. A comforting warmth enveloped him as she wrapped him in the towel and threw her arms around him.

He luxuriated in the tenderness of her embrace. He was home. He delighted in her scent.

"Lavinia, I..., " he began.

"Coo-eee!" Evangeline's orange and black-clad figure wobbled towards him, arms outstretched, her voice piercing the air. She seized him in a bone-crunching hug. Gazing at him in adoration, she fluttered her eyelashes. "My darling!" she cried. "You brave angel! How magnificent you were, cutting through the waves! How I feared for your life! I could scarcely bear to watch! I would have been at the water's edge to greet your triumphant return with that poor girl, but terror for your safety had rendered me unable to move." She licked her lips, and he noticed a smear of jam at the corner of her mouth.

Lavinia had withdrawn and was heading back up the beach.

"I was in shock!" Evangeline's voice grated on him. " I had to seek sustenance with which to revive myself, but never fear, I am now quite restored." She waved her arm towards Lavinia, Mrs Bubb and the others. "See how soon they have forgotten you! They leave you here, my dear one, at the water's edge, all alone and forlorn, but never fear - I am here! Your little Evangeline is here to be your succour and your strength! Kiss me, you brave, selfless creature!" She puckered her lips.

Timmins recoiled, but to his horror, she did not let this deter her. She made a long, loud kissing noise and cried, "Darling, darling man! So modest!" before singing a song he recognised - Gilbert and Sullivan, again!

"From the briny sea," she warbled,
Comes young Samuel, all victorious!
Valorous is he -
His achievements all are glorious!
Let the welkin ring
With the news we bring.
Sing it - shout it - Tell about it

Safe and sound returneth he
All victorious from the sea!

"Please Madam, unhand me!" he said. "You are making a spectacle of both of us!"

Evangeline ignored him. "There is no-one to see, and besides, I care not who knows of my love for you!" she exclaimed. "Oh, you dear, darling man! You showed such bravery, dashing into the briny ocean to rescue that poor infant! I am sure that even the great G and S would forgive me for the little liberty which I have taken with their words!" She gave a little giggle. "Oooh, how I envy that little girl!" she said. "To be wrapped in your arms and carried like that!" She shivered. "I go weak thinking of it!" There was a short pause, then she licked her lips again, tilting her head to one side in mock shyness. "Perhaps one day," she said, walking her fingers up his chest, "you will carry me in your arms... over the threshold?"

'Madam!' Timmins cried, jumping back in alarm. 'You go too far!'

"Oh, you are so shy - and I love you all the more because of it," she purred, wrapping her arms about him. He attempted to disengage himself, but it was no good. The woman was like an octopus - each time he released an arm from round his waist, it grasped him again, determined not to let him go.

"Please Madam, unhand me!" he said. "This will not do!" What would Lavinia think when she saw Evangeline clinging on to him like this? With one last effort, he wrenched himself free and pushed her away from him. "Your behaviour is inappropriate! What will people think?"

Had Lavinia noticed? She must have done - how humiliating! What would he say to her that could excuse either his apparent intimacy with Evangeline or his less than gentlemanly behaviour in pushing her away? He let out a long sigh and shook his head.

"I understand, my dear. You are not ready yet to share the news of our love with others." She giggled. "Well, let it be our secret for a while longer. I shall leave you." She blew him a kiss and made her way back to the rest of the party.

Timmins did not move. Overcome with exhaustion and emotion, he stumbled his way up the beach in a daze, scarcely aware of his surroundings. He barely noticed someone throwing a second towel around his shoulders and pulling it tight. Then Lavinia's voice cut through his stupor.

"Darling Samuel! You brave, brave man! I am so proud of you!"

A sudden memory came to him of what she had said to the Bishop. "So, you do not find me tiresome any longer?"

"Pardon?" She frowned. "I don't understand."

"You were discussing me with Bishop Archbold after the Choosing of the Beard," he said. "Selfish and heartless, I believe were the words you used."

Her brow furrowed. "I have never called you that - why would you think...?" Her expression changed and she laughed. "Oh no, Samuel!" she cried. "We were not discussing you! We were talking about the Amélie books! We were discussing the Duc d'Évergne!"

"But then why did you say that you had tried to make him less selfish? How could you change a character in a book?"

"Can you not guess, Samuel? I am Blossom Madgwick, my dear."

He stared at her. What? Her words made no sense. She was Blossom Madgwick? How could she be? He had always imagined the writer of those books to be someone altogether more worldly - a celebrity, living the high life amongst the literati. How could this quiet, unassuming person be Blossom Madgwick? He remembered all the times he had seen her scribbling away in her notebook, recalled the business appointments in town and her collection of Blossom Madgwick books. Then there was the time they had argued - and she had quoted lines from a book which was so hot off the press that he had wondered how she had had time to read it. Good Lord, could it be true?

"I... I..." he mumbled, overcome by a sudden immense lassitude. 'Oh,' he gasped, "I feel most peculiar. I have such a headache!'" All energy drained from him, the world darkened, and he felt himself sink on to the sand.

CHAPTER SEVENTEEN

ON THE MEND

The next few days were a strange limbo for Timmins, a period of whispering voices, shadowy figures looming over him, wild dreams, and the vague awareness that he was at home in bed. He thought he heard Lavinia's voice, soothing and loving, and once or twice he felt his face being licked vigorously by a large, wet tongue. Reassuringly, the slobbering kiss was accompaniedby her voice issuing the command "Poffley! Stop that this instant!"

When he awoke, he was more tired than he could ever remember. For some time he lay still, alone in the room and aware that his whole body ached. He dared not move a muscle. His skin burned, his head pounded, his mouth was dry and the jug on the bedside table was empty. Never had he felt so weak. He tried to summon enough energy to shout for Mrs Whibley who, judging by the banging and clattering coming from the kitchen, had arrived, and begun her day's work. She would not thank him if she had to run up and down stairs after him. "I'm not a bloomin' nursemaid!" would, he imagined, be her likely response and Mrs Whibley in a bad mood was the last thing he needed at this moment.

If only he could get out of bed, he could fill a glass from the bathroom tap. But oh, how tired he was, and how far away the bathroom! A vision of his father shimmered into being at the foot of his bed. "Look at you, boy, malingering in your bed. If you had an ounce of grit about you, you would be up and about, not languishing like some damned consumptive damsel!"

Anger and resentment boiled up in Timmins. ""Scold me, will you Papa?" he muttered. "When I have risked my life to save that poor child? Nothing I can do will ever earn your approval. You are - were - a..." For the first time, he could speak the word, "a bully. A successful soldier you may have been, but as a father, Sir, you were a failure. Even in death you cannot alter your ways." He lifted his head from the pillow and wagged his finger as if scolding a miscreant child. "You have made my life a misery, Papa, but I no longer need your approval. Good day to you, Sir." As he spoke, the vision of his disapproving parent grew fainter, disappearing with a little "Pfft!".

Timmins, elated, attempted to sit up. "I shall get myself a drink!" he declared to the empty room, but the effort was too much. He fell back on to his pillow. "Steady on, Samuel," he muttered to himself as he gingerly stretched out his legs, pointing and flexing his feet. It hurt. It was no use. He had no energy at all, and besides, he found himself hemmed into a small part of the bed by its other occupant. "Oh dear, Poffley," he groaned.

Curled up with his back to Timmins and his head on the pillow, Poffley thumped his tail. Timmins pushed against the animal and Poffley, with a yelp of protest, awoke, sat up and scratched himself vigorously, then jumped off the bed, his claws clicking on the linoleum as he nosed open the door and, with a reproachful glance at Timmins, exited the bedroom in search of breakfast.

Timmins lay back on the pillows. He was hot and uncomfortable. The blood was rushing in his ears, his head felt as if it was being held in a vice and his lips were dry and sore. Everything irritated him - the sheets rumpled and uncomfortable, the pillow hot and lumpy. The sunlight filtering through the half-drawn curtains was too bright, and the birdsong grated on his nerves.

"Vicar? Are you awake?" Mrs Whibley's voice as she called up the stairs was like fingernails scraping a blackboard. "Don't you dare try to get out of bed! I'll be with you in half a tick!"

Wincing, he tried to open his mouth and shout that all he wanted was a glass of water, but all that came out was a croak.

He tried again, but it was no use. The effort exhausted him, so he lay back on the pillow. Swirling blobs of green, purple, and red made patterns behind his closed eyelids, and he felt himself drifting...

"Vicar?" It was Mrs Whibley. She must have come into the bedroom. "Vicar, are you alright?"

He did not - could not - answer. He was back on the beach again, the sound of the crashing waves drowning out all other noises as seagulls wheeled and screamed overhead, and the sun burned down upon him. An enormous dread permeated his entire being and the feeling that there was something vitally important he should remember. What was it? Something dwelt at the periphery of his vision, but each time he tried to identify it, it vanished, only to reappear seconds later as a vague shape at his side, barely visible. He turned his head this way and that in an unsuccessful and frustrating effort to discover what haunted him. "Who are you?" he murmured - although he was unsure if the words left his mouth or whether he imagined that he uttered them. "What do you want? Who are you?"

Did the creature speak? He strained to hear what he imagined were its words - or was it merely the sound of the sea rushing and splashing on the shore? "Ssshhh! Sssshhh! Sssshhhh!"

"Mousie? Is that you?" Whatever had been shadowing him was no longer there. Still, he had an overwhelming feeling that he had a task to complete - how could he complete it unless he knew what it was?

A voice interrupted his rambling thoughts. "I'm here, dearest!" it seemed to say. "I'm here!" A woman's voice - but whose? It seemed to come from a long way off. Gazing about him, he saw for the first time the enormous rocks, jagged and black. The waves thrashed and boomed against them, swirling violently. Fear overcame him and then he realised who had spoken. It was... Amélie Delacour! It was she... abandoned to her fate by the vengeful Alphonse. And there, twirling his moustache at the water's edge, was the sneering Duc! He bore a strange resemblance to someone Timmins recognised, but who? And then it came to him. Alphonse, Duc d'Évergne looked just like Claude Augustus!

"No! No!" he cried in his dream. "You shall not win! Amélie, my beloved one, I am coming for you!" and he realised that he was no longer Samuel Timmins; somehow his identity had merged with that of Guy, Comte de Chalfontaine, the one true love of Amélie Delacour's life. "You shall be mine, my love!" And now the sand no longer dragged him down as he raced down to the water, plunged in, and swam effortlessly towards the rocks. "Dearest one, where are you?" he cried, heaving himself on to the crags, and her voice came back with the answer; "Here I am, darling!"

With some effort he scaled the forbidding precipice and there, sitting on a seaweed-covered rock, was ... not Amélie Delacour, the raven-haired young beauty, but Lavinia Bellamy, in her lilac cardigan and tweed skirt.

"Where have you been, Samuel?" she whispered.

Timmins shook his head. This was wrong - where was Amélie? And why did Lavinia call him Samuel, when he was Guy, Comte de Chalfontaine?

"Amélie?" he whispered. "Where are you, my beloved?"

"I am here, Samuel, my love - waiting for you!" Lavinia's voice was nearer now, and louder. "Oh, darling, come back to me," she said, and he blinked in the light, to see Lavinia sitting by his bed.

"Lavinia?" he croaked. "What are you doing here?"

"Ssh, dearest," she said, "do not speak." She leaned over him and planted a gentle kiss on his forehead. "Welcome back, Samuel. We have been so worried about you. You have been so very ill. Try a little drink of water." Smiling, she poured a glass of water from the newly filled jug and offered it to him, supporting his head as he sipped and then allowing him to rest back on the pillow. "Oh, Samuel," she said, and her voice cracked with emotion. "Where else would I be?" She held the palm of his hand to her face so that it cradled her cheek. Her skin was cool, and tears spilled down her cheeks. "You have suffered a heat stroke, dear Samuel. It has been a week since you took ill after our day out at the seaside - a week in which we feared for your life!" There was a catch in her voice. "Oh, I was so worried about you, darling!" She kissed his hand again.

A week? He had lain here all that time? No wonder he felt so feeble. "I was dreaming," he said, struggling to remember the details. "I... I was swimming out to the rocks ... Amélie was in danger ... but then... you..."

"You were being my brave hero - my very own Guy de Chalfontaine!" she whispered. "And I..."

There was a short silence before she spoke again. "I am not Amélie, dearest - I am no longer young, and have never been the beauty she is." Placing his hand gently back on the bed, she smoothed her skirt and folded her hands in her lap. "But she is part of me."

"I don't understand," he said.

"I am Blossom Madgwick, my dear. I tried to tell you that on the beach. Are you disappointed in me?"

"Disappointed? I can still scarcely believe it, but no, I am not disappointed. I am in awe of your talent." He licked his lips and she poured him another glass of water. "But why have you kept it such a secret?"

"Because of Papa," she said. "He felt that the Amelie books were not quite the thing for a Vicar's daughter to be writing, although, as you know, he would never have tried to stop me doing anything. The early publicity made them out to be quite shocking, so he asked me to use a pseudonym." She paused. "I know you like the books, Samuel. Does it shock you to think that I wrote them?"

"No. No! Never believe that! I adore your writing! I thrill to the adventures of Amélie and Guy! How can you doubt it? Why, even the Bishop is a fan!" He tried to heave himself up in the bed, but the effort was too much.

"Calm yourself!" she cried. "You must give it time, dearest Samuel, before you attempt the slightest exertion. Mrs Whibley and I shall nurse you until you are better. And, Samuel, you will keep my little secret, will you not? I am not ashamed of my books but now they have become so popular there is the danger that, were my true identity to be revealed, it would threaten my quiet little life in Quillington Parva. Autograph-hunters would plague me."

With great effort, he took her hand. His heart flooded with emotion. "For as long as you wish, my love. You are, and always shall be, my Amélie," he whispered. "I love you, dear Lavinia, with all my heart. I always have and I always shall...." The dryness of his throat caused him to cough and splutter, and Lavinia busied herself with pouring another glass of water and offering it to his parched lips. He sipped, then pushed the glass away. "Lavinia, I wanted to ask if you would...."

The door burst open and Poffley bounded in, barking, and wagging his tail. He ran up to Lavinia, jumped up at her and attempted to lick her face.

"Oh, Poffley! You silly creature!" She put the glass down on the bedside table and took the animal's front paws in her hands. "No, I don't want you to kiss me! Get down, you bad, bad boy!" She let go of his paws and as she did so, another figure appeared in the doorway.

"Who's being a bad boy? Is dear old Sammy up to his tricks again? Is he trying to kiss you, Lavinia, old scout?" It was Claude Augustus, carrying a large bunch of roses. He strode across the room towards the bed, wagging a finger. "Tut tut, Sammy. And I thought you were at death's door! Ha! Glad to see there's life in the old dog yet, dashed if I'm not!" He bowed to Lavinia, winked at her in what Timmins thought was a very inappropriate manner, and sat down on the end of the bed.

"Oh no, I..." Timmins protested, but Claude Augustus interrupted him.

"Just teasing, old lad, just teasing. You know me! No, don't sit up, dear boy - I didn't mean to upset you." To Lavinia he said, "Either of you. Think I've done that enough, don't you?"

Timmins lay back on the pillow. What was his brother up to now? Trust him to come lumbering in at the wrong moment!

Claude Augustus thrust the flowers at Timmins. "Here, brought you these. Bit soppy and all that, but it's the thing to do, it would seem, when one visits an invalid. Besides, I had to pop into the florist's." He took off his hat and hung it on the bedpost at the foot of the bed. "I'm taking Miss Honeybell out this evening for a spot of dinner, and you know how the ladies like a bloom or two. Makes 'em feel special and then - well, need I say more?" He chortled, and Timmins frowned at him.

"They are lovely, aren't they, Samuel?" Lavinia said, before Timmins could reply. She gathered up the bouquet. "I shall ask Mrs Whibley for a vase while you two have a little chat." As she left the room, Timmins saw her cast a warning glance at Claude Augustus. "He is still very weak..."

Claude Augustus nodded. "Don't worry old girl, I won't stay long, and I promise not to upset him."

Lavinia left the room, and they heard her light step on the stair as she descended, calling Poffley to follow her. As the dog scampered out of the room, Claude Augustus spoke.

"What have you been up to now, eh?"

"I... we..." Timmins croaked, but before he could say more, and to his enormous surprise, Claude Augustus seized his hand and patted it.

"Don't speak, old lad!" He cleared his throat. Still holding on to Timmins' hand, he said, without a trace of his usual jocularity, "I'm not talking about you and Lavinia! I was referring to your heroics at the seaside! Plunging into the briny seas to rescue a damsel in distress and all that - it's the talk of the county! You're quite the hero of the hour. You're in all the newspapers, don't you know!"

In the newspapers? Surely not! Timmins sighed. Long experience told him that his older brother was very good at lulling one into a false sense of security, only to drive home a mocking taunt or cruel barb. "Don't..." he croaked. "Please, Claude..."

Claude Augustus shook his head vigorously. "No, Samuel, I mean it." His voice cracked and his pale blue eyes were, Timmins noted with astonishment, brimming with tears. This was an unfamiliar Claude Augustus, serious, intense, and clearly emotional - what was he up to? Timmins withdrew his hand from his brother's clammy grasp, waiting for, and dreading, the teasing that was sure to follow - he would not allow himself to fall into another of Claude Augustus's little traps.

"It's true, Samuel. You risked your own life to save that little girl. You were never a strong swimmer - you might have drowned!" His voice faltered. "Oh, dear!" He took out a large blue and white spotted handkerchief from his top pocket and blew his nose with an elephantine trumpeting that made Timmins recoil. "I admit, Samuel, that, in the past, I have ... once or twice, behaved in a... less than kind fashion towards you. I saw you as a weak, puny specimen."

Timmins frowned.

"You were always so timid and afraid of standing up for yourself. Frankly, I shared our dear Papa's misgivings that you would never amount to anything much."

"Oh, I say..." Timmins croaked in protest, but Claude Augustus held up his hand and shook his head. "Still yourself, dear brother; we were quite, quite wrong. Allow me to continue." His voice husky with emotion, he continued. "I admit, brother, that I had long thought you unfit to bear the distinguished name of Timmins."

Timmins bristled, but before he could reply, Claude Augustus reached out and grabbed his hand, squeezing it so that Timmins yelped in pain. "Dearest Samuel - my dear old chum" Claude Augustus's voice was cracking with emotion. "Mama and Papa would have been so proud of you! Your sisters are proud of you... and I... I am proud of you! Damn and blast it, Sammy, you risked life and limb to rescue an innocent young maiden, a poor, dear waif! Forgive me for my past behaviour. You are a true Timmins." With that, he took out the handkerchief again and blew his nose with another thunderous snort.

Timmins stared at his brother, open-mouthed. Never had he seen Claude Augustus display such emotion; he half expected the older man to burst out laughing. "Ha! Had you there, old lad! Hook, line and bally sinker!" He waited to hear those words, words he had heard so often when Claude Augustus had caught him out. But Claude Augustus, for once, said nothing. Silence reigned in the bedroom, save for his snuffling.

Finally, when Timmins realised that there was to be no humiliating jest, no insult, he reached out and patted his brother's hand. "Thank you. That means a lot."

Claude Augustus flinched at the touch and frowned momentarily before clearing his throat. "I... Er... No need for... Oh... I say, get down, boy!"

Poffley had come bounding back into the bedroom and hurled himself excitedly at Claude Augustus, determined to lick his face. 'Ugh! No! Get off!' Claude Augustus protested, pushing the dog away. He cleared his throat and took out his pocket watch. Glancing at it, he frowned, stood up and snatched up his hat. "Well, that's all I came to say. Can't hang around the sickbed for too long, don't you know? Sun's over the yard arm now. I must be going."

He put his hat on at what Timmins thought was a ridiculously jaunty angle, then prodded Timmins' leg. "You should be up and about too, you know. Dear old Lavinia's downstairs - carpe diem, I say, if you get my gist. Alone in the house with the object of your affections..." He whistled. "Ideal opportunity to breach the defences, don't you think?" In the doorway he hesitated. "I have an appointment with a little lady - the aforementioned, delectable Evangeline. She has resisted my charms, but I shall prevail! She's a juicy little morsel and worth a bob or two, I should think."

Timmins shuddered.

"And besides, I like a challenge! Now, I'm off. Mustn't be late, old lad." He clicked his fingers at Poffley, who had flopped down by the side of the bed and took no notice of Claude Augustus. With an exasperated 'Tch!' Claude Augustus strode back into the room, grabbed the dog's collar, and gave him no choice but to follow. Together they left the room and as they descended the stairs Timmins could hear Claude Augustus urging the dog to "Come along, you blasted hound!"

His brother's visit left Timmins feeling more exhausted than before. For the next few days Lavinia and Mrs Whibley ensured that nothing disturbed him, and a week later Timmins had recovered enough to take Poffley out for a gentle stroll around the village. "No gallivanting off around the fields now," warned Mrs Whibley, wagging her finger at Timmins in a manner which once would have irritated him, but which now warmed his heart. She had been so upset at his illness and, he now understood, cared about him rather more than he had ever realised.

"Do not fear, my dear," he said, fastening Poffley's lead. "I shall enjoy a brief stroll about the village, and Poffley here will take care of me."

"Woof!" said Poffley, scenting the fresh air that drifted through the open front door. He tugged on his lead, his tail wagging.

"We had best be off," Timmins said. "Mrs Whibley, I shall probably need only a small snack this evening - perhaps a roll or two, some of that delicious cheddar cheese, a little of your apple chutney and perhaps one - or two - of your sausage rolls. I may call in at the Fat Rascal for a slice of Mrs Manifold's Victoria sandwich... and perhaps, a scone with cream and jam. Do you know, I have eaten so little during my period of illness I feel quite skeletal."

Mrs Whibley snorted. "Well, I am sorry that my steak and kidney pudding and that jam roly-poly and custard you had for lunch seem to have left you wanting, I'm sure. And there was me thinking I'd done me best to build you up, but I shall do as you say." With that, she made her way back to the kitchen, her slippers slapping on the tiled floor. "Oh, and Vicar, there's a letter on the hall stand there - came this morning, by hand." She disappeared into the kitchen, letting the door slam behind her.

Timmins frowned. "Oh dear, Poffley, I seem to have upset her," he said. He picked up the letter. "Stop pulling! Stop it, I say! I know you are eager to be on your way, but...Oh, very well, I shall read it on our return." He threw the half-opened letter back down on the hall table. "Now, off we go, but slowly, boy, please!"

They set off down the driveway of the Vicarage at a pace, Poffley pulling on the lead and Timmins struggling to keep up and to keep his straw hat on. The sun was shining, bees buzzed, and a warm and gentle breeze smelling of newly cut grass brushed his cheeks as they made their way past the little cottages with their flower-filled front gardens. It felt good to be alive, Timmins thought, inhaling the summer air. It was good to be out of his bed.

"Vicar! Oy! Vicar!" Arnold Bubb, in his vest, braces hanging in loops down by his sides, was sitting in the doorway of his cottage, waving.

Timmins nodded and hurried past. He did not feel strong enough for an encounter with Bubb. The fellow was always so belligerent. He would surely ask how his little girl had clambered on the rocks unsupervised, and what Timmins thought he was playing at by allowing it to happen. It was a question Timmins had been asking himself.

As they entered the High Street, Timmins noticed Harold Bungay locking the door of the offices of Bungay and Biggs, Solicitors. "Ah! Timmins, you old reprobate!" Bungay called. "Wanted to have a word with you." He made his way over to Timmins, puffing and wiping his face with a large white handkerchief. "Glorious weather, eh?". He put his handkerchief away and bent to pat Poffley on the head. "Looks as if this old boy is enjoying his walk." Glancing up at Timmins, he bit his lip and shifted his weight from one foot to another. "Thing is, Timmins - and I am not a man who finds it easy to say this - I owe you an apology." He took out his handkerchief again and dabbed at his nose. "Blast this hay fever! Ruins my summers for me. I cough and sneeze and splutter...Harrrummmphh!"

Poffley barked and pulled on the lead.

"Steady," said Timmins. "I'm sorry to hear that, Bungay. I should go home if I were you. Stay indoors."

"Yes, yes, I know all that," Bungay said. "Thing is though, I wanted to..."

"Is it Parish Council business you wish to discuss? Because I know I have been incommunicado of late, but I intend to organise a meeting and we..."

"Well, yes... but that is not..."

"I have been unwell," Timmins continued.

"I know it!" Bungay exploded. "Good Lord, let a man get a word in edgeways! AAAATCHOOO!"

The violence of the sneeze sent Bungay tottering, and Timmins reached out to steady him. When he had recovered himself, the solicitor grasped Timmins' hand, squeezed it and clapped him on the shoulder. "The thing is, Timmins, I feel I owe you an apology. I own that, in the past, I may have been a little unfair to you - teased you rather a lot. Fact is, it turns out you are a decent chap - seems you have guts, going out and rescuing that little girl - so I apologise. There, that's it done and dusted." He nodded. 'I've been beastly to you, Timmins, and I don't like myself for it. I am sorry." He blew his nose. "Best be off now, out of this sunshine. AAATCHOOO!" With another great sneeze he set off down the High Street, calling out as he went, "Cheerio - see you at Millicent's after church on Sunday?"

Timmins frowned. He did not recall having made any engagement at Hatherley Court. The solicitor must be mistaken. An unaccustomed feeling of superiority put a spring in his step as they continued along the High Street. Bungay had always made him feel inadequate and uncomfortable, with his air of confident entitlement, but today things had changed. It was Bungay's turn to be uncomfortable. "Well, Poffley,' he said. 'What do you think of that then? Shall we celebrate with a cup of tea and something tasty at the Fat Rascal?"

Poffley barked.

"Come along then." Together they made their way to the tearoom. The door was open and from within came the sounds of china rattling, laughter, and the buzz of conversation. Timmins was about to tie Poffley up outside when Dorothy Manifold appeared in the doorway, fanning her face with a tea towel.

"Vicar!" she cried. "How lovely to see you! And dear Poffley here!" She stooped to make a fuss of the dog. "Don't leave him out here - I'll take him through to the back where he can have a little nap in my sitting room. I might even have a little treat for him. What do you say to a bone and a drink of water, Poffley?"

Timmins followed Dorothy Manifold and the retreating dog, taking a seat at his favourite table. When she came back, she sat down opposite Timmins, lowering her bulk on to the cane-bottomed chair. "Ooof!" she exclaimed. "My poor old legs are no better, Reverend! And this catering lark is blooming hard work when all's said and done. You don't mind if I take the weight off my feet, do you? I've told the girl to bring you one of our special teas, on the house."

Before Timmins could say anything, she reached out and patted his hand. "You deserve it, Vicar! The way you dashed into the sea to rescue that poor mite, and you're not a young man! I said to Edna Dobson when we heard, I said, 'That Reverend Timmins might seem as if he couldn't fight his way out of a paper bag but he's a real hero - our very own Douglas Fairbanks!'"

"Well, now, I don't think I am quite deserving of such praise..." Timmins began.

Dorothy Manifold shook her head. "No, it's no use you being all modest, Vicar. Edna's got quite the crush on you now! She says you can throw her over your shoulder any time you want! Mind you, I'm not sure exactly where she thinks she might need rescuing, or how she thinks you could do it!" She let out a peal of laughter. "Edna's a dear, but it'd take something to sweep her up into your arms!" She patted Timmins on the knee and got up. 'I'd best see where that girl's got to with your tea. Shan't be long!

Here's Miss Bellamy to keep you company! I'll make sure there's enough for the both of you." So saying, she disappeared, still chuckling, into the kitchen.

"May I join you, Samuel?" Lavinia's gentle voice was a welcome relief after Dorothy Manifold's raucous jollity. She was a picture in her pale blue linen dress.

"Lavinia - dearest Lavinia!" His heart filled with love for her. "You are most welcome, my dear girl."

She slid into her seat and took off her white cotton gloves. "How are you, Samuel? Not overdoing it, I hope?"

"Not at all, my dear. Poffley and I have taken but a short stroll today, so I might regain a little strength in my legs. He is at present enjoying a butcher's bone in Mrs Manifold's sitting room while I, as you can see, have sought the shade of the tearoom."

"I am glad to hear it, Samuel. And how was your walk?"

Timmins recounted his meeting with Harold Bungay. "He said something about going to Millicent Gore-Hatherley's on Sunday after church. Do you have any idea what may be going on?"

"Yes, dear," Lavinia replied. "Did you not get her letter? She has invited a great number of the villagers to lunch at Hatherley Court to celebrate your recent heroics." She hesitated. "You will be well enough to attend, won't you, Samuel? She has invited the Bishop."

Timmins nodded. "There was a letter on the hall stand, but I am afraid I did not open it. She did not need to go to such trouble - I only did what anybody would have done in the circumstances. But I shall attend - I am almost fully recovered, and that I am is due to your tender care whilst I was on my sickbed."

Lavinia blushed. "There is no need to thank me, Samuel, darling - I am glad I could help."

"You gave me strength to get well, and hope for the future, my beloved Lavinia," Timmins replied, overwhelmed with emotion. This woman - this lovely, clever, kind, strong woman - cared about him! He had not dreamed it. "Darling Lavinia!" he exclaimed. "Before Claude Augustus came into the sickroom and interrupted me, there was, as you may recall, something I wished to say to you..."

"Yes, Samuel?"

"My beloved - I wanted to ask you... "

"Here we are - a Fat Rascal special for you both!" Dorothy Manifold loomed over them, bearing an enormous, fully laden tray. "I must go back for the milk and the sugar," she continued, putting the tray down on a neighbouring table and transferring everything over to the table occupied by Timmins and Lavinia. "Couldn't fit it all on one tray. Phew!" She arched her back and grimaced. "Now, you've got ham and mustard, cheese and pickle, sardine and tomato, chocolate cake, Victoria sponge, two scones, jam, cream and a couple of Fat Rascals each for luck. That do you?"

Lavinia gazed at the enormous spread. "Well,' she said, 'you seem to have regained your former appetite and no mistake. That is a ridiculous amount of food to order."

"I assure you, my dear Lavinia," he replied, stiffening, "that it is entirely Mrs Manifold's doing. She took it upon herself to pre-empt my order with one of her own. And you heard her say she has brought enough for you too." He frowned. "In fact, I rather resent the implication. Will you have some tea?"

Lavinia nodded. "Yes, thank you Samuel. I cannot stay long. I have business to attend to."

Timmins poured tea for them both. "Where is Mrs Manifold with that milk? The tea will be cold."

"You had something to ask me, Samuel?"

"Yes." He paused. "Will you... will you have a sandwich?" he said, his voice clipped. There was all that food spread out in front of them and now, with that one remark, Lavinia had turned its beauty to ashes before him. It was too bad of her.

She took a ham and mustard sandwich and nibbled it as Dorothy Manifold reappeared with the milk and sugar.

"You did seem to have something on your mind, Samuel?'

Timmins shook his head. "It doesn't matter." He took a bite of his sardine and tomato sandwich. Silence reigned between them. When he had finished his sandwich, he reached out and took two more, which he ate in quick succession, although they had suddenly seemed to lose all taste. How dare Lavinia criticise him? How could he help it if Dorothy Manifold had taken it into her head to lavish all this food upon him? Left to his own devices he would, he assured himself, have ordered a simple toasted tea cake... And then for her to accuse him of gluttony in that fashion! It was most unjust! He avoided Lavinia's gaze, preferring instead to study an interesting print of Queen Victoria on the wall to his left. He knew that she was regarding him. She was waiting for him to speak.

The silence continued, prickling in the air between them. Finally, as Timmins defiantly helped himself to a fourth sandwich, Lavinia spoke. "Very well. I feel it is only fair to let you know that I have some important business matters to deal with. I shall be away for a few days." She finished her tea and picked up her gloves. As she put them on, she said, "I appear to have offended you, Samuel. I did not intend to upset you - I thought we understood each other better than that. I am sorry that you have taken an innocent remark to heart in quite the wrong way. However, I must go now. Thank you for the tea. Do not get up."

At this comment, Timmins half raised himself from his chair and when she had gone, he sat back down. What had just happened? Damn and blast it! He had thought he and Lavinia had found a new understanding. He had been about to ask her if she would consent to... And now this!! It was most frustrating. Still, it would be a shame to let all this good food, provided at Dorothy Manifold's own expense, go to waste, he thought. He would have just one or two more sandwiches, and then perhaps a slice of cake. Or two.

CHAPTER EIGHTEEN

THE DAY OF RECKONING

Back at the Vicarage, Timmins first let Poffley out into the garden then, remembering the letter, collected it from the hall stand. It was, as Lavinia had suggested, an invitation to attend a lunch party in his honour at Hatherley Court that Sunday. "No need to RSVP," it said, in Millicent's loopy black handwriting. "Bishop attending - your presence is mandatory!"

Just like Millicent, he thought, steamrollering her way through everyone else's arrangements without consultation. Since his little disagreement with Lavinia he had quite gone off the idea of a party, but there was to be no getting out of it. Resigned, he put the opened letter back on the hall stand and was about to make his way into the garden for a spot of dead-heading the roses when the telephone rang, its shrill sound splitting the silence. He picked up the receiver to find Bishop Archbold on the other end of the line. His heart raced. Perhaps the Bishop was so impressed with his recent exploits that he would allow him to remain in Quillington Parva regardless of the state of the church bells?

"I trust you are well, Your Grace?"

"Yes, yes. Never mind all that nonsense. I hope you're better? Can't have my chaps out of action for too long, you know, even if it is because they've been rescuing damsels in distress, like the knights of old!"

Timmins joined in with the Bishop's energetic laughter. This sounded promising! The Bishop was in a good mood.

"Now, the thing is that the six months I gave you to sort yourself out are pretty much up. I propose to trot along to Quillington Parva on Sunday, have a quick chat about the books. That sound all right to you? Timmins! You still there?"

"Er, yes, Your Grace. That will be ... fine." Timmins felt sick. It was, he thought, anything but fine.

" Good Lord, man, you could summon up a little enthusiasm! Never mind, I will be with you on Sunday at 9 o'clock sharp. Cheerio."

Replacing the receiver, Timmins regarded his reflection once more in the hall mirror. "That's put the tin hat on things. There's not enough cash in the coffers to fix the bells and the church is rarely more than a quarter full on a Sunday - you'll be out on your ear, shuffled off to the outer reaches of Quillinghampton or somewhere even worse. You won't know anyone, Lavinia is avoiding you and it's your own silly fault." He went into the garden and spent an hour taking out his disappointment and frustration on the roses.

"Vicar! What on earth are you doing?" Mrs Whibley hurried across the lawn towards him and stood gazing around her with a horrified expression on her face. Leaves, dead flowers and severed branches littered the ground. "You've made the place look like a blooming battlefield! Old Jim'll go berserk!"

Timmins sighed. "It'll grow back," he grumbled. "Put these away for me, will you?" Thrusting the shears into Mrs Whibley's hands, he stomped into the house, went into the sitting room and threw himself down on the sofa. He gazed about him. This was his home. He loved it, and he did not want to move. It was not fair! A tear rolled down his cheek. Why did things always go wrong?

When Poffley came bounding in, leaping up onto the sofa, Timmins grabbed hold of him and hugged him, stroking the shaggy fur. "Dear Poffley," he said. "You still love me, don't you, boy? To think I didn't want you!" A tear rolled down his face and Poffley removed it with a thoughtful lick.

Timmins passed the rest of the week in a state of abject misery. His ill-temper and low mood clouded the atmosphere in the Vicarage, and although he knew that his behaviour was unacceptable, there was nothing he could do about it.

Old Jim had, as predicted, been thunderous when he saw the damage to the garden, muttering comments under his breath about "Folks as should know how to control themselves and not go about spoiling things." He threatened to resign, to which Timmins responded with a terse comment that the gardener could do as he pleased - there were plenty of others who would take on the job.

Mrs Whibley pointed out that Old Jim needed the income, that he would not, at his age, find it easy to find another post, and that he had cared for the Vicarage garden since the early days of Reverend Ambrose Bellamy's ministry. "He loves that garden - he's worked on it his whole life and you want to dismiss him? It's not right, Vicar."

Timmins relented and Mrs Whibley had smoothed things over with Old Jim by giving him a pot of her strawberry jam. From then on, however, she took umbrage at every remark Timmins made, taking it out on him by burning his toast in the mornings and refusing to cook anything but offal - which he loathed - for dinner each evening. Lavinia was still absent and even the adventures of Amélie Delacour held no attraction for him, knowing, as he did, that they were the product of her imagination.

Sunday dawned bright and clear, the sun shafting down into the bedroom and a fresh breeze causing the curtains to billow. Timmins woke early and lay in bed, listening to Poffley's snoring. It was odd, but now the day of judgement had arrived, he felt more at peace than he had done since the Bishop's telephone call. "Well, this is it," he remarked to the sleeping dog beside him. "Nothing I can do about it. Although I suppose one more quick prayer might help." He got out of the bed and knelt, his hands clasped. "Dear Lord, I know that I have been a fool, and I accept what may come my way. Thank you for these years in this lovely place, and I promise that, I will try to do better in the service of Your Church, wherever the Bishop sends me."

As he finished, he felt a waft of warm air on his face. His heart missed a beat. Was this a sign? Opening his eyes, he met Poffley's steady amber gaze. The dog twitched a hairy eyebrow and tilted his head to one side.

"Ouch!" said Timmins as he stood up. "It would appear, Poffley, that I am becoming too antiquated to be getting down on my knees. Either that, or I do not do it often enough for my poor old bones and muscles to become accustomed to the movement. Now, I shall perform my ablutions and we shall go forth together to face the day." He patted Poffley's head. "Wish me luck, my dear friend!"

The first hurdle awaited him in the kitchen. Mrs Whibley glanced up as he entered the room but did not greet him with her usual cheerful "Mornin' Vicar!" Instead, she sniffed, took his breakfast from the range and plonked it in front of him. A collection of pallid-looking devilled kidneys atop some soggy bread gave off a nauseating aroma, and Timmins sighed. Offal again! He had little appetite, but he dared not offend Mrs Whibley by refusing the meal she had prepared. As he ate, washing the food down with long draughts of lukewarm tea, Mrs Whibley clattered about, tidying the kitchen. Timmins felt her disapproval in every movement she made.

At last, he put down his knife and fork. "Mrs Whibley, I can stand no more of this. Please sit down. I have something I wish to say to you."

She stopped what she was doing, wiped her hands on her apron and complied. 'Well?"

"My dear Mrs Whibley," Timmins said. "I owe you an apology for the way I acted in the garden..."

"Yes, well..." she shifted in her chair and bit her lip.

"I realise that I acted badly and that probably I frightened you by my actions. I have been short-tempered with you since then, and although I note that you have registered something of a protest against my behaviour by furnishing me with nothing but offal since that incident..."

Mrs Whibley folded her arms.

"... food which you know I abhor," he continued, "I wish to tell you I accept the criticism implied by such ... unpalatable meals. I apologise. I was boorish and have been so for most of this week."

Mrs Whibley sniffed and opened her mouth to speak, but Timmins held up his hand to stop her.

"Please, Mrs Whibley, allow me to continue. I have appreciated your loyal and sterling service over the years, and I feel blessed to have had your help. I also should say how grateful I am for the way you nursed me through my recent sickness. You are a treasure, and I shall miss you when I have to leave this house and this parish..."

"Leave?" Mrs Whibley frowned. "Where are you going?"

Timmins told her of the Bishop's impending visit and his own dread of being found wanting. "I must prepare myself, my dear, for the distinct possibility that, having studied the finances and when he sees that the church is, as usual, rather empty today, he will fulfil his promise." He gave a wry laugh. "I fear Miss Gore-Hatherley's party this afternoon will be rather a bittersweet affair. Still, it will at least allow me to say goodbye to everyone."

Mrs Whibley stood, removed her apron, and hung it on the back of the pantry door. There was determination in her eyes and a sense of purpose about her every move. "Well, Vicar. I accept your apology, and I thank you for it. If you will excuse me, I have to go out. You won't mind washing up your own dishes?"

Without waiting for a reply, she picked up her handbag and left.

Timmins washed his cup and plate, then dried his hands on the tea towel. Where on earth had she gone? Would she return in time to cook his dinner? At this moment, the doorbell rang. Timmins jumped and his heart beat faster. Bishop Archbold! This was it! He must face the music. His insides fluttered as he made his way to the front door.

"Ah, Timmins!" Archbold boomed, bounding into the hallway where Poffley greeted him with enthusiasm. "Lovely day, what? Been for a stroll around the village - did me the world of good, I can tell you. Nothing like rising early and getting out in the dawn of a new day. Hello, old boy!" He stroked Poffley vigorously, whereupon the dog hurled himself to the floor, lay on his back and waved his long legs in the air. His belly made a dull, drumming sound as the Bishop patted it. "Now, to business. In here?" He pointed to the sitting room and when Timmins nodded, he strode in and threw himself down into the armchair.

Timmins followed, perching on the edge of the sofa. "Er, would you care for a cup of tea, Bishop?" he enquired. Anything to put off the dread moment.

"No, no... Time for tea later, after the service, perhaps."

"The...er, the service? You are coming to church this morning?"

"Good Lord, man, of course I am. You've gone quite pale. No need to worry! I'm sure you have a masterful sermon for us all. Good gracious, if you can brave the briny deep to rescue a maiden in distress, then I am sure you can stand up to the prospect of having your Bishop see you in full flow in the pulpit. Cheer up, Timmins old sport! Now, about these books..."

Timmins steadied himself. This was it!

"You have not, as I requested, raised the required amount for the repair of the bells." the Bishop began, his bushy ginger eyebrows knitted. "Which is a failure on your behalf."

"I..."

"No. Make no excuses, please. You have not reached your target, but you have made a significant improvement upon previous years and collected more money than I expected." His booming voice bounced around the sitting room. Poffley barked in response.

Timmins stared at Bishop Archbold. "I... I do not understand..." he stuttered.

"It's simple," the Bishop said. "You could never, in the time allotted, raise the sort of cash we will need to repair or replace the bells. That will take a serious amount of money, but you needed a real kick up the backside, so I set you an impossibly high target. The way I saw it, you would either prove yourself a complete laggard by failing even to try meeting the target or you would stir your stumps and get on with it. And you did not let me down. Bungay tells me he is quite prepared to release Mrs Prout's money, and that is a major achievement on your part." He roared with laughter again and slapped his leg. "Your expression! Don't worry, Timmins! You jolly nearly did it!"

Timmins stared. "Does this mean I can..."

"Stay in Quillington Parva? That remains to be seen, old boy. Remember, I also challenged you to increase your flock. I am looking forward to the service. No doubt the church will be full?" He raised a questioning eyebrow, but before Timmins could reply the bells rang out. "Ah, well, we shall soon find out!" he said, springing to his feet. "Come along, let's meet your public!"

With a sinking feeling, Timmins followed the Bishop out into the hallway and through the front door. Together they made their way down the gravelled drive and across the grass to the little green door that separated the Vicarage garden from the churchyard. This was it, thought Timmins. There would only be a handful of people in the congregation, as usual. People would pay to have fun but were far less likely to donate to the collection plate in return for being preached at.

"Mornin' Vicar!" A cheery voice called to him. He blinked in the early sunshine. Standing by the church door was Arnold Bubb, spruced up and shiny in his Sunday best suit. Beside him stood his wife and their children, and next to them the Bearded Lady and others whom Timmins recognised as belonging to the circus. "Looking forward to your words of wisdom, Vicar - you've got quite a crowd in today!" A throng of people were negotiating the lych gate. "There's more inside." said Bubb. "Come along, kids - we'd best go in or we'll not find a seat at this rate!"

"Well, you're a popular chap!" the Bishop grinned. "Tell you what, you nip off and get togged up, while I find myself a place!" He gave the astonished Timmins a little push. "Hurry along!"

When Timmins emerged from the vestry into the church, the first thing he noticed was that the usual echoing emptiness of the building had gone. Instead, there was a buzz of anticipation and a few coughs as he stood before the packed congregation. Not one pew remained empty! Mouth open in astonishment, he gazed about him, his eye falling on Mrs Whibley in the front pew. She smiled, and beside her, Arnold Bubb surreptitiously stuck a thumb up at him. They were all on his side! Mrs Whibley had clearly made it her mission to rally the crowds, helped, to judge from his air of jaunty satisfaction, by Arnold Bubb. There was little Ethel Bubb, none the worse for her adventure. Cissie Bubb clasped her daughter's hand and mouthed the words, "Thank you!"

Timmins' spirits lifted as he uttered the greeting, "This is the day which the Lord has made; let us rejoice and be glad in it." During his sermon, for which he had taken as his topic the Parable of the Lost Sheep, Timmins searched the congregation for a sight of Lavinia. She was not there. "Just as the sheep in the Parable was lost, and little Ethel Bubb was almost lost to us, so I, dear friends, have strayed far from you all when I should have been the shepherd. With joy and thanks in my heart, I can truly say that I have learned the error of my ways."

The congregation sang lustily, roaring with laughter when he made even a passing attempt at humour, and bellowing their responses to the prayers, but all he could think of was Lavinia. Afterwards, as he stood with the Bishop at the Church door, everyone wanted to shake hands with him.

Arnold Bubb was the most enthusiastic. "We enjoyed that a great deal, Rev. We'll all be here again next week for a repeat performance, won't we, Cissie?"

His wife nodded and nudged Bubb. "Go on, Arnie; you've got something to say to the Vicar, haven't you?"

Bubb bit his lip and looked down at his feet. He shifted from one to the other. Cissie Bubb nudged him again and he looked up at Timmins. "You saved my little girl. If there's anything I can do for you, Vicar, you've only got to ask."

Timmins was about to reply, but Bubb continued. "Turns out you've got guts. More than I have. So, thanks, Vicar, and I'm sorry for the way I've behaved towards you. I got in with a bad lot when I palled up with Nobby and Reg. Thought they were mates, but they weren't." He paused, biting his lip. "If...if you want the honest truth, Rev, they were just messing with me - egging me on to muck you about - and I went along with it because I thought being with them made me look good. I was wrong. When I heard how you risked your life for our Eth, I thought, that man might look like a bit of a twit, but he's OK, so I told Nobby and Reg I wanted nothing more to do with them. You're all right, you are."

When they were alone, the Bishop himself thumped Timmins on the back and burst out, "Jolly well done, Timmins! What a cracking service! Thoroughly enjoyed it. And you seem to have won them over! Who would have thought it?" He paused, and for a moment all was silent save for the piping song of a robin somewhere nearby. Timmins breathed in the sweet-smelling summer air and waited. This was it - the moment when Bishop Archbold would decide his fate.

"I know that your congregation had made a special effort this morning. I am not such a fool as to believe that the church is always that packed!"

Timmins' heart sank. Bishop Archbold would order him to leave this village, these people! His shoulders slumped, and he mumbled his reply. "Yes, Your Grace. Oh dear, oh dear!" He sighed. "I shall pack up my belongings this afternoon and shall await further instructions as to the -"

"Hold your horses! You pre-empt me. Incorrectly, I might add. I said it was for my benefit. What I meant is that the fact that so many people came to church to support you is a proof they value you. It would be a disservice to the parishioners of this ancient church were I to move you on. No, Timmins - here you shall stay!"

Timmins' jaw dropped, and he stared at the Bishop. He felt suddenly lighter, almost dizzy, and he gasped. "You... you mean I have not failed? I can stay here, in Quillington Parva?"

The robin, which had been sitting on a nearby tombstone, regarding them with a bright, beady stare, flew down and landed at Timmins' feet, tilting its head quizzically. Then, as the Bishop spoke, it flew off, singing. "Now then, Timmins, don't stand there with your mouth open, gawping like a landed fish! What do you say?" Bishop Archbold wore an amused expression.

In a sudden, overwhelming rush of gratitude and relief, Timmins lunged forward and grasped his hand, shaking it vigorously. "Oh, thank-you! You don't know how much this means! I promise I shall not let you down!"

"Steady on - you'll have my arm off at this rate! I shall keep my eye on you though, Timmins, and there is still a deal of work to do if you are to get those bells mended. But now, for goodness' sake take off your vestments - I am ravenous and from what I hear of Miss Gore-Hatherley I imagine she will have laid on a splendid lunch for us!"

When they arrived at Hatherley Court, Sproat showed them into the Great Hall, wheezing news of their arrival to the assembled guests. They were all here - Harold Bungay, Claude Augustus, Dorothy Manifold, the entire Bubb clan, Mrs Whibley, Edna Dobson and even Poffley, sporting a vivid emerald and white spotted neckerchief - all, save Lavinia. Where could she be?

Millicent Gore-Hatherley, clad in an unflattering mustard chiffon frock, came striding towards them, the frills on her sleeves fluttering. "And here they are, our guests of honour!" she cried, enveloping first the Bishop and then, much to his embarrassment, Timmins, in an energetic embrace. She smelled of dog. "Sproat!" she cried, when, at last, she released Timmins. "Fetch these two gentlemen a glass of champagne each and let us all raise a toast to the hero of Winkleton-on-Sea, our dear Reverend Timmins, who plunged into the briny deep and swam to the rescue of a damsel in distress!"

The toast was drunk and then, much to Timmins' dismay, Arnold Bubb stepped forward and sang. "For he'sa jolly good fellow, for he's a jolly good fellow, for he's a jolly good feeeellllloooww! And so say all of us!"

One voice soared above the rest. Evangeline Honeybell! There she was, clad in pea-green and puce, glass held aloft and quivering as she sang. When the song finished, she raised her glass to Timmins, and took a sip of champagne, running her tongue over her top lip.

Timmins cleared his throat and looked away. He could feel his face burning.

Bishop Archbold put down his glass and clapped his hands. "I would like to say a few words. Thanks to our hostess for her generous hospitality, and to Miss Honeybell for lending her voice to this joyous occasion. Thanks to all of you for coming to honour this brave man here." He took hold of Timmins by the shoulder and drew him forward. "It is due to his bravery that little Ethel Bubb is still among us."

Where was Lavinia? Why did she not come?

"And so..." Bishop Archbold was reaching the end of his speech. "When I took up my post as Bishop of this Diocese, I found that things in Quillington Parva were not all they might have been. Church attendance was low, there was little or no community involvement, and the fabric of the building itself was falling into disrepair. It concerned me that Reverend Timmins had let go his hold on the parish, so I issued him with a challenge to put things right or I would have to move him out of the parish. I am sure it will delight you when I say that Reverend Timmins will remain as your vicar for the foreseeable future."

A loud cheer went up, and Millicent stepped forward. "Thank-you, Bishop dear,' she said. 'And now, please make your way to the dining room where the buffet awaits."

The guests needed no further invitation but surged towards the dining room, funnelling through the doorway in a tide of excited bonhomie. Several of them came to congratulate Timmins. In his heart of hearts, however, he had little appetite either for their kind words or for the buffet which awaited him. Where was Lavinia? Surely she was not still angry with him? She had said something about having business to attend to, but that was days ago. She must have returned to Quillington Parva by now.Why had she forsaken him?

Timmins felt no hunger. He took a plate and helped himself to a sausage on a stick, a fish-paste sandwich and a gherkin. He was about to take a bite of the sausage when a voice boomed in his ear, startling him.

"Cheer up! You look as if you've lost a pound and found a penny!"

Claude Augustus drew deeply on his cigar and exhaled the smoke at his brother, making him cough. "There's someone over there who is keen to speak to you." He gestured with the cigar, leaving a thin trail of smoke dancing sinuously in the air.

And there she was, more lovely than he had ever seen her, in a rose-pink and white floral tea dress. He thrust his plate at Claude Augustus, and pushed his way through the crowd towards Lavinia, who reached out and took his hand, leading him out of the dining room. They crossed the great hall to the library, where she drew him in and closed the door behind them.

"Oh, Lavinia!" Timmins cried. "My dear girl! How glad - how very glad, I am to see you! Where have you been? I have missed you so. Oh, Lavinia, I was so foolish, taking umbrage at your words in the tea-room the other day - I should have known you meant no criticism of me."

"Sssh!" Lavinia put a finger to his lips. "Dear Samuel, you have done nothing for which you need to apologise! I did not realise that my words would upset you. You have always loved your food - who am I to change you? There are far worse vices, and I would rather have you happy and, shall we say, plump, than miserable and thin as a rake!"

Was she calling him fat? He bristled, but..., she was right, might as well admit it, he was well-covered. He laughed and patted his stomach. "Perhaps," he said, "with you at my side to bring me the happiness I have lacked in my life, I will not need to seek solace in such pleasures."

Lavinia blushed and bit her lip and with a mischievous twinkle in her eye said, "There are other pleasures, Samuel."

"Lavinia!" Joy bubbled up in him and he reached out, took both her hands, and kissed first one and then the other. "Dare I hope that... Does this mean you will...?"

"Yes, Samuel, but only when we are married!"

"Oh, my darling! My dearest, beloved, clever, wonderful, beautiful Lavinia!" He gathered her in his arms and kissed her as he had kissed no one before. The softness of her lips, the warmth of her body and the sweetness of her perfume were an intoxicating mix. He wanted to hold her forever, never to let her go.

Finally, however, she broke away, grasping his hands in hers and holding him at arms' length. "Oh Samuel, my darling boy! Why did we let a stupid misunderstanding come between us!"

"It was all my fault, Lavinia! I was foolish to believe that you had abandoned me for Claude Augustus - I know you better than that. You are the most loyal, honourable, loving, darling..."

"You might be describing Poffley!" she said and squealed as he once again pulled her towards him and kissed her.

"Lavinia Bellamy," he said, "you are the best woman - the best person - in the entire world, and I can think of nothing better than to have you as my wife. Let's tell everyone!"

"But first, Samuel, I have to make myself presentable. You have quite messed up my hair! Join the guests, I shall find you in a short while." Ignoring his protests, she slipped out of the library.

In the Great Hall, he found himself surrounded by people, all asking questions. Where had he been? Had he had anything to eat? Was he recovered from his recent illness? He answered them all politely and was glad to feel an arm slip through his.

"Here I am, darling," a voice whispered - but it was not Lavinia. Evangeline fluttered her eyelashes. "Have you missed me? I have missed you!" She walked her fingers up his arm. "You are a naughty boy to run away from us - from me. And after I sang for you too!"

Timmins disentangled himself. "Miss Honeybell," he said. "I am flattered by your attentions, although I cannot for the life of me see what I have done to encourage you to lavish them upon me in this fashion. You are an admirable woman, but..."

Evangeline giggled. "Oh, you charmer!" she replied. "I told you; I have always had a soft spot for a clergyman! There's something beguiling about a man who has to be good all the time! What, I wonder, lurks beneath that veneer of goodness? That, for me, is the intrigue! And you are such a mystery, my dear man! You constantly rebuff me and appear so ... repressed ... so impervious to the charms of a woman. You are quite unlike that brother of yours, who is so...ardent." She cast a glance in Claude Augustus' direction. He blew a kiss and raised his glass. She giggled, then turned back to Timmins. "You fascinate me, Samuel. I long to..."

"No, Evangeline," Timmins interrupted before she could say any more. "You are correct - I have lived a lonely bachelor life, believing, until today, that I was happy. Things have changed, however. I have realised that my happiness can never be complete until there is a Mrs Timmins."

Evangeline's mouth dropped open. For a moment she reminded Timmins of an enormous carp his father had once caught in his lake - fat and shiny, with bulging eyes and mouth agape. He stifled the urge to laugh, then clapped his hands loudly and called out for silence. "I have something to say to you all - dear friends," he said. "This is a joyous occasion for me - in part because I am surrounded by such kind, generous, and forgiving friends, but mostly because I have determined that I shall marry!"

Uproar greeted his announcement. He held up his hand for silence. Beside him, Evangeline gasped, tottered, recovered herself and simpered, fanning her face with a lace handkerchief. "Words cannot express," he said, noticing that Lavinia had appeared through the doorway at the other end of the room, "how proud I am of the talented, wonderful woman who will be my wife. Ladies and gentlemen, I have the honour - the great honour - to present to you the future Mrs Timmins. Come here, my dear."

To the sound of a strangled gasp from Evangeline, he reached out to Lavinia, who made her way through the crowd to take his hand and stand beside him. "Lavinia Bellamy has consented to share her life with me and has made me the happiest man alive!" He raised her hand to his lips and kissed it, to the delight of the assembled crowd, which surged forward to congratulate the happy couple, leaving Evangeline to stalk off towards the drinks table.

The rest of the afternoon passed in a whirl until, one by one, the guests left for the peace and quiet of their own homes. When only a few guests remained, Timmins turned to Lavinia and told her about what had happened with Evangeline. "I feel bad about it, darling," he said. "She clearly believed that when I said I was taking a wife I was referring to her, and I am afraid that I rather enjoyed misleading her."

Lavinia wagged a finger at him. "That was very remiss of you, Samuel," she said, laughing. "However, I don't think you need fear that Miss Honeybell will waste away, pining for you!" She nodded her head toward the dining room. There, in the doorway, stood the Bishop, an expression of horror on his face, while beside him Evangeline fluttered her eyelashes and walked her fingers slowly up his arm. Nearby, Claude Augustus looked on, jealously. "I think you have had a lucky escape. Now, shall we say our goodbyes, darling?" Lavinia fondled Poffley's ears. "This boy could do with some fresh air and then his dinner."

"Am I your darling, or is he?" Timmins enquired. "And which of us is it who needs his dinner? I can see that I have competition for your affections!" He kissed her forehead. "I can think of nothing better," he said, "than a quiet walk home with you two."

ACKNOWLEDGEMENT

Thanks to Roddy Phillips, whose workshops kickstarted my writing and showed me that ideas for
stories can spring from just about anywhere. Thanks
to the tutors and my fellow students on the Creative
Writing Programme 2015-2017, who gave such
insightful feedback on my work, particularly
Victoria Benstead-Hume and Dr John Herbert, who
both ploughed through my entire – very long! -
early draft of the book and whose advice was invaluable. Thanks
to my lovely husband, Tony, who drew
initial designs for previous book covers and, finally,
thanks to friends and family who have listened to
me banging on about it for too long and have given
their advice and encouragement

ABOUT THE AUTHOR

J E Horth

ABOUT THE AUTHOR

J E Horth is a former English teacher and the author of Timmins Rings the Changes, her first novel about the inhabitants of the little village of Quillington Parva. Whilst holding down a full-time teaching career and bringing up two boys with her husband, Tony, she also managed to fit in time as an actress with Wired Theatre, devising performances for Brighton Fringe Festival which reflected her enjoyment of quirky characters. Since leaving teaching she has been exploring her creative side, writing short stories and painting. It was when both her sons beat her into print that she finally got her act together and finished this book.

Printed in Great Britain
by Amazon

46066223R00148